*Every Month Original
Novels, Stories, and Articles*

MONTHLY

USA Today Bestselling Writer
Dean Wesley Smith

TABLE OF CONTENTS

SHORT STORIES

FULL NOVEL

SERIAL BOOK

NONFICTION

Smith's Monthly Issue #29

The Writings and Opinions of

Dean Wesley Smith

Introduction
STILL GOING STRONG

Sometimes I am stunned at the fact that there have been twenty-nine issues of this magazine.

And I will be putting issue thirty together this next week or so.

I honestly had no plans or thoughts beyond trying to get this magazine to last for two years, or twenty-four issues.

The reason for that seemingly random number came right out of my own history.

The first magazine I edited and partially owned was *Pulphouse: A Fiction Magazine*. That magazine started off with grand ideas, settled into a monthly for a while, and then became very erratic near the end.

Counting an issue zero to start off with, the magazine didn't make it past twenty issues over a four-year period.

Then I was hired to be the fiction editor at a computer tech magazine called *VB Tech*. Now the magazine was focused on a form of technology I flat didn't understand, but the publisher wanted two science fiction stories from major authors every month, and they illustrated the stories and always had one of the illustrations as the cover of the magazine.

VB Tech had over twenty-five thousand readers, and two original science fiction stories every issue, and no one inside the world of science fiction would even give it a notice. I published original stories from Harlan Ellison, Jack Williamson, Kristine Kathryn Rusch and many, many other top writers of the time.

The magazine never got any traction inside the field of science fiction or even notice, and thus the publisher cut including short stories after eighteen issues.

So I've never had a magazine that I edited that got past the two-year monthly level. Even my editing on *Star Trek: Strange New World* only had ten volumes over ten years. So when I started this magazine, the goal was to get to at least twenty-four issues.

Thanks for the Support

Dean Wesley Smith

I had no thought past that point.

But it seems I have blown right through that goal since you now hold issue twenty-nine. That means twenty-nine novels and way past a hundred short stories, plus the other features.

And I am still having fun.

So I see this just continuing on for some time now.

In this issue is the full new novel of *Dead Hand* in my Cold Poker Gang series of twisted mystery novels. And, of course, the issue opens with a Poker Boy story.

I've also put a side story in my jukebox series in here called "He Could Have Coped with Dragons." The Richard in the story is the eventual owner of the Garden Lounge in the jukebox series.

Also in this issue is the second installment of my first published novel, *Laying the Music to Rest.* Do remember that even though Doc is the main character, it's not the same Doc in my novel *Dead Money* or in the Cold Poker Gang series. And the Garden Lounge is not the jukebox series Garden Lounge.

I wrote that novel in 1987 and it was published in 1989. So almost thirty years ago now and I think it still stands up just fine. I'm not changing a single word of it.

I hope you are enjoying these stories and novels in this magazine as much as I am in writing the stories and putting the issues together. I try to keep things diverse even though I wrote everything in these pages.

I hope you will remain with me on this journey into the future.

—Dean Wesley Smith
February 20, 2016
Lincoln City, Oregon

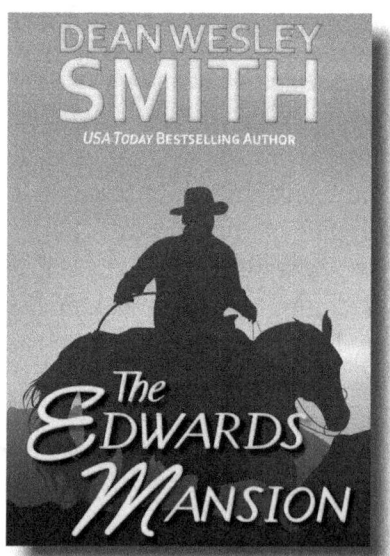

Two Thunder Mountain Novels
Available at your favorite booksellers.

Coming Next Issue in *Smith's Monthly*

THE IDANHA HOTEL

A Thunder Mountain Novel

Smith's MONTHLY

NUMBER THIRTY
MARCH, 2016

Original Stories, Novels, and Articles

DEAN WESLEY SMITH

THE IDANHA HOTEL
A Thunder Mountain Novel

Poker Boy and his team must stop a possible war between fairies and trolls. A war guaranteed to start at a poker table in the hidden Okey-Doke Casino.

So everyone figured who would be better to stop it than Poker Boy.

One problem: Poker Boy didn't even know fairies and trolls existed.

SHOOTOUT IN THE OKEY-DOKE CASINO
A Poker Boy Story

ONE

IN MY FEW, short years working as a superhero for the gambling gods, no one had ever bothered to mention to me that fairies and elves and trolls and all those sorts of things actually existed.

Of course, until I became Poker Boy, I had no idea that just about everything that existed had gods that ruled over that area of the world. Gambling gods, gods of food, gods of hospitality, gods of mathematics, and so on. So I suppose it wasn't much of a jump to realize fairies were real as well. I had just honestly never thought about it.

It was a Monday night, just after nine, and I was playing in a small, two-hundred-dollar buy-in tournament at my local Spirit Winds Casino in the mountains in Oregon. The eleven-table poker room had the three remaining tournament tables tucked off in one corner, with two real-money tables on the other side of the room. I planned on moving to one of the regular tables if I got knocked out of the tournament, and playing until eleven when my girlfriend got off work.

I owned an old double-wide about a half-mile away from the casino, tucked in the back of an old trailer park. I liked playing in the Spirit Winds' small poker room when I wasn't out chasing bad guys or saving dogs – even though I am a super-hero in the gambling universe, I seemed to save a lot of dogs. No one could really explain it, beyond it just happened.

I was about to fold a ten-nine-suited to a raise in front of me when someone tapped me on the shoulder.

I glanced around to see Stan, the God of Poker, standing behind me in black slacks, white shirt, and dark sports jacket. No one seemed to notice him.

Actually, Stan was one of the most unnoticeable people I had ever met. His square-jawed face seldom showed emotion and he could disappear completely from just about any crowd without using any superpower at all.

I had on my usual superhero costume of black leather coat, black Fedora-like hat, and jeans. The coat and hat helped focus my powers when I was near or in a casino.

Stan leaned in and said, "Get your team together. Half-hour at The Diner."

Then he turned and headed out the door before I could even ask a question. At the exact spot where there was a three-foot dead spot in camera feeds to security, he vanished.

No doubt something bad was happening. When Stan came in person to Oregon to get me, things were urgent.

I mucked my hand and pushed back from the table, pretending to get a call on my cell phone, the very same phone I never turned on and never used. Then I turned to the dealer after pretending to listen for a moment to a call. "Blind me off. Got to run."

The dealer nodded and a couple of the players actually looked relieved I was leaving.

I waited until I was outside the casino in a blind camera spot before I jumped to another blind camera spot in front of the MGM Grand Hotel and Casino front desk on the Strip in Vegas.

I loved that I knew how to teleport. Teleporting was, at the moment, my favorite superpower. I had just learned how to do it a month or so ago, and it was startling how often it came in handy. Especially when I lived in Oregon and often had to work or rescue people in Las Vegas.

My girlfriend, Patty Ledgerwood, aka Front Desk Girl, is a superhero working under the gods of hospitality. She was standing behind the counter smiling at an overweight woman customer when I arrived in front of the counter beside the customer. I instantly slid Patty and myself out of time, leaving the women who had been trying to register standing with an open mouth full of yellow teeth and eyes half-closed in a blink.

Being able to slip out of time and freeze everything around me was my second-favorite superpower. I had learned how to do that back during the fight with the Slots of Saturn. It never got old.

The noise of the large lobby and the casino down the hall instantly stopped, as did everyone in the lobby except Patty and me.

"Knocked out of the tournament already?" Patty asked, smiling and reaching across the wide counter to take my hand and give it an affectionate squeeze.

Her big brown eyes and wonderful smile could melt an iceberg, and every time she turned that smile and that wonderful gaze on me, I melted right along

Now Available
from all your favorite booksellers
in trade paper and electronic editions.

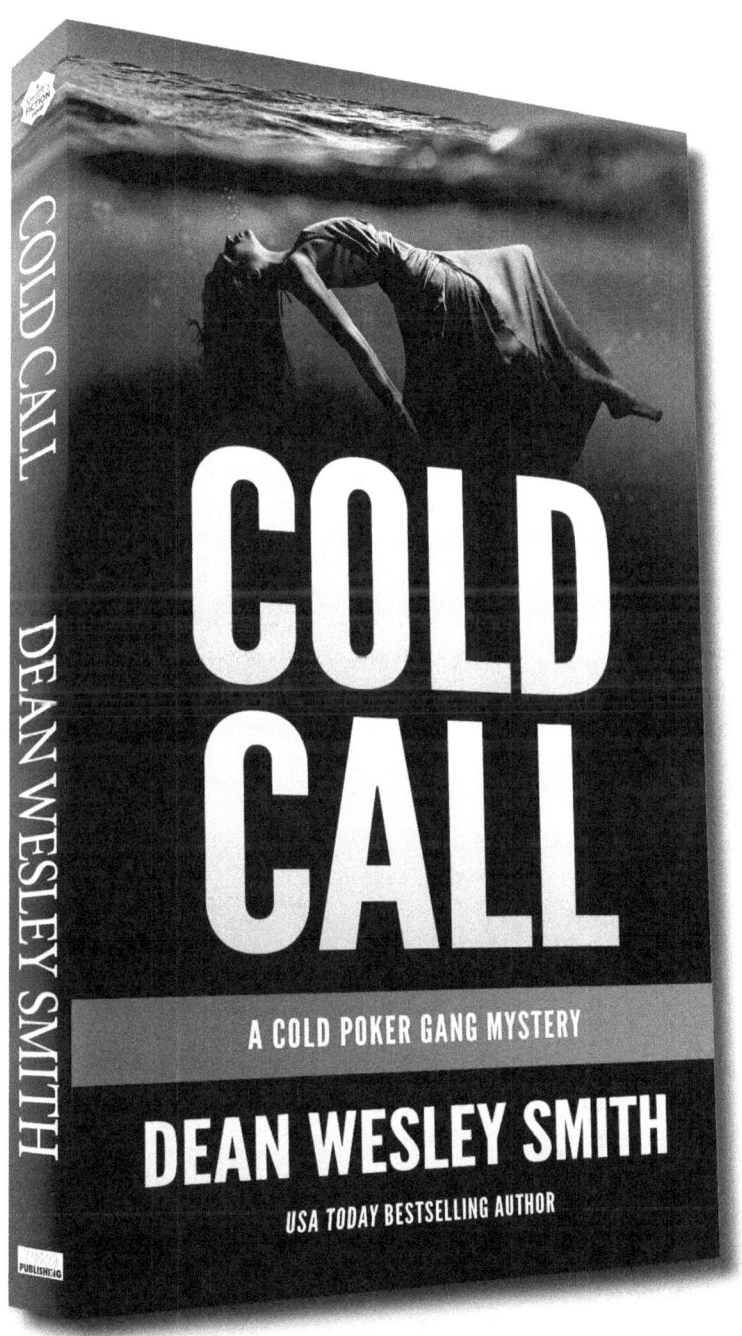

with the berg. She had her long brown hair pulled back and had on the standard white blouse and black slacks of the MGM front desk, where she worked.

"Stan came and got me," I said. "We have some sort of mission. He didn't say what kind, but it sounded urgent."

She nodded, reached into her pocket, and slid me her cell phone, knowing mine was only a prop. "It will take me a minute to finish with this customer," she said, indicating the open-mouthed woman who really, really needed a dentist. "Then I'll be ready to go. Give Screamer a call."

"Is The Smoke in town?"

"No," she said. "Off working a case of bear-killings in Alaska."

I slipped us back into real time as I turned and walked away from the counter. The noise of all the people and tourists talking at the same time as I crossed the stone and high-ceilinged room rammed into me again.

I dialed Screamer's number and then stood against a stone pillar to stay out of the traffic lane.

"So what's up?" Screamer asked.

"Stan called us together," I said. "You free in a half hour?"

"I'm out at the airport," he said. "Got about fifteen minutes to finish the case here with airport security."

"Call when you are done and I'll jump you to The Diner."

"Got it," he said and hung up.

Screamer worked as a superhero for the gods of law enforcement. His main power was being able to crawl inside a person's head, and transfer thoughts from one person to another. It came in very handy in more ways than can be imagined.

He got his nickname when he got a serial killer to scream for mercy by letting

him experience what he had put others through. Screamer got the guy to tell the police where he had buried a woman alive and the police got there in time to save the woman.

It took the killer an hour to stop screaming from whatever Screamer had put in his head.

The fourth member of our team was The Smoke, a werewolf who had complete control over which form he was in and who could also walk through walls. He worked as a superhero for the animal gods.

Our team was the only team I knew about that crossed over four areas of gods, and we had done our share of saving humanity since we formed.

I sure hoped the mission tonight was a more mundane one, but with Stan coming to get me, that wasn't likely.

Patty vanished into the back area behind the counter. About one minute later she came out into the lobby, headed for me.

She kissed me, then hand-in-hand we turned and headed for the parking garage.

"We got time to drive?" Patty asked as we started down the staircase.

"Yeah," I said. "Stan said thirty minutes, it's only been less than fifteen."

So we got to The Diner in downtown Las Vegas the old-fashioned way. We drove.

TWO

THE DINER WAS a small hole-in-the-wall restaurant downtown on a side street about a half-block from the Horseshoe Casino. It had fantastic milkshakes that almost matched its fake 1960s décor. And Madge, the waitress, ran the place. She was a superhero working for the gods of food and beverage, and she didn't mind us jumping in and out as long as her other customers didn't notice.

Madge was a large woman in many ways, and always wore a uniform two sizes too small for her build, which meant watching her walk away in her tight skirt wasn't something anyone wanted to do.

Just like my black leather coat and hat was my uniform and gave me extra power, her tight skirt and too-tight white blouse was clearly hers. Not sure what powers it gave her, or if those powers were worth it, to be honest.

"Been a week," Madge said as Patty and I walked in the door, "since the last time you guys saved the world. I figure, since you are walking this time, whatever is going on now can't be that important."

"Nice seeing you as well, Madge," I said, smiling at her as she popped her gum.

"Who else is joining you lovebirds?" she asked as we took our normal booth. Patty and I slid in beside each other leaving the other side open for Screamer. No one else was in the place and Madge looked almost happy to see us.

"Screamer and Stan," Patty said. "Milkshakes."

Madge nodded. "Let me know if there's anything I can do to help you guys this time around. What you did for all those dogs a while back was really special."

"Thanks," I said.

She turned away to go make milkshakes as Stan appeared.

"Where is everyone?" he asked, looking worried as he pulled up a chair in front of the booth.

"Screamer is finishing up at the airport and needs a jump here when he's done. The Smoke is in Alaska on another case."

"The moose-shooting thing by the ex-governor," Stan said, nodding.

"Bear," Patty corrected.

Stan nodded again. "He might need some help on that when we finish with this one."

At that moment, Patty's cell phone buzzed and she took it out of her pocket and glanced at it. "Screamer," she said.

Before I could jump to get him and bring him back, Screamer was sitting across from Patty and me, his cell phone still to his ear.

"Thanks, Stan," he said, snapping the phone closed and putting it in his dark shirt pocket.

Stan hadn't left the table. Looks like I had a lot more to learn about teleporting – I didn't know that stunt was even possible.

"So what's happening?" Patty asked Stan as she put her phone away.

"The fairies have challenged the trolls again," Stan said.

Patty suddenly looked worried. "The Curse of the Bayback Bridge."

"I thought we had another twenty years before that hit," Screamer said.

"We all did," Stan said, the look of seriousness on his face making my stomach twist. "But someone rebuilt the bridge damned fast this time around."

Well, I knew that was all in English, but just because Stan said it like I should understand it didn't mean I did.

But Patty clearly did.

And so did Screamer.

Sometimes being the new kid in the superhero neighborhood just sucked. I knew Patty was a good hundred years older than I was, and I had never asked Screamer how long he had been around. Stan remembered Atlantis, and once mentioned he had been born there.

Me, I was born in 1950, and sort of stopped aging around thirty-five when I got hired as a superhero by the gambling gods. I had been told I wouldn't age for a very long time, which I honestly liked the sound of. But having a girlfriend a hundred years older than I was sometimes felt just intimidating.

"What are they fighting about this time?" Screamer asked, shaking his head.

"Is this normal?" I asked, afraid to mention I didn't know who the trolls or the fairies were. Or what the "Curse of the Bayback Bridge" even was. At that moment, it hadn't occurred to me they were talking about kids' books trolls and fairies. I thought they meant some sort of teenage gangs or something.

"About every thirty to fifty years," Stan said, "the curse makes them fight again. This time it seems the fight is over which group is a better no-limit poker player."

"You're kidding?" Patty asked, almost laughing.

"I wish I was," Stan said. "And it's up to us to make sure the tournament they are staging is settled and doesn't explode into a bigger battle. Direct orders from all our bosses while they find and blow up that damned bridge again. Our job is to control the fight and make sure it's fair if they can't find the bridge before the tournament starts."

"Fair with trolls' dark magic and fairy fancy magic?" Screamer asked, shaking his head. "Now that's going to be a real trick."

"There is no magic in poker," I said, still not having a clue what I was really talking about.

"Exactly," Stan said. "So we have to figure out a way to keep magic out of this tournament completely. And we have two hours until it starts."

"What starts?" Madge said as she arrived with our milkshakes.

"The trolls and fairies are fighting again, in a poker tournament this time," Stan said, pulling his chocolate milkshake closer to him.

"The curse again?" Madge asked, clearly disgusted. "Count me out of this one. Two or three battles back those ugly, smelly, little trolls trashed my restaurant in a food fight against the fairies. I'm afraid if I see any of them again they may get even shorter."

With that she walked off.

Both Stan and Screamer were laughing.

"Okay, I admit," I said, "I'm the baby here, so I'm going to need a little help. What exactly are trolls and fairies?"

All three of them were starting to sip on their milkshakes and all three stopped and looked at me like I had lost my mind, which I was starting to think I might be doing.

"You ever read any fairytales when you were a kid?" Screamer asked.

It finally, at that moment, dawned on me. "You're telling me that fairies and trolls are real?"

"Yeah," Screamer said, laughing.

Patty patted my hand and pushed my milkshake closer to me.

"Very real," Stan said. "And don't believe that Tinker Bell fairy stuff the movies show. Real fairies are tall, skinny, and pranksters. Mean pranksters. And the trolls are short, but not that short. They tend to smell like two-day-old fish, and they are naturally as rude as an angry landlord. But they don't live under things. In fact a lot of them in this area live in a big condo complex out by the university."

"And some of them are married to fairies," Patty said.

I took a deep breath and tried to let all that sink in. Then, after a wonderful, cool sip of my vanilla milkshake, I asked the next question. "What is this curse, and why is their poker tournament so important, and why do we care that the trolls and fairies are fighting?"

I guess that was three questions, but shoot me. I was confused.

"Far before I was born," Stan said, "a God of Domestic Happiness named Roger Bayback got into a really nasty divorce from his fairy wife after she had an affair with a troll. He put a dark magic curse on all fairies and trolls. The curse actually flows from the bridge his wife and the troll had sex under. As long as the bridge stands, the two races must fight."

"You remember reading about World War Two?" Screamer asked.

I nodded.

"Hitler was a troll," Stan said. "He took over Germany after the bridge was rebuilt. It's been destroyed many times over the centuries, and he did everything in his power to clear out all fairies. And he did his kind and fairy-kind deep harm."

"Not counting what he did to everyone else," I said.

All three nodded at that and Stan went on. "Hitler's attitude was that if he killed everything and everyone in Europe who might be a fairy, eventually he'd get them all."

"Thankfully, he failed," Screamer said.

"But because of that," Stan said, "all the gods stepped in and destroyed the bridge. And we keep destroying it every time it rebuilds in a new location. And we brokered a long-term peace between the fairies and the trolls."

"But since the fairies and the trolls must fight whenever the bridge is up, because of the curse," Screamer said, "part of the truce is that the fighting be in a contained way, like a poker tournament."

"So we have to figure out a way to stop both their magic, and just let them play poker?" I asked, "Or it might escalate into something much bigger?"

"Exactly," Stan said.

"Why don't the gods just break the curse forever?"

Stan shook his head. "Can't do that unless we can find Roger Bayback, and he has been missing for thousands and thousands of years."

"So how are we going to contain both fairy and troll magic so they can just play poker?" Screamer asked.

I just stared at my milkshake, trying to wrap my mind around fairies and trolls being real. Let alone some ancient curse on them.

Stan shrugged. "That's what we have less than two hours to figure out if the gods can't find that damn bridge."

No one said a word.

The image of Hitler as a troll just kept flashing through my mind. Not an image I wanted to keep.

THREE

A HALF-HOUR LATER, after Stan and Patty explained troll and fairy magic to me, I knew there was no chance that this coming tournament would even last through the first fifteen minute round.

Alone, without magic and curses and other fairytale issues, poker was a game of emotions and frustration and cold, hard calculations. The first bad beat put on a troll by a fairy would send the room into full-fledged war, magic or no magic, curse or no curse.

"Whose idea was it to fight in a poker tournament?" I asked. "Anyone who knows poker knows that it's a guaranteed way to escalate a fight instead of contain it. Even blocking or taking away all the player's magic won't matter in the slightest."

"I said the same thing to Laverne," Stan said. "But it was decided that a poker tournament was the form of combat this time, unless the bridge can be found first."

Laverne was Lady Luck herself, one of the most powerful of all gods.

Something was really bothering me that I couldn't put my finger on. This staged fighting thing had been going on since after the Second World War.

"Who decided that?" I asked. "Who suggested a poker tournament?"

Stan stared at me for a moment, then said simply, "I'll find out."

He vanished and then came back less than ten seconds later.

"The poker room manager at the Okey-Doke suggested it," Stan said.

I think I just stared blankly at him.

He laughed when he saw my look and said, "The Okey-Doke Casino and Hotel is where all the fairy-folk gamble. It's magically hidden from real people. It's out on the old highway headed toward the dam."

That wasn't why I was looking blank. I couldn't understand why a poker room manager had suggested the battle? Poker room managers know how impossible it can be at times to keep even normal human poker players under control, let alone races with magic forced to fight under a curse. Again, nothing about this was making sense.

I sat back for a moment and just stared at the ceiling, trying to ignore all the stuff I didn't understand, or had just learned. Instead I tried to make sense of all this from a very human viewpoint.

Point one: An angry ex-husband wanted to take out revenge on his ex-wife and her new lover's peoples. Okay, a little over-the-top, but understandable, considering the sex under a bridge part.

Point two: If I was the very screwed-up angry husband, I would want to watch every battle to get my emotional satisfaction.

Suddenly I had an idea.

"What does this Roger Bayback look like?" I asked.

"No one really knows anymore," Stan said. "This is a very old curse. And besides, he's a god, he can disguise himself completely."

I nodded. I had a hunch I knew exactly where Roger Bayback was, but I didn't dare trust my instincts alone, so I turned to Stan.

"If we have to fight this battle, here's how you set up the tournament. Two brackets, equal number of players in both.

Equal chips. Trolls only in one bracket, fairies only in the other bracket. Winner of both brackets face off in a showdown. One on one. That should keep the chance of violence down."

Stan nodded. "Great idea."

He started to move, but I stopped him before he jumped. "Tell Laverne and Patty's boss and a number of other gods to watch me carefully, then jump me and Patty and Screamer to the Okey-Doke poker room and support us."

Stan looked as confused as Screamer and Patty looked.

"I have a hunch I know where Roger is, and if I'm right, it's going to take a bunch of gods to contain him."

Stan, still puzzled, nodded and vanished.

If anyone could contain this Roger-god, it was Lady Luck.

I turned to Screamer and Patty. "We might need to be hooked up, Screamer, if I am wrong on my first guess of who Roger is."

"Hooking up" was when Screamer touched us both at the same time so all three of us could be connected and acting as fast as we could think.

"Why?" Patty asked.

"We're going to need to quickly screen a lot of bystanders," I said.

"Laverne and everyone is ready," Stan said, appearing again on his chair.

"If my first ploy doesn't work," I said to Stan, "we're going to need to take a large number of people in a large area around the tournament set-up out of time. If Roger is in the area, will he know he's been taken out of time?"

"Yes," Stan said. "But by jumping out of a time bubble like that, he can be traced."

"Okay, then if he's not in that area, Screamer, we go to the second backup plan. You and Patty and I are going to need to be linked to check everyone close by to see if we can spot in their minds where this poker idea was planted and by who."

"Still confused on plan one and the first backup plan," Stan said.

"You'll see plan one when we get there," I said. "If that fails, the backup plan is to trap him and make him jump."

"Got you," Stan said. "But why do you think he's there?"

"If you were as pissed-off as he has been for thousands of years, wouldn't you be there to watch the bloodshed?"

Stan and Patty and Screamer all nodded slowly.

For an instant Stan seemed to look up, then he was back in his eyes. "Laverne and the rest are ready."

"Then let's go," I said.

FOUR

STAN JUMPED US right into the front area of a large poker room that held a good thirty tables. Around the rail a large group of faintly-blue fairies stood in a group, talking. They were tall and thin and laughed a lot among themselves.

Not a one of them had wings that I could see. Not sure why I expected wings, but I did.

I stared for a minute, still working to get past my shock that fairies were real. Then I looked around to the other side of the room to a group of trolls, trying to get the image of Hitler out of

my mind but failing. They all looked like fireplugs with human bodies and greasy black hair.

At first glance, The Okey-Doke Casino and Hotel seemed very much like any other casino in Vegas, except for the unicorns carrying drinks on their backs among slot machines, and the giant ponds and streams that wound through a huge forest, dividing the blackjack tables from the slots and making the entire thing look like it was a casino parked in an ancient forest. Even the carpets looked like pine needles.

And the place smelled like no other casino I had ever been in. No cigarette smoke, but a distinct odor of sour milk.

All my warning superpowers went into high gear. This was not a friendly place for most humans or superheroes. But after studying the place for a moment, I suddenly had a backup plan three.

I nodded to Stan and then walked toward the poker room counter. It looked again like any other main counter in any poker room, with sign-up whiteboards behind it on the wall showing all the tables and possible games. Right now all the boards were wiped clean as everyone got ready for the tournament.

I walked up to the guy who was clearly the poker room manager. He was short, but human, with gray hair and a long gray beard that made him look more Gandalf-like instead of a poker room manager. He had on a white shirt, with a green vest over it, and black pants. That was the traditional uniform of most dealers and brushes that worked poker rooms.

"I'm Poker Boy," I said, coming up beside him as he stacked racks of blue and red tournament chips on a table. I motioned at the other three of my team behind me. "We're here to help keep the tournament under control."

"Great to have you," the guy said, not looking up. "We should be ready to go in about fifteen minutes."

"Great," I said. "We'll be over by the rail."

He nodded and kept counting. I turned and started to walk away, then winked at my team and turned back.

"Oh, Roger, one more thing."

He looked up without thinking. Then I could see in his eyes he understood what I had done.

An instant later he froze in place, solid as a rock, before he could even think of jumping. In fact, he looked like he had actually become rock, like a carved Greek statue holding a rack of poker chips.

Lady Luck appeared, wearing a power suit of black silk with silver stripes. She was smiling, staring at the rock that had been the god, Roger Bayback.

After a moment she turned to all of us. "We finally got this guy. Great job, Poker Boy. Everyone. Now we just have to find that stupid bridge one last time."

I pointed to the middle of the casino. A short bridge, styled like an ancient European bridge, crossed over a large pond to a high-stakes slot area. She turned and saw what I was pointing at, then just shook her head.

A moment later the bridge was gone in a cloud of smoke, stranding a bunch of elfin-looking old women on the island of high-stakes.

The Curse of the Bayback Bridge was gone forever.

"You don't know how many lives you might have just saved," Laverne said, smiling at me. "Thank you and your team once again."

Every time Lady Luck had smiled at me, I got chills, and this time was no exception. I was a poker player, after all. You didn't take something like that lightly.

With a slight nod to all of us, she and the now-stone-god vanished to cheers from all the fairies and trolls standing around watching.

The cheers and celebration were so loud that I couldn't even hear the bells on the slot machines.

Trolls were kissing trolls.

Fairies were kissing fairies.

And trolls and fairies were kissing each other.

Now every warning power in my body was off, and I could feel this wonderful feeling of welcome and warmth.

It looked like the poker tournament had just been cancelled. And I had to admit, this was the first time I had been happy about a tournament cancellation.

Stan smiled, looking around. "Poker Boy, it seems you have a new room you are welcome to play in."

I glanced around at all the laughing and cheering and dancing fairies and trolls. "Thanks, but no thanks. I have a hard enough time reading human faces."

What I didn't say was that I just couldn't shake the image of Hitler as a troll.

A moment later the four of us were back in The Diner.

And this time the burgers and fries and milkshakes were paid for by Lady Luck.

~

Dean Wesley **Smith**

USA Today Bestselling Writer

Deciding to Change
Can Sometimes be
the Hardest Fight
of All

He Could Have Coped With DRAGONS

A JUKEBOX STORY

Have you ever wondered what your life would be like if you had made a different decision?

A bar napkin with a strange saying and a dragon gives Richard Cone just that: A second chance.

Bestselling writer Dean Wesley Smith returns to his popular Jukebox series with the origin story of the new owner of the Garden Lounge.

HE COULD HAVE COPED WITH DRAGONS
A Jukebox Story

ONE

RICHARD CONE STOOD in the doorway, feeling completely out of place in his construction clothes, and gaped at the medieval castle decor of the new hotel bar. Crest-covered satin banners draped over the fake stone walls above the booths. A gigantic wood and fake-candle chandelier hung in the center of the room above high-backed cloth chairs and wood tables. He was glad he hadn't been hired for the building crew. Just hanging that chandelier must have been a nightmare.

The two waitresses wore long, peasant dresses that seemed as out of place as he felt among the suits and modern outfits of the few hotel guests scattered around the bar this early in the afternoon. The hostess wore a brown dress that forced her moderate-sized breasts up into a huge mound of cleavage.

Richard would have bet anything that it was uncomfortable. She glanced up over the ornately printed, "Please Wait to be Seated" sign and Richard noticed she barely held back a frown. "Can I help you?"

Richard glanced up at the place in the ceiling where the cables holding the chandelier were anchored and then down at the empty tables under the huge wood fixture. No way could sitting under that be comfortable. "I'd just like to sit at the bar."

The hostess nodded and without a word led the way. She helped him get settled on one of the huge, high-backed bar stools before she went back to the door.

Everything about the place looked and smelled brand new. Not the normal smoky, thick smell of the old Garden Lounge. This bar smelled of paint and new carpet, which did nothing but clash with the effect of old-England they were trying for. Directly behind the bar above the rows of bottles was a huge display of crest-covered shields and swords. Someone had tried to make the swords and shields look old, but it was obvious they too were brand new.

Richard looked around. Coming in here had been a mistake. He had such fond memories of the years in the Garden that somehow he had hoped a little of the Garden's magic would carry over into the new bar here. But it was clear it hadn't. No one could be comfortable in this place. And certainly none of the old gang would be caught dead in here.

Richard sighed. He had missed his chance. He had wanted to buy the Garden from Stout, the former bartender and owner, but didn't have anywhere near the money. When Stout said he was moving to live with Jenny, his old love down in California, he offered the bar to any of

his regulars who wanted it. But none who could afford it wanted to own a bar, and those who did want the Garden couldn't come up with the money.

So Stout sold it to a land developer, who tore down the Garden Lounge and the two buildings beside it and built the new hotel. It was a sad day when Stout took some special drinking glasses, the old jukebox, and left town.

A bartender wearing green tights, a long-sleeved shirt and a green vest placed a napkin in front of Richard. "What can I get for you?"

"Bourbon water." Richard said. "Very little water."

The young man nodded and went back to the well as Richard just shook his head. Back before he started working construction and driving truck, he had done some part-time bartending. But if his boss had ever forced him to wear green tights he would have quit in an instant. This poor guy must have been really desperate.

He glanced down at the white napkin. An ornate sword filled the center of the napkin with a dragon holding onto the sword. Above the sword were red letters in ornate script.

There are no dragons
Only small spiders
and stepping in chewing gum
Could you cope with Dragons?

It wasn't funny.

All bar napkins were supposed to be funny, weren't they? Otherwise what was the point? Of course, nothing in this bar seemed intended to be funny.

The bartender placed Richard's drink square in the middle of the red letters and hesitated. Richard dug out a twenty-dollar bill and slid it at the bartender. "Hold this for a tab and let me know when you need more."

The young guy seemed almost relieved as he nodded and headed back down the bar toward the cash register hidden inside a fake wine barrel.

Richard took a sip and let the strength of the first swallow seep down his body and heat his insides. He could almost feel his fingers tingle against the cold wet glass. He had needed this drink all afternoon, wished for it, longed for it hour after hour. Driving that damn truck back and forth from the dust-covered construction site to the gravel pit always made him thirsty. And the thought of the first drink always kept him going until quitting time. Now that he had the cold glass in his hand, he intended to savor it.

He took another sip and nodded appreciatively in the direction of the bartender. The kid poured a real, solid drink. Almost like Stout at the old Garden. Stout used to call a drink this strong a "Cone Drink." Today it was exactly what he had needed.

He was about to set the glass back on the napkin when he noticed that it had changed. Words now filled the space across the bottom of the napkin below the sword and dragon.

IF YOU REALLY THINK
YOU COULD HAVE COPED
WITH DRAGONS
TOUCH THE SWORD

Richard glanced at the bartender and then around to see if anyone was watching, or even close by. But not even the hostess, who stood behind her small podium, seemed to be paying any attention at all. Someone must have switched the napkins. But why would anyone bother?

He picked up the napkin and glanced at the back.

Nothing. He dropped it back on the bar. What kind of joke was this and just what the hell did it mean about dragons? He was just about to signal for the bartender when the sword started to strobe in bright red flashes.

Richard grabbed the wooden edge of the bar as he felt himself being pulled up and out.

Away from the bar.
Away from his drink.

TWO

RICHARD CONE SAT at the metal-legged kitchen table and spread brown sugar on his hot Cream of Wheat. With his spoon he broke up some of the larger chunks as they turned gold against the white of the cereal. His mother stood at the sink. She wore a brown dress that stopped just above her ankles, brown slip-on shoes, and a flowered apron that tied around her neck.

"Richard," she said, "have you decided what you want for your birthday yet?"

"Huh-uh." He slowly stirred the cereal, blew on a spoonful and then tasted it. Too hot and almost too much sugar.

"You're going to have to help me. I just have no idea what a seventeen-year-old boy would want."

"Nothing, Mom. Really." Silence filled the kitchen, broken only by the sound of a neighbor warming up his car and the clinking of Richard's spoon against the bowl. He was going to have to tell her sooner or later. Maybe this morning would be as good a time as any. Sure, she'd be mad, but he'd made up his mind. He'd move out if he had to.

He stirred the cereal hard, took another quick taste and then laid the spoon down. "Mom, I've got something you should know."

His mom wiped her hands on the towel and pulled the drawer beside the sink open. "I'm listening."

He watched the bun on the back of her head as she dug through the drawer and pulled out a peeler. She plucked a carrot from the sink, turned the water to a slow stream and started peeling the carrot.

"Mom, I've decided I'm going to quit school." He took a deep breath and went on. "With all the men getting called back for Korea, old man Jensen says I can get on down at the Mill."

She turned from the sink, frowning, still holding the carrot and the peeler. "You know what I've said about you quitting school. You only have one year left."

"One-and-a-half. And I hate it. I could make a lot of money working."

"I don't care how much money you could make. I want you to finish school. A high school diploma is important."

He picked up the spoon and without looking at her stirred the cereal. "Yeah, I know. I've heard that a hundred times. But I've already told Mr. Jensen that I would start next Monday. And I'm going to do it."

"You can just un-tell him. If your father was here, he wouldn't—"

"Dad's gone. Besides, even if he was here, he would agree with me."

"That's not true. Your father wanted you in school and you know that."

Richard looked up at her, holding her gaze. "Yeah, then why didn't he finish?"

"Things were different. He had to work and—"

"And that's exactly what I'm going to do." He gave his cereal one quick vicious stir and then stood. "I've got to be going."

His mother remained in front of the sink, carrot in one hand and peeler in the other, watching. He reached for the handle of the back door and suddenly felt himself being pulled.

Away from the kitchen.

Away from his mother.

THREE

THE DOOR HANDLE turned into a wet, cold glass in his hand. Richard glanced down the bar at the bartender in green tights and then at the napkin in front of him. That had been the craziest thing that had ever happened to him. Hell, he hadn't thought of his mother in years.

He took a long, hard gulp out of the drink, his heart pounding like he had just woke from a bad dream. The sword was still flashing, blinking red at him, calling for him to pay attention.

Somehow, he knew, without a doubt, that if he touched that sword, he would have a chance to go back and change the decision to quit school. He didn't know how or why he knew, but he just knew. He could feel it.

If he touched the sword.

If he picked up the challenge it offered.

He killed the drink and set the glass on the inside edge of the bar, signaling for the bartender to bring him another.

The question on the napkin was fading. Did he really want to go back and change? What would be different? Would he be sitting here right now if he did?

Richard shook his head, trying to clear the thought. He was being stupid, that was all. It had been a long day and now he was just daydreaming. Nothing more.

The blinking of the sword slowed and the words below the sword became lighter and lighter. What a joke, him going back to school. He hadn't thought of that in years.

The sword stopped blinking at him and the words below the sword were gone.

He reached over and picked up the napkin, looking at both sides and then unfolding it to make sure. Nothing but a bar napkin. No trick inside to make it blink like that. Now he was sure he was imagining things. Maybe he should take tomorrow off.

"Sorry for the delay," the bartender said as he picked up Richard's glass and moved to the well to refill it. He poured the drink and set it back on the napkin in front of Richard.

Richard gave it the customary one quick stir, laid the straw beside the first and downed half the drink.

"You sure are thirsty," the bartender said as he learned against the back bar across from Richard. "Rough day or something?"

Richard set the glass on the bar beside the napkin and studied the words above the sword again. "Nope. Just thinking about something I can't do anything about."

"What's that?"

"Nothing important, really. Just thinking about finishing school."

The bartender leaned forward, a large smile on his face. "Hey, that's great. I'm third year in engineering at the University. How much longer you got?"

Richard just smiled. "Years."

Sharp laughing broke the background music of the bar and Richard glanced around as five college-age kids entered the bar and took the front booth. The bartender waved and patted the bar in front of Richard. "Be right back."

Richard nodded and again glanced down at the napkin. Maybe it was better he hadn't finished school. He never really liked the know-it-all college types anyhow.

Slowly, the sword started blinking again. Red. Red. Red.

Demanding that he pay attention to it. He rubbed his eyes, but it didn't stop.

And below the sword was the question.

The same question.

IF YOU REALLY THINK
YOU COULD HAVE COPED
WITH DRAGONS
TOUCH THE SWORD

Richard grabbed his glass and took a quick drink as again he felt himself pulled out of the bar.

Not up. Not back.

Just away.

FOUR

RICHARD PUSHED THE knob on the dash forward and let the black, remodeled '47 Ford coast the last fifty feet in the dark. He nudged it slightly against the curb in front of the white, two-story house with the porch light on, then reached around the steering wheel and turned the key off. The motor idled slowly to a stop and silence filled the car, flowing through the windows from the quiet street like a river overflowing its banks.

Richard glanced over at Janice where she huddled beside the passenger door. Usually she sat beside him, holding his hand. But tonight she had her hands folded in her lap as she stared forward through the windshield. She had on a light gray blouse and gray-blue skirt. Her long blonde hair was pulled back over her ears and Richard thought that tonight she was as pretty as he had ever seen her.

"Look, I'm sorry," Richard said. "All right?"

She didn't say a thing, but just kept staring down the dark street.

"How come it's such a crime that I'm not ready? I want to marry you, but just not yet."

Janice glanced down at her hands and then back out the window. He could see her short nose and strong chin outlined against the light coming from the porch. She was eighteen, almost nineteen. They had been going steady for ten months and planning on getting married for two. But he still had a lot of things he wanted to do. Janice wanted kids and that simply scared the holy hell out of him.

"So what would be so bad just going steady for a while longer? I mean, we've only known each other for less than two years. That's really not that long."

Again Janice didn't answer. She'd been giving him the silent treatment for the last hour, ever since he told her what was bothering him.

Richard rolled down the window and laid his head on the door, staring sideways up the tree-lined street. Two houses down was where Jeff Perkins had grown up. He used to go steady with Janice, but Richard had broken them up. Now Jeff was in the Navy and, from what everyone said, was doing real well.

The cold evening air cut at the tension between them. Richard took a deep breath and glanced over at Janice. He knew he was doing the right thing. It wasn't that he didn't love her. He did, very much. He loved everything about her; the smell of her perfume, the way she held her head when she laughed, the feel of her soft hand in his. He was proud to just walk down the street with her.

But he wasn't ready for marriage. Marriage meant changing diapers, paying bills, and being unhappy. Every married couple he knew was unhappy. His parents had been unhappy right up to the day his father died. Why couldn't he and Janice just go steady for a while longer? Have some fun?

Janice's tears caught the reflected light in shimmering stabs through the darkness. He reached across and gently touched her arm. He could feel her shaking.

"Janice? Please? It's not that bad. Really. I still love you. I just want to postpone getting married a little, that's all. Just for a while."

"No." She took a deep breath and tried to straighten her back. A sob shook her shoulders.

"Why? I don't understand?"

"Because you promised me that—"

Richard pounded his fist against the steering wheel. "Damn it. Why marriage? Why can't we just be happy? Why go and spoil everything?"

"Because I want to marry you. I want all of you."

Richard looked at her tear-filled eyes glistening in the faint light. "Or none of me. Right?"

Janice turned her head toward her house and Richard turned back to face the dash, both hands on the steering wheel.

Not even the cold air blowing through the open window could now break the thickness between them. She wasn't giving him any choice. He couldn't marry her now and because of that he was going to lose her.

He gripped the steering wheel hard as the darkness of the road ahead swallowed him.

FIVE

RICHARD OPENED HIS eyes to tinkling of bar glasses and ice mixed with low music and talking. Both hands gripped the padded edge of the bar, his knuckles white, his fingers almost punching holes in the new leather.

He let go, flexed his fingers and then grabbed his drink. The cold bourbon felt good against his hot, dry throat and seemed to push the memory of Janice just a little farther into the background.

The bartender stood at the well, making drinks and laughing with one of the cocktail waitresses who stood across from him.

"Touch me. Touch me," the sword on the napkin invited in laughing red flashes.

"Touch me if you dare. Accept my challenge."

What would have happened if he had married Janice? That was a question he always wondered about for years. He hadn't ended up marrying anyone at all, but now this napkin was mocking him, letting him believe that he could change all that by simply touching the sword printed on it.

With shaking hands he carefully adjusted the napkin exactly straight. Its ink was fading again. The flashing slowing down. He didn't have much more than a few seconds.

He'd loved Janice and he still loved her, or the memory of her, after all these years. He'd heard she and Jeff Perkins had gotten back together.

Touch the sword.

Nothing more. What could it hurt? It was only a stupid bar napkin making him into a fool.

Simply touch the sword.

"Ready for another?"

Richard glanced up at the bartender and then back at the napkin. The sword had stopped flashing and the question was gone.

"Yeah," he said and pushed the empty glass at the bartender. Then he wiped his sweating forehead with the sleeve of his shirt. They really kept the heat up in this bar. Maybe it was so new they didn't have the heating system adjusted yet.

He opened one more button on his shirt as the bartender set his new drink down and headed back toward the well.

Damn, that had been so real. He could still smell the lingering sweetness of her perfume and feel the softness of her arm. He gave the drink a quick stir and laid the straw with the rest. Then he picked up the drink, flipped the napkin over and set the drink back down on the plain white of the back side.

Coping with dragons? Hell, he couldn't even cope with bar napkins.

He took a long drink and then noticed he was starting to feel the booze. The kid made a strong drink and he was into his third. Three straws on the bar and it wasn't even six p.m. yet. Usually it took him until at least seven before he had three straws on the bar. He was going to have to slow down or get something to eat real soon.

The white edges of the napkin looked helpless sticking out from under his drink. He thought he could see parts of the red letters fighting to bleed up through the exposed corner. He twisted the glass a half-turn without taking the pressure off the napkin.

"You all right?" the bartender asked, again leaning against the back bar. For a moment he looked beyond Richard at the other customers in the bar, then focused back.

"Yeah." Richard took another quick swallow and put the glass back before the napkin had a chance to move. "You ever regret anything?"

The bartender shrugged. "Sure. Who doesn't?"

"No. I mean really regret something so much that you wish you could go back and change it? Something that was maybe a turning point?"

"Yeah, I suppose. Why?"

"You're not married, are you? No ring?"

The bartender nodded in agreement. "Not yet."

"So you must be at least twenty-one, maybe twenty-two. How come?"

The bartender laughed. "Thanks. Actually I'm twenty-six. And I came close once, over in Idaho. Her name was Jody and there was nothing I could have changed or done. We were just wrong for each other."

"Would you go back and marry her if you had the chance?"

"Shit, no! If I'd have married her I'd still be in Idaho, chances are with two or three kids. I hate kids." He laughed again. "I was lucky to escape with my life."

Richard raised his glass as a half-hearted toast. "I felt the same way once. For a short time."

"You ever married?" the bartender asked.

Richard studied the glass and the trapped napkin. "No, close once like you." He didn't say anything more and he could tell the kid was getting uneasy in the silence.

After a moment he tapped the bar in front of Richard. "Be right back."

Richard picked up his drink and held it out at eye level. The light broke into rainbows inside the brown and white of the bourbon and ice. Hell, having kids with Janice wouldn't have been so bad. Maybe they'd even have grandkids by now. Maybe the napkin would give him another chance.

He took a quick sip and put the drink beside the napkin. Another chance with Janice. That's exactly what he needed. Slowly, as if he were turning over a dead body, afraid of what he would see, he eased the napkin back face up.

The saying was still there, the red even brighter, like blood from a fresh wound.

Slowly the sword started blinking and the question faded back into view.

Maybe the sword would give him another chance with Janice?

He took a deep breath and glanced at the bartender as something pulled him away from the bar.

And away from the thought of Janice.

SIX

The office of plant manager sat to the right of the small front door and opened onto an outer reception area and a glass wall overlooking the main floor of the plant. Richard pulled open the door between the plant and the outer office and nodded at the secretary. "Mary, got any idea what he wants?" He cocked his head in the direction of the main office.

Mary glanced up from the letter she was typing. "Something about a replacement for Jim, I think." She pushed her glasses back up her nose as she finished speaking.

"Got any idea who?"

She shook her head. "Nope."

He knocked on the door marked "Jim Barrens, Plant Manager."

"Come," echoed from the other side.

Richard glanced back at Mary. "I'll let you know if I find out anything."

The smell of sweet, orange-tasting pipe smoke caught Richard as he pushed open the door. Behind the huge wooden desk that filled the left-hand side of the office sat a small, bald man with a long-stemmed pipe lodged in the side of his mouth. He wore a button-up, yellow golfer's sweater and a white shirt. It was old man Hallahan himself sitting in the plant manager's chair.

"Grab a seat," Hallahan said, pointing to the only available one in the room.

Richard pushed the door closed and sat quickly. He had worked for Hallahan for almost fifteen years and he still felt as if he stood in front of a school principal every time he saw the man. Richard loosened the collar of his shirt slightly and then rubbed his hands along the tops of his legs as Hallahan finished writing on the form and looked up.

"Well, Richard," he said, smiling and leaning back in his chair. "With Jim moving to California on us it looks as if we need a new plant manager. You got anyone you think might be good for the job?"

Richard shook his head. "Not right off. Can't say as I do."

"Well, then, to come right to the point, I've been thinking about you for the job."

For a moment Richard felt as if he had floated off the chair. The room was spinning and he gripped the arms of the chair to hold on.

Hallahan didn't seem to notice. He just went on. "You've been senior shop foreman for years now, doing me a good job. Hell, you know more about this plant than I do and I built it."

Somehow Richard managed to say, "Thank you, sir."

"Don't thank me just yet. I haven't given you the job and before I do I want to get one thing cleared up."

Richard frowned and took a deep breath. "What's that?"

"Your drinking. I can't have a plant manager who comes to work three mornings a week hung over."

"Sir, I—"

Hallahan held up his hand for Richard to stop. "I understand that you do a damn good job for me as shop foreman. And I'm not saying that your drinking hurts your work. It's just that I can't take the chance with someone I put in as plant manager."

Richard felt as if he had been punched in the gut. He didn't even realize his drinking was a problem, or that anyone even noticed except Stout and the gang down at the Garden. He usually had a few after work, but who didn't? He only tied a real bender on once or twice a week, but not once had he come to work drunk. So how did old Hallahan know?

Richard blinked hard a few times, trying to clear the blurring that filled both his mind and his eyes. Hallahan was watching him, his pipe held in one hand.

"Well, Richard. What do you say? You want the plant manager's job enough to give up drinking. Be a lot more work and a lot more money."

Richard gripped the edge of the chair hard.

What could he do?

What could he say?

SEVEN

THE BACKGROUND MUSIC seemed even louder as Richard opened his eyes and let go of the edge of his bar stool. He cradled his glass with both hands and then downed the entire thing in one long swallow.

The sword blinked at him, demanding to be touched.

Touch me and be the plant manager. Touch me and never get fired by the new plant manager.

Touch me and get a raise.

Touch me and stop drinking.

Touch me and change your life.

He wiped his forehead with the back of his sleeve. Why did they keep it so hot in here? It had to drive customers away.

The sword blinked.

He had a second chance. How many people got that? Never mind that it made

no sense at all. Never mind that it wasn't possible. He had to touch the sword. He couldn't let it fade again.

He pulled the napkin closer to him. Did he really want to be plant manager? When he had told Hallahan what he did on his free time was his business, Hallahan had hired someone else.

Richard had kept drinking.

He glanced down the bar at the bartender and then back at the napkin.

The question was fading.

He didn't have much time.

Quickly he tried to suck the last drops of bourbon off the ice. Plant manager? Why would he want to be plant manager? Stupid job with a lot of headaches. And if he had taken the job he would have had to put up with old man Hallahan every day.

The red letters of the question were now a light pink. The blinking of the sword was down to less than one per second. He wiped his forehead again with his sleeve. All he had to do was touch the sword.

A second chance.

Everyone wished for a second chance. But now that he was offered that chance, what should he do? Having a second chance seemed harder than the first time around.

Should he have finished school?

Or married Janice? Would his life be more exciting if he had? His life wasn't that bad as it was. He had a good job and good friends.

He held his shaking hand over the faint sword.

All he had to do was touch it.

Quick, before it faded.

His hand stayed suspended.

The sword faded.

With a deep, sucking breath he jammed his hand down on the sword, grinding it into the bar as if crushing out a cigarette.

Slowly the bar around him blurred.

The shields and swords behind the bar shimmered and appeared to melt down the wall.

He felt dizzy.

He felt pulled.

God, what had he done?

EIGHT

"RICHARD? RICHARD? YOU all right?"

Richard opened his eyes and glanced around at the familiar surroundings of the Garden Lounge. The old jukebox sat dark against the wall and there was a country-western tune on the tape player. The special Christmas drinking glasses were still in their locked case above the jukebox with the newly added picture of Stout. The red vinyl booths and center tables were empty of customers.

"What does it take for a fellow to get a drink around here?"

Richard glanced up at the huge frame of big Carl who was holding onto Richard's arm and trying to smile.

But Richard could tell he was concerned.

Ben, the overweight bar supplies salesman beside Carl was also looking worried. Ben's supply case was open on the end of the bar and straws, fruit picks, and other items were spread out on the polished wood.

Richard took a deep breath and sort of shook himself. "Must have got a little dizzy is all. I'm all right now."

Carl nodded, but the look of concern didn't leave his face as he moved back to his bar stool beside Terry. They were the only two regulars in this early in the afternoon.

"You been to the doc lately?" Terry asked. Terry worked nights as a male nurse and always worried about the gang's health around the bar.

"Last month," Richard said. "Gave me a clean bill all the way."

"Maybe you need something to drink," Ben said. "You might be just flushed. Was a warm day out there today."

Richard nodded. Maybe he did. He moved around behind the bar and quickly poured himself a bourbon water.

"What are you doing?" Carl asked. The sound of disbelief in his voice was so strong that Richard looked up into Carl's now seriously-worried face.

"Getting myself a drink," Richard said, glancing down at the glass. "Why?"

Carl slowly looked at Terry and then at Ben before he looked back at Richard.

All three men were looking very upset. "Is something wrong?"

Carl nodded slowly. "You don't drink."

Richard shook his head and tried to clear the fuzzy pictures mixing together. He could remember coming into the Garden every night for years and never once breaking his promise to old man Hallahan. He always drank soda with a lime. Not once had he touched a drink since he took the plant manager's job. And when he bought the Garden last year from Stout and quit the plant he hadn't started drinking again.

But it seemed that somehow, somewhere, he had just had a drink a few moments before. He could even remember the taste of the bourbon. He hadn't thought of that in years.

But he didn't drink. He knew that. And he wasn't going to start again.

Ever.

"Not sure where my head is," he said and dumped the bourbon down the sink. With a new glass he poured himself a soda and then squeezed a lime in it. The clean sharp taste cleared his head a little more and he took a second long swallow.

Carl shook his head and glanced at Terry.

"All right," Richard said, taking a deep breath and moving back down the bar to Ben. "Where were we?"

Stout held up a napkin with red letters and a sword. "You were looking at these."

Carl laughed. "Ugliest napkins I have ever seen."

"Yeah," Terry said. "They look like they belong in a restaurant."

"A hotel bar," Richard said, having a clear feeling he knew exactly where those belonged. He tossed the sword napkin upside down back into Ben's sample case.

"Give me a funny one. Bar napkins in the Garden Lounge are supposed to be funny."

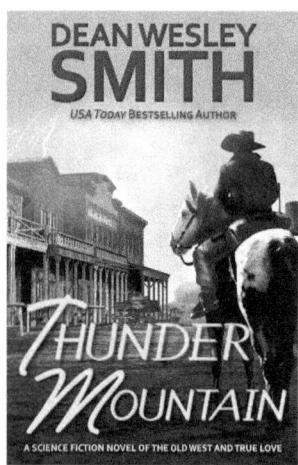

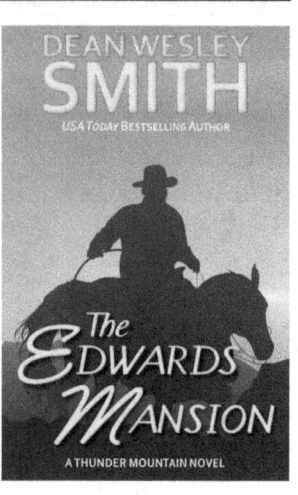

Now Available
from all your favorite booksellers in trade paper and electronic editions.

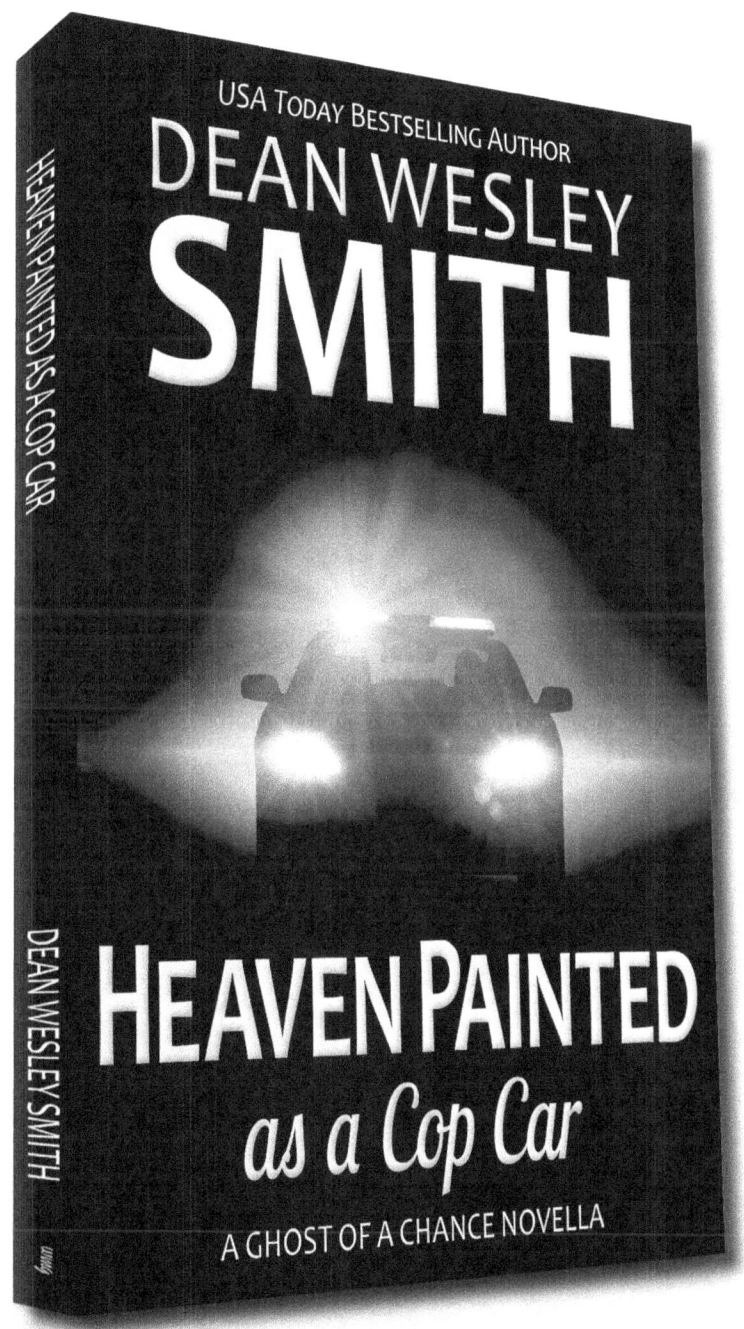

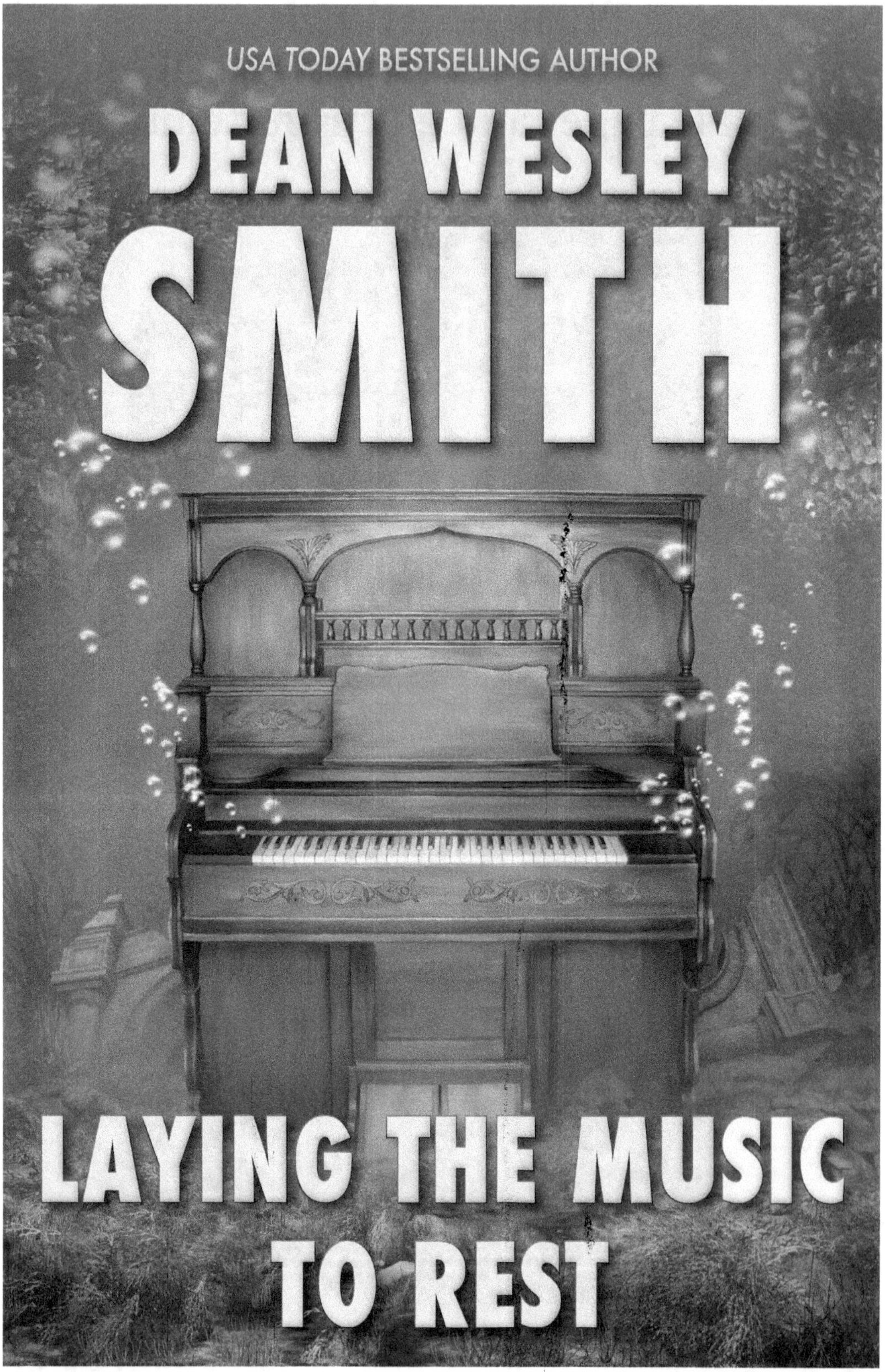
USA TODAY BESTSELLING AUTHOR
DEAN WESLEY
SMITH
LAYING THE MUSIC
TO REST

A former college professor turned bartender, Doc finds himself trying to save his friends from a ghost under a lake in the wilderness of Idaho.

From diving into a ghost town buried under a lake to trying to stay alive on the sinking deck of the Titanic, *this time-travel science fiction novel reads like a roller-coaster ride with all the twists and turns.*

First published in paperback in 1989 from Warner Questar Books, Dean Wesley Smith's first published novel gives a lot of hints of his future series and his bestselling career spanning over a hundred and fifty novels.

Published here in its original form, without any changes, just as Dean wrote it almost thirty years ago.

LAYING THE MUSIC TO REST

Part 2

CHAPTER TWO

Stibnite, Idaho
June 26, 1990

FOR THE LAST five hours I had watched Constance handle her four-wheel drive Jeep as if it were an extension of her right arm. She feathered into graveled corners, accelerated without a jerk, and knew exactly when to downshift to keep the best power to the wheels. In other words, she was a damn good driver.

Five hours of winding, mountain roads from Boise to the ghost town of Stibnite and not once had she taken a corner too fast. And never too slow. Never. There had been a few hundred times when I'd grabbed for the armrest while looking at the fast-approaching hillside or cliff. But each time she'd known the corner and her speed had been perfect. Of course, it always took me a few seconds to catch my breath after those corners, but I knew an amazing show of driving skill when I saw one.

Now we were on the flat ground of the old town of Stibnite and she was still making me grab for the armrest. She cut close to the remains of a large wooden building, swerved around two weathered piles of rock, and started the Jeep bouncing across a small meadow on what looked like no more than a vague memory of a road.

"Old town hall," she said, pointing back at the building we had missed by a door handle, her voice clear even over the constant drone of the engine and the rattling of our diving equipment. "Last building to be actively used in Stibnite. Abandoned somewhere around 1948, I think."

I nodded. For the last few miles I had been getting a lecture on the history of Stibnite. In its prime, during World War II, thousands had lived here…now it looked like an abandoned battlefield. Tumbled and ruined buildings, piles of dredged rock, and open mining pits half-filled with stagnant water dotted the obviously leveled valley floor. The site of the town itself stretched up the narrow, steep-walled valley. Before the mining boom, the valley must have been spectacular. Now it was nothing more than a monument to what human beings could do to something beautiful if given a free hand. It was no wonder everyone had moved away when the mines shut down. They probably all went looking for other valleys to destroy. With any luck, they'd all left Idaho.

The goat path Constance was using as a road veered suddenly to the right past a stand of pine and merged into what actually was a road, albeit a low-quality logging road. From the looks of it, the road was only maintained for fire access.

"It'll be fairly quick from here," she said. "About eight more miles to the summit. All up hill."

The road stays this good?" I said, joking. The thought of eight miles on this poor excuse for a logging road seemed no small distance.

"It gets a little washed out toward the top. But no worry. We'll make it."

"People find their way into your place?" It didn't seem possible that, even with the best of directions, I would have recognized those faint tracks across the field as a road, let alone the right road in the maze of old buildings and mining pits called Stibnite.

"Oh, really it's simple," she said. "I just took you on the scenic route. We tell our customers to stay on the main road heading up the river out of Yellow Pine. The gravel turns into this logging road about a mile beyond the point I turned and went into Stibnite. There are real clear signs pointing the way. Haven't had anyone get lost yet. Of course, customers we sign up pretty much know what they're getting into. That's why they want to stay at our place. It's away from things."

"I'll drink to that," I said, and Constance laughed.

"See what you've been missing not coming up all these summers?"

I glanced out over the tops of the pine trees as we climbed away from the valley floor on a road that was becoming no wider than the Jeep plus two door handles, with dirt brushing the handle on Constance's side and high-flying eagles pecking at the one on mine. There was no doubt that the stunning beauty of the Idaho mountains could make a person stop and stare for hours. But like all beauty, danger went hand-in-hand with it, and right now I was more concerned about the wheel on my side not dropping off into space.

I did the only thing I could do without letting Constance know how scared I was. I grasped my seat belt just below the seat on my door side while forcing my left hand to stay calmly on my leg. And the higher we climbed, the more I hoped she knew how to fly a plane.

Constance didn't seem to notice the road any more than she had the paved, two-lane road out of Boise. She took each corner at what seemed to be the maximum possible speed, her left hand steering and her right hand resting on the stick shift.

"You know, don't you?" she said, "that Fred's really happy about you coming up? I think if this mess with the ghost hadn't come up, he would have invented something just to drag you away from that plant-filled bar."

"Did he invent the ghost?"

Constance turned to look at me for a quick moment before darting the Jeep through a dry streambed. "No, I'm afraid it's there," she said. "And it's as real as a ghost can be."

She didn't look happy. This ghost thing had her worried far beyond anything I had ever seen Constance concerned about before. I forced myself to look out over the valley without glancing at the edge of the road flashing by, inches from the front wheel.

These were my two best friends and they were hurting. I wanted to help, but what could I do against a ghost? What could anyone do?

Especially this far from anything. It suddenly occurred to me that in the last three hours of driving, we had not met a single car. Not one. As Constance said, this was away from things. A long damn way away.

Below I could see the faint outline of a mountain stream as it cut through the pine and brush. Back down the valley I could see a mountain range that faded into the distance on the clear, summer day. Ahead, there was only up.

***

My ears popped seven times in eight miles.

And, as Constance had warned, the road didn't get better, it got worse. At one point we had to get out and move fallen rock out of the way. At another tight switchback, Constance had to back up two nerve-destroying times to keep the front end from banging into the hill. The second time she ground into reverse I swore she was backing right out into space.

"Last switchback and we're on top," Constance shouted over the noise of the engine as she cut the corner hard and at the same time shifted into low and let the Jeep's tires eat at the road, spraying dual fishtails of sand and dirt out behind us.

I had completely given up on hiding my fear and was holding on to the dash with both hands. I always thought that as I got older, I would fear death less and less. That basically had come to pass, but what I hadn't counted on was my increased fear of accidents. Death no longer bothered me. Accidents scared me something awful. Especially when I wasn't in control. This road would have bothered me even if I had been driving. But sitting in the passenger seat, the eight miles had been pure and simple torture.

I glanced at my watch. Forty-five minutes since we had left Stibnite. We must have gone through twenty switchbacks, across five streambeds, and straddled six miles of washed-out gullies down the center of the two tire tracks. From the first mile I had kept looking up thinking that the summit was only a little bit farther. But with every turn it never came any closer. The mountain just seemed to grow as we climbed it.

But finally, mercifully, the road widened and then cut up on top of the ridge. Constance leisurely wound the Jeep in and out of trees. The summit could have passed for Mid-western flatland, if not for the fact that if I looked real hard through the trees on either side, I could see blue sky and mountaintops for fifty miles in all directions.

The road ended in a widened turnaround with a large Forest Service sign blocking the remains of a trail continuing off through the trees. The sign said,

FRANK CHURCH SALMON RIVER
PRIMITIVE AREA. NO VEHICLES
ALLOWED PAST THIS POINT.

Constance pulled the Jeep off under the pines to the right. Two other rigs were parked among the trees. One I recognized as Fred's rebuilt pickup truck. The other was a blue Ford two-door sedan. It looked like any standard airport rental car and felt incredibly out of place sitting up here on the edge of the primitive area. I had trouble believing that anyone could even get it up

the road. But, short of having it airlifted in, someone must have, because there it sat.

Constance honked two long blasts on the horn, then cut off the engine. The silence seemed louder than the engine. I let go of the dashboard one finger at a time as Constance laughed, then unsnapped my seat belt, and pushed open the door.

The mountain air was as welcome as opening a refrigerator on a hot summer day. I took a deep breath of the freshest-tasting air I could ever remember and let it slowly out, along with five years of built-up tension. The crisp, cold feel of the air let a flood of memories back in. Memories of dives into cold Canadian lakes and the taste of hot coffee while sitting beside the fire afterward. Memories of camping as a kid, helping Dad put up the tent while Mom fixed lunch. Memories of the first nights with Carla at the retreat and how golden her skin looked in the faint starlight.

I took a few more deep breaths to let the memories drift their natural course, then did a few deep knee bends to loosen some of the tense muscles. Ten seconds of mountain air and I was starting to understand why Constance and Fred came up here every summer.

Constance scooted around to the back of the Jeep and started unloading the equipment, piling it on the thick carpet of pine needles.

"It'll take Fred a few minutes to get the horses and get them here," Constance said, as I joined her. "I hope he heard us coming up the mountain and got them ready."

"You weren't kidding when you mentioned me riding a horse, were you?" I pulled one of the double scuba tanks out of the back and stood it against the wheel of the Jeep. "You know how long it's been since I rode a horse?"

"Do I win something if I guess right?"

"No."

"Then what's the point of guessing?" she asked as she pulled out a large sack of groceries.

"So you won't laugh when I fall off."

"I'll still laugh."

Before I had a chance to answer, there was a loud snapping of branches and Fred appeared out of the trees on the left side of the clearing. He was riding backwards on a medium-sized brown horse while leading seven other horses.

It was the funniest sight I had seen in a long time. His long legs dangled down the side of the horse, his feet only loosely caught backwards in the stirrups. He looked like Ichabod Crane, except he had on blue work jeans, a red plaid work shirt, and the most beat-up excuse for a baseball cap I had ever seen. He even had the damn cap on backwards.

Constance looked over at me. "He does that all the time. Says it works better when he has to lead more than three horses. I'm waiting for a low tree limb to knock him on his nose."

I just kept laughing. Fred smiled and tipped his cap as the train of horses filled the small turnaround. He was still the same old Fred. Down in town, he had lost some of his craziness over the past few years. But up here, it was clear that he was his old self. Probably the thin air did things to his brain.

Constance moved to help him with the horses and I followed.

"Glad to see you could make it, barkeep," Fred said as he dismounted, somehow without kicking the horse in the head. His handshake was firm. His skin felt hard and calloused against my bartender-soft hand.

"Wouldn't have missed seeing your trick riding for all the money in the world. Besides, that Sunday drive up the mountain is a real thrill a minute."

Fred chuckled as he unhooked two horses from the string and tied them to a tree. "Constance doesn't believe in wasting any time, does she?"

"It wasn't that bad," Constance said as she led two other horses toward the Jeep.

I held up my hands, fingers curled. "Permanent white knuckles."

Some Classic Jukebox Stories
Available at your favorite booksellers.

"Comes with age," Constance said. "And you certainly aren't getting any younger. Besides, I got us here, didn't I?"

"And just in time," Fred said. "Lunch is cooking and I wasn't planning on waiting for you two."

I glanced at my watch. It was only eleven in the morning yet it seemed like we'd been on the road a full day. Or more like a full lifetime.

We spent the next half hour packing all the dive gear and supplies on the horses while chatting about everything except the ghost and the lodge. By the time we were done, I was sweating and a little out of breath from the high altitude. But I felt better inside than I had in years. There was something about being out in the mountains with close friends that surrounds a person with a warm glow of belonging. Maybe it was the openness of the air and the trees. Or maybe it was the lack of the confines of buildings that reminded us of our pasts. All I knew was that working there with Constance and Fred made me feel good.

Fred's "cooked" lunch consisted of ham sandwiches and cold lemonade, with the promise of a better lunch once we reached the valley floor. We ate quickly and before I knew it, I was on a horse for the first time in too many years and headed off into the Idaho primitive area.

***

Two and a half hours later we reached the Monumental Valley floor. My back ached, the insides of both legs were rubbed raw, and my face felt as if it were coated with three inches of dust. I had completely lost any feelings of wellbeing

I had had about the trip. Now all I wondered was why anyone would want to do something like this for fun.

Not that it hadn't been fantastic at the start. The trail along the summit had stayed wide, winding its way along the ridge for about a mile through open meadows and stands of pine. The clear smell of the air, the warm sun, the power of the horses had made everything seem so easy.

The trail had turned to the right and headed down the side of a ridge into a picture-postcard valley. The steep walls on both sides cut upward to end in linked chains of rocky mountain peaks. Patches of snow still dotted the walls of the valley, reflecting the sun like slivers of mirrors. Far below I could see flashes of deep blue as a stream wound its way through the trees.

At that point in the trail I could look back and see where we had been riding. The cars were parked on a low saddle between the mountain ridges. The valley we were dropping into seemed to dead-end into that saddle.

"It's nothing but downhill from here," Fred had said at that point. He hadn't been kidding. The trail became so narrow and so steep, that I found myself leaning into the hill for fear of sliding off the horse and not hitting the ground for hundreds of feet. Fred and Constance didn't seem to mind, even the two times we had to stop, dismount, and lead the horses across places where mud and rocks had slid down the mountain and wiped the trail away.

About a hundred yards beyond where the trail bottomed out, Fred led us down into a small meadow beside what he said was Monumental Creek. I let Fred take my horse and the packhorse I had been leading and tie them up while I found a nice, solid rock next to the stream and proceeded to alternate taking a drink and washing my face off with the icy water. By the time I felt refreshed enough to wander back up to the meadow, Constance had a fire going in a ring of rocks near a small grove of trees and Fred had a hammock strung and was already stretched out in it.

"Looks like you two stop here regularly," I said, pointing at prerigged hammock hooks on the trees.

"Every time," Constance said. "We take turns cooking and lying in the hammock. Doing the entire trip to the summit is just too much without a rest. We usually stop here for an hour or so. Gives the muscles time to loosen back up. Plus we figured our guests would like it here."

"And the creek there has a little color in it," Fred said. "I show the guests how to work a pan. They get a kick out of it."

"You're kidding," I said, glancing back at where I had washed my face.

"Don't let Fred get you going," Constance said. "There's very little gold left in that stream. And besides, the water will freeze your hands blue after only one try."

"Not if you do it right," Fred said. "Trust me, there's gold in there. I don't have the source spotted yet. It's somewhere above here, but I haven't had the time to go searching, what with building the lodge and everything. Bet you haven't dipped a pan in years. You want to give it a go?"

"Next time," I said, more interested than I let show. I sat on a cut-off stump and watched as Constance expertly built us a quick snack.

"You know," I said, finally breaking the unspoken rule that we wouldn't talk about the ghost or the dive until later. "What I would really like to know is more about this old town. What are we going to find down there? You got any idea?"

Fred shook his head. "Not much, I'm afraid. They didn't believe in securing buildings to foundations in the old mining towns. And since all the buildings were made of logs, everything floated, broke apart, and jammed into where the stream

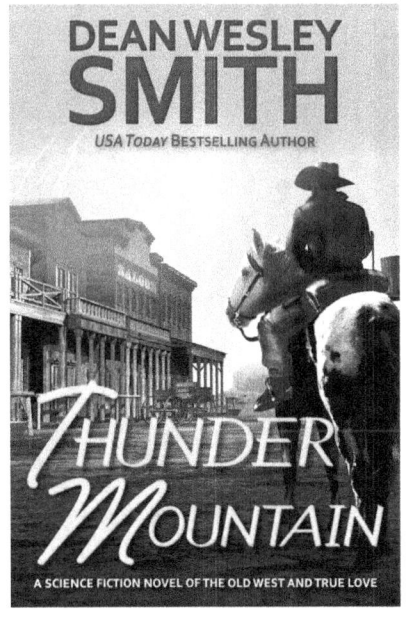

USA Today *bestselling author Dean Wesley Smith weaves a science fiction tale of love and survival of two modern professors dealing with the past.*

Offered a free trip into a remote Idaho wilderness that she loves and studies, Professor Dawn Edwards can't refuse. On the trip she meets Professor Madison Rogers.

But living in the Old West proves to be a brutal task. Somehow, Dawn must survive to rescue herself, her friends, and the man she has come to love.

topped over the slide. There's a huge log-jam there. The water is as cold as that stream and with the long, frozen winters, I doubt if there will be much down there but old foundations and a lot of junk.

"So what's the point? Won't the old site be covered with two or three feet of silt?"

Fred shrugged. "Most of the town site is in about seventy to eighty feet of water. There's going to be some silt, but not as much as you might guess. The lake is relatively near the top of this valley and the stream doesn't have much time to pick up the mud and sediment that would fill in the lake. What sand and stuff the stream does pick up is dropped near the upper end. There's a pretty good sandbar built up there over the years. It has some color in it too."

"So how big was this town?"

"During the peak mining seasons," Constance said, "over five thousand people. The last few years before the flood, the gold boom had started to die off and on the day the slide buried the town,

there were less than seven hundred living there. Of course, that was in the spring and the summer influx of miners hadn't yet returned."

Fred shook his head and the hammock with him. "That town was an amazing place. It was famous for its saloons, wild summer nights, and pianos."

"Pianos?" I asked. "Why would a town be famous for its pianos?"

"Because there were seven of them in town," Fred said. "All in the main saloons."

"So?" I couldn't figure out why pianos in a 1909 town were such a big deal. I always figured there were a lot of them around.

"You just came down the main trail," Fred said, gesturing at the hill above us. "That trail hasn't changed much in seventy years. Can you imagine getting a piano down that?"

"You're kidding?"

"Nope," Constance said. "There are two other trails in the area. Both worse.

One comes in over the summit up Mule Creek. That's where the Dewey Mine was. The other comes up Monumental Creek from the River of No Return area of the Salmon. There was never a wagon in Roosevelt that wasn't built there. Yet somehow they had seven pianos."

"Amazing," I said, glancing up at the tall mountains that towered above us like huge walls.

"Sure is, isn't it?" Fred said. "And the music's pretty amazing, too."

The voice in the back of my head screamed at me not to ask. But I was already into this mess past the point of turning back, so I did anyway. "Music?"

"Damn it, Fred," Constance said. "Give him time to get used to the ghost before springing anything else on him."

"It's part of the ghost," Fred said.

"There's more than the ghost?" I asked. I didn't like the sound of that.

"We're not sure the music is caused by the ghost," Constance said.

"I think it is," Fred said. "Makes lots of sense."

"Would someone please tell me about this music?"

Fred looked at Constance and then smiled. Constance shook her head in disgust and went back to working at the food. "Every so often," Fred said, "usually in the evenings, someone starts playing a piano."

"And I assume you're going to tell me you don't have one and neither do the neighbors." This entire thing was starting to stretch even my belief in Fred. They had to be suckering me into some big joke that they'd spring when we got to the lodge. Angie was probably involved in it too, and they would be laughing at me for months.

"That's right," Fred said with the straightest face I had ever seen. He had a good poker face. But after all the years, I knew when he was wearing it. This time he was being dead serious. And he looked embarrassed about it.

I turned to Constance. "Is he kidding?"

She shook her head no. I could see in her eyes she too was telling the truth.

I just sat there. A ghost that roamed around a lake. And someone playing piano music in the middle of the Idaho wilderness. It was all too much. If it hadn't been Fred and Constance I wouldn't have listened to it for a moment.

Constance handed Fred, then me, a cup of coffee. The smell was like a comforting hand that said I hadn't yet left the world of reality. Coffee was civilization and civilization was still here, at least for the time being.

"Why don't you tell him about the legend?" Constance said.

"There's a legend, too?" I asked. "No, don't tell me. Big Foot drops by every twenty years and he's due this week. Right?"

Fred laughed. "Believe it or not, there really is a legend about the music. Constance found it down at the historical society after our first visit up here. It's in some book—"

"*Legends of the Frontier*," Constance said, "by Nelson. A great book."

"Yeah," Fred said. "It is. The one about the music is called *The Legend of Lake Roosevelt*. I got a copy of it here somewhere. It'll be just as easy if I read it to you." Fred climbed out of the hammock and rummaged in one of the saddlebags they'd brought over to the clearing. After a short moment, he pulled a few folded sheets of paper out and opened them up. He didn't get back into the hammock, but instead sat in it like a chair and rocked as he studied the paper in his hands.

He took a sip on his coffee, then looked up. "You ready?"

I shrugged. "Couldn't be any wilder than some of the things I've heard so far."

He laughed. "True. Here goes: 'To hear the pianos of Roosevelt, the listener must follow instructions.'"

"A legend with instructions?" I tried not to snicker. "What do you have to do, climb the third tree from the lake and put your ear to the trunk?"

"You really don't have to do anything," Constance said. "You can hear the music all over the valley."

She said it so matter-of-factly, it made me shudder. I suddenly had a great desire to stand and move back out into the warm sun of the meadow and let the heat on my shoulders remind me I really hadn't gone crazy. But I sipped my coffee instead as Fred started reading again.

"The listener is to make camp at the upper end of the lake where Monumental Creek has laid a fine carpet of sand and rock, overgrown in places with light brush. The valley walls on both sides will be steep, climbing almost vertically for thousands of feet. The slope to the left as you face the lake will be tree-covered and thick with brush."

"That's where the lodge and cabins are," Constance said. "About three hundred feet above the water. Had to clear a massive amount of scrub."

"She's not kidding there," Fred said, holding up his hand. "Remember those thick callouses we used to show you every fall?"

I nodded.

"Bush and logs," he said. Then he went back to reading.

"The slope to the right, the West, will be mostly free of tall pine. Instead it will be covered with large rockslides and cliff faces."

"Is that where the slide came from?" I asked.

Constance shook her head. "Nope. It was on that side of the canyon all right. But the slide was completely mud and whatever else it picked up along the way. The slide came down Mule Creek which drains into Monumental right below the town. A lot of the mining was up Mule Creek, so that's why they built the town where they did. Besides that, it was the widest place in miles."

"You know," Fred said, "there's still two cases of dynamite unexploded under that slide? They tried to blow it to stop the slide, but it didn't go off."

"You mean they had time to fight it?"

Fred nodded. "Lots of time. The accounts of what happened that night say the slide was moving about as fast as a man could walk. It started three miles up Mule Creek, right below the Dewey Mine."

I just shook my head. "Could the dynamite still be dangerous?"

"I doubt it," Fred said. "Would take something pretty strong to set it off, even if it was still any good after eighty years in the ground."

"Amazing," I said, again.

Fred nodded and went back to reading the legend.

"The sand flat above the lake will be marked with stone fireplace rings, black pimples against the white sand. The listener should choose to camp to the right of the trail that leads to the lake from Monumental Summit and at the nearest fireplace ring to the lake and the rock slope."

"A few people still camp there every summer," Constance said. "But they rarely stay for longer than a night. The place spooks them."

"I can understand that," I said. "It spooks me and I haven't even seen it yet."

"The listener should have dinner early. Then, as the light slowly drains from the sky between the towering ridges the listener should let the crackling of the camp's fire die down."

Fred looked quickly up as Constance set his lunch beside him on a stump.

"The listener should then beware. His ears will pick out other sounds from the forest twilight. Birds fluttering in the branches. Fish jumping after one last insect. Maybe even the sound of a chipmunk clattering up among the rocks. The listener must try to push those sounds into the background."

As Fred read, I found myself becoming aware of all the sounds around us. The fire's soft cracking as it licked the bottom of the large water pot Constance had sitting across two rocks. The slight breeze clipping the tops of the trees with a light brushing sound. The clear, but distant background bubbling of the creek as it tumbled over rocks on its way toward the submerged town. And every so often, the cawing of a distant hawk cut through the clear air of the valley and echoed off the mountain walls.

"The listener must now try to focus his attention completely on the cold water of the lake. He must try to imagine the old Main Street spread out at his feet. He must see the miners as they celebrated the end of the day and their success or failure in the saloons that framed the street like nails in a coffin lid. Then, and only then, will the listener hear the music of Lake Roosevelt."

Fred looked up at me with a raised-eyebrow sort of look.

"Some crazy legend." I took another sip of coffee. Damn, it was getting cold in this shady little nook. The sunlight that filled the meadow looked like water to a thirsty man. I took a big gulp of the hot coffee and let the heat work its way toward my stomach. Fred and his damn ghost stories. If this was all a joke, I was going to kill him.

"There's still more to it," Fred said as Constance handed me a plate filled with corn, potato chips, and a great-smelling hamburger.

Constance filled her plate while Fred and I took big bites of our hamburgers. Then Fred went back to reading from the papers in his lap.

"If the listener hears the music, he must understand the reason is a simple one. The town submerged before him prided itself on one aspect more than even the gold it fought out of the hills and streams. Its pianos."

Fred glanced up at me, then over at Constance. Then he continued.

"Seven pianos, one for each of the famous saloons along Main Street. Every night, the seven battling pianos filled the narrow valley with sound, pouring from their gun-barrel saloon doors. And for years, the pines took every song and held it in their sap and their needles. The rocks let the notes seep into their cracks and crevices like water, then trapped them. The great mountains, Thunder to the west, Monumental to the east, took the music and laid a net of echoes between them until the songs supported themselves in the night without touching the stars.

"The listener must be alert, for the concert only lasts a short time. The mountains and the rocks and the trees are jealous of their songs. Also, the listener should not be surprised if all but one of the pianos drops out of the musical war. The listener who hears this should consider himself treated to a special concert, for the remaining piano's music will be

clear and crisp, as if the listener were standing right outside the saloon door. The playing will be fine, practiced. But the song will feel sad and somehow lost. The listener should look around as the dim night shadows of the pines will seem to sway to the melody of the solo.

"And, if the listener still has the courage at this point to not throw an extra log on the fire and start whistling his own tune, he just might recognize the song."

Fred stopped reading and folded the paper.

"You might get to hear the music tonight," Constance said.

"Lovely," I said. "Just lovely. And we're going to make a dive down into that lake?"

Fred nodded. "Crazy, huh?"

I nodded and took a bite of my hamburger. Crazy didn't even begin to describe what we were going to do.

CHAPTER THREE

Monumental Lodge
June 26, 1990

"ALMOST THERE," FRED said over his shoulder as we rounded a curve and started to climb. "You'll be able to see the lake in another hundred yards or so."

I nodded and tried to adjust my position in the saddle for the thousandth time in the last four miles. There wasn't a spot left on my ass that wasn't sore or bruised. Four o'clock in the morning had been a long time ago.

The sun had dropped below the edge of the high mountains and over the last few hours the line between bright light and dark shadows had worked its way up the steep slopes like the waterline in a filling bathtub, leaving the tops of the mountains tinted pink. The moment the direct sunlight had left the valley floor, the air had turned a crisp, biting cold. Three miles back I had put on both my sweater and light jacket, and if the ride went on much farther, I was going to ask Fred to stop so that I could dig out my ski parka.

The main trail branched to the left and climbed hard up the left side of the valley away from the streambed we had been following. Fred took the high road and after a short distance pointed down. Through a gap in the trees I could see a small section of the lake and the part of the sandbar the legend had talked about. In the shadow-filled light, the water looked black, as if the valley was filled from side to side with a pool of ink. Every so often a ripple spread out on the glass surface as an insect or fish broke the calm.

At first nothing about the small lake seemed unusual as I studied it through the branches of the trees. No ghost walked its banks. No music stirred from its black depths. It seemed like any of the hundreds of other small mountain lakes I had seen over the years.

Almost. The more I studied it, the more the lake felt different. Colder. Alien.

I pulled my jacket tight in front and tried not to shiver. The thought of diving into those black waters seemed ludicrous. Granted, Fred and I had pulled a lot of crazy stunts over the years. And by and large got away with them. But somewhere, sometime, there was going to be one we couldn't do.

Up ahead, Fred turned left off the main trail, kicking his horse to move straight up the steep slope. The two packhorses he was leading scrambled to follow.

Through the trees farther down the main trail I could see a two-story log structure built into the side of the steep hill. Two large windows on the main floor stood guard over a wide clearing and the black lake. Both windows gave off a yellow glow that lit the deck railing around the front of the building. Smoke curled from the top of a rough stone chimney on the near end, giving me a sense of warmth that cut through the chill.

At the same spot, I turned to follow Fred. As firmly as I could, I coaxed my horse up the steep slope, at any moment fearing that either a cinch would come loose and I would slide right off the back to be trampled by the packhorse, or that my horse would just tip over from being on too steep a slope and smash down on top of me. I'd seen that happen in a dozen old movies and it always made me flinch.

Miraculously neither happened and I made it up to the log stable behind the main building, breathing hard, but still seated on all the spots the saddle had rubbed raw.

Fred dismounted and tied his horse to a long bar outside the back door of the lodge. I nudged my horse into place beside Fred's packhorses and then did my best to dismount without kicking anyone or anything.

I'd thought I was sore while sitting. Getting down, I felt so stiff it was a wonder I could move at all. My legs felt weak, almost as if my weight was too much for them. I leaned against the horse and took turns shifting from one foot to the other to give each a fair shot at recovery.

"Here we are," Fred said. "That wasn't so bad, now was it?"

Constance moved her horse into place beside my packhorse and slowly dismounted, obviously feeling some of the same aches that I did.

"Ask me in the morning," I said. "Assuming that I live that long." I rubbed the back of my legs and then my shoulders. My body was so full of kinks I didn't know where to rub first. My face felt like it had two inches of dust on it and if I smiled too hard, it would all cake right off, taking the first four layers of skin with it.

Fred moved around to help Constance with the two packhorses she had been leading. "Believe it or not," Constance said, leaning against the rail and brushing one layer of dust off, "we feel exactly the same way the first few trips in and out every spring. But you almost get used to it."

"Don't let her kid you," Fred said. "You'll be able to hear her groan clear across the valley when she crawls out of bed tomorrow morning."

"It will be a duet, I'm sure," I said.

Both of them laughed. The thousand aches that made up my body didn't think it was so funny.

"Twenty minutes to get this all unloaded and the horses taken care of." Fred said. "Then you can hit the hot shower. Guaranteed to work wonders on horse-type aches and pains." He looked over at where Constance was pulling a saddlebag off one horse. "Whose turn is it to cook?"

"You know whose turn it is," Constance said, as she carried the saddlebag over and dropped it with a loud thump on the wooden back porch of the lodge. "And it's not going to even get started until I get into a hot shower and then some clean clothes. Besides, if I cook, you do the horses. Remember?"

Fred patted the neck of the horse he had been riding. "How could I ever forget?"

***

It took closer to an hour before we had all the gear stored, my bag up in my room on the second floor of the lodge, and my body standing under a hot shower washing away the smell of horses. Fred made me promise that no matter how good it felt, I would make it quick. Hot water was scarce since all they had was one water heater powered by a generator. He didn't want to take a cold shower.

I promised him. But it was a hard promise to keep.

After far too short a time, I fought my way out of the shower, put on a fresh pair of cotton work pants, my most comfortable shirt, and a thick wool sweater. I carried my shoes and padded in my socks down the wooden stairs.

The Monumental Lodge was one of those big, open-roomed places where the minute you walked in, you just knew deep down inside that you'd found the home you'd always wanted. The walls and rafters were all made of large, rough logs, filled in between with a light brown chinking. The kitchen sat in the right back corner as you entered from the main door. Directly to the right of the main door, in front of a large, small-paned window that overlooked the lower end of the lake, was a huge wooden table with a dozen chairs around it.

A stone fireplace filled the left wall, surrounded by a number of handmade couches and chairs padded with an abundance of throw pillows. The stairs went up the back wall to the one bathroom and two bedrooms upstairs. I dropped my shoes by the front door and walked slowly around the room, glancing at a few of the old pictures and odd knickknacks. The room made me feel cozy and warm, even with only a small fire in the massive mouth of the fireplace.

Constance had been first in the shower and she was now preparing dinner.

"Feel better?" she asked as I wandered into the kitchen.

"Six thousand percent," I said. "Anything I can do to help?"

"Sure is. See that cabinet there beside the back door?"

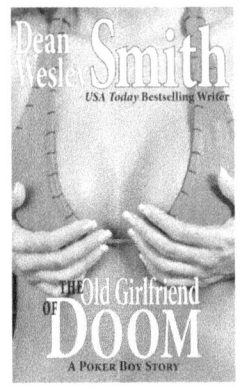

I nodded. It was a rough wood cabinet with no sign of a lock. An old picture of six miners standing with shovels in front of an open mine shaft hung beside it.

She slid a ceramic mug across the counter. "Pour a little rum in that for me. Then fix yourself whatever you want. Figure I might as well let you do what you do best."

I picked up her mug, enjoying the heavy feel of the stoneware in my hand. "What's this for? Rum toddy?"

"Hot buttered rum."

"Sounds too good to pass. Toss me a mug too."

She slid another across the counter and I went to the well-stocked liquor cabinet.

"You folks sure know how to spend your summers," I said, inspecting the supply of booze that would have made a small public bar proud.

"It's been a lot of work."

"Obviously. All a person has to do is look at this place to see that. Have I told you how impressed I am with all this?"

Constance looked at me with one of those very serious expressions reserved for marriages, funerals, or corporate boardrooms. "You mean it?"

"Of course I do. This place is fantastic."

"That means a lot to me," she said. "Really. Make sure you tell Fred. He's afraid you'll think this is all stupid. What with the ghost and all."

"It's far from stupid. And I'll make sure Fred knows that. All right?"

"Thanks," Constance said. She gave me one of her light-up-the-room smiles and went back to working on dinner.

"In fact," I said, "even if you can't think of a better way to get me in here than on some stupid horse, I think you've made a regular customer out of me. Assuming, of course, I survive the ride out."

"You will," Constance said. "Wait until you see the cabins. They're really cozy. Perfect for that getaway with your current lady. And that reminds me, just who is your current lady these days?"

Three Seeders Universe Novels
Available at your favorite booksellers.

"No one," I said, and then kneeled down in front of the liquor cabinet. That was one topic I really didn't feel like talking about. In the years since Carla had died, I had spent very little time with any other woman. Somehow, I would end up comparing every one to Carla and that would be the end of that. For most of the last year I'd been keeping company only with myself and almost enjoying it. At least, that's what I kept repeating to myself. Just as I kept telling myself I enjoyed tending bar at the Garden.

I finished putting the rum in the two mugs and went back to the counter. "Mix?" I held up the mugs.

"In the fridge. And the water should be almost boiling."

I dug the mix out, added the hot water, and then sat down on one of the bar stools facing across the counter into the kitchen as Constance began her standard quiz about my invisible love life. For years she had been trying to set me up with one woman after another. None of the ones she had picked had ever lasted more than a date or two. But she showed no signs of giving up.

Fred came down the stairs at the same time footsteps sounded on the front deck, the front door opened, and two people came in without knocking.

I turned around on my stool, cradling my hot buttered rum in my hands, and studied the two new arrivals as they took off their heavy jackets and hung them on hooks beside the front door. They did it without hesitation, as if they were very used to doing so.

The man looked to be in his late thirties, about my height, maybe six foot one, with a full head of graying black hair, and a sincere smile. Clear across the room, I liked the guy. I didn't want to like him.

But for some reason, on first glance, I did. Annoying. Damned annoying.

That happened once in a while with a customer in the Garden. I would like certain people even before they said a word. The ones that I had been lucky enough to get to know ended up following along with my first impression. It had also happened a lot back when I was teaching. There was always one, sometimes two, students in the class that I would instantly like. It had been hard not to give the favorites too much extra attention. Angie had been one of those students.

The woman was young, maybe middle twenties. She had striking silver hair, cut in a short, page-boy haircut. She wore a "University of Idaho" sweatshirt and Levi's as if they were the most natural things in the world. I could tell that her small green eyes didn't miss a thing. The feeling I had about her was one of distrust. No more reason for it than for my liking the guy.

Fred, now wearing a thick baggy sweater and a wool stocking cap on his bald head, did the introductions and I again assumed my role as bartender. Susan Rule wanted a touch of gin with a lot of soda. A very unusual combination. Professor Steven Jerome wanted scotch, a splash of water, lots of ice. He was a drinker's drinker. Another reason I liked him.

I handed Steven his drink, then slid Susan's across the table to where she had sat with her back to the now-dark window. As I did, I noticed she was staring at me as if trying to remember something and not really being able to.

"Fred said your name was Kellogg Jones?" she asked after I sat back down on my stool at the counter. "Do you happen to go by a nickname of some sort or another?"

I nodded.

"Sure," Fred said as he sat down at the table with a can of beer. "Everyone calls him Doc. Why?"

Susan's face drained of color and she looked quickly down into her drink. Then, as if deciding that the drink would help, took a deep gulp of it.

"Why?" I asked, after I got over shuddering from the thought of how bad gin and soda must taste. "Have we ever met?" I knew we hadn't. I'd have remembered her. With or without the silver hair.

"No, we haven't," she said after a quick moment in which all of us looked at her. She smiled a weak smile. "The name reminds me of someone out of my past, that's all."

"I hope it's not a bad memory," I said. Judging from her reaction, there didn't seem much hope of that.

"No, it's fine. Your name just caught me a little off guard, that's all."

I nodded, not believing a word she was saying. "I'd change it if I could, but you know."

She laughed. "No, really. I like the name a lot. Honest." She looked me square in the eye and we held the pose for a moment. I didn't know what to think by the time she looked down into the depths of her drink and her own thoughts. There was a lot more to this woman than what showed through the surface. And she was not as young as I had thought. No one had old eyes like that without having lived awhile. No one.

***

The rest of our informal cocktail hour and dinner was filled with laughing conversation and short history lessons about everyone involved, except Susan. She steered the conversation expertly away from anything about herself, always directing it back to someone else. She was a master at it, like a good teacher who could keep the students talking.

The meal was one of those fun meals between friends and strangers where everyone was relaxed and seemed to share a common sense of adventure. Being that far back in the wilderness made everyone friendlier, more open. In my trips to mountain lakes, I always found that occurrence interesting. And I was not immune to it.

It wasn't until after Fred and I had the dishes cleared up and everyone was sitting in the big living area around the built-up fire that the topic of the ghost came up.

I started it.

"Steven," I said, trying to keep my voice as conversational as I could, "what do you think of this ghost I've been hearing about?"

Steven shrugged and took a sip of his after-dinner drink, Constance's lodge-made eggnog. He looked no more concerned about the question than if I had just asked him what time it was. "She's just a trapped spirit," he said. "And damned unhappy. One of the clearest cases in recorded study."

"Clearest what?" I asked.

"Oh, sorry," he said. "She makes more obvious appearances than any other spirit I have ever seen or read about. Very regular and very consistent."

"So this is a real ghost, then?" I asked, then glanced over at Constance and shrugged. I couldn't help it. She smiled at me.

"In the common definition of the term ghost, yes. She is very real. By the way, her name is Gretchen."

I didn't want to ask how he knew that yet, so I turned to Susan. "And you've seen this ghost? She's real as far as you're concerned?"

"Very much so," Susan said. "And anything possible should be done to free her so that she can move on. It makes me really sad every time she walks."

I sat back against the pillows of the couch and stared into the fireplace. My intellect was saying go ahead and buy it, but my stomach and all my years of believing in only the here and now was yelling at me.

"I know it's hard to understand," Steven said. "Especially when you haven't seen her yet. You obviously don't believe in ghosts. Am I right?"

I nodded.

"What kind of afterlife do you believe in?"

"None," I said. "When you're gone, you're gone. Six feet down and cold. Nothing more." I told him the truth, but lately I had been wondering. I had figured that the questions I had been asking were a natural function of getting older and having that cold end come closer and closer. But there was no way I was going to get religion. To me it made no sense. I had lived a good life. If some God did exist, and was even half of what all those churches claimed, He or She would see that. If there wasn't a God, then I certainly wasn't going to go wasting time on an insurance program of pray now, collect later.

"The simplest way to understand a habitual spirit, a ghost," Steven said, "would be to give the brain some credit. From what Fred has told me, you spent a lot of years teaching college. Right?"

"Too damn many."

"I'll drink to that," Fred said.

"So then," Steven said, "just think of a spirit as a brain that's too powerful to die. For some reason, a spirit usually has such a strong feeling for something that the power of that feeling alone does not allow the essence of the person to either dissolve, as you believe, or pass on to the next life, as the religions teach."

I had to give him credit. What he was saying made an odd sort of sense. "So then why is this Gretchen spirit still hanging around here?"

"Something happened to a man by the name of Alex and she felt he would return for her. She's been waiting since the day the town was destroyed."

"You'd think she would realize that this Alex is, in all likelihood, dead."

Steven shook his head. "Maybe not. There's a lot of evidence that trapped souls have no sense of time. And no idea who has died and who hasn't. In a few cases in the past, it has been necessary to summon spirits from the other side to help the trapped soul."

"I bought your 'power of the mind' idea," I said. "But now you're getting way past my gag level."

Steven shrugged. "Doesn't really matter with Gretchen. But I'd be glad to show the facts of other cases where such an occurrence has happened. That is, if you're interested."

I wasn't. "Maybe sometime," I said. "So tell me, why the dive into the lake?"

Steven looked over at Fred and Fred nodded for him to go ahead. "As I said, this spirit is waiting for someone named Alex to return for her. I got that much from her just in thoughts. She radiates it over and over. There is something down in the lake that is very important to her and to her search. I am unable to sense what that something is, but know for certain it is there."

"Do you believe her?" I asked.

"I have to admit," Steven said, "that I do."

"You think we might be able to help her?" Fred asked.

Steven shrugged. "We'll have to see what it is that's so important to her. If you can find it."

"What about the chance this may be some sort of trap?" I tried to mentally stop the shivers from running up and down my spine from the thought. I could see Fred shift on his seat. He didn't look too happy with the idea, either.

"I doubt it," Steven said. "But, of course, there's no way of knowing. It's not like habitual spirits to take any kind of action against the living. When some harm does come to someone, it's usually because the spirit is doing something related to its own time and the living get in the way. Evil spirits are the invention of fiction."

"But you said this Gretchen was different. Right?"

Steven nodded slowly while looking first at me, then over at Fred. "That she is. But I got no sense of animosity from her. None. She's just lost. And waiting."

I looked over at Susan and Constance. "Any opinions?" I asked. Both women shook their heads. I could tell that Constance was upset, but she wasn't going to say anything. I could imagine the arguments she and Fred must have had over this.

I turned to Fred. "What do you think we should do?"

Fred shrugged. "Doesn't seem like there's much choice. We don't stand a hell's chance of keeping this place the way we want it without getting rid of the ghost. It looks to me like the best hope we have of doing that is on the bottom of that lake."

"It's been a long time since we've made a dive," I said. "Think we're up for it?"

"Why not?" He smiled the half-smile that I knew meant we were in trouble. "Besides, when were we ever known for doing sane things?"

"Ten years ago, almost never. And this time certainly won't be any exception."

Fred nodded as his smile disappeared. "That it won't be."

An uneasy silence dropped over the room, leaving only the crackling of the fire and the very loud stillness of the mountain night. I listened hard, expecting to hear the faint sounds of piano music drifting in from the direction of the black water.

It was obvious I wasn't the only one listening.

To be continued...

Now Available
from all your favorite booksellers
in trade paper and electronic editions.

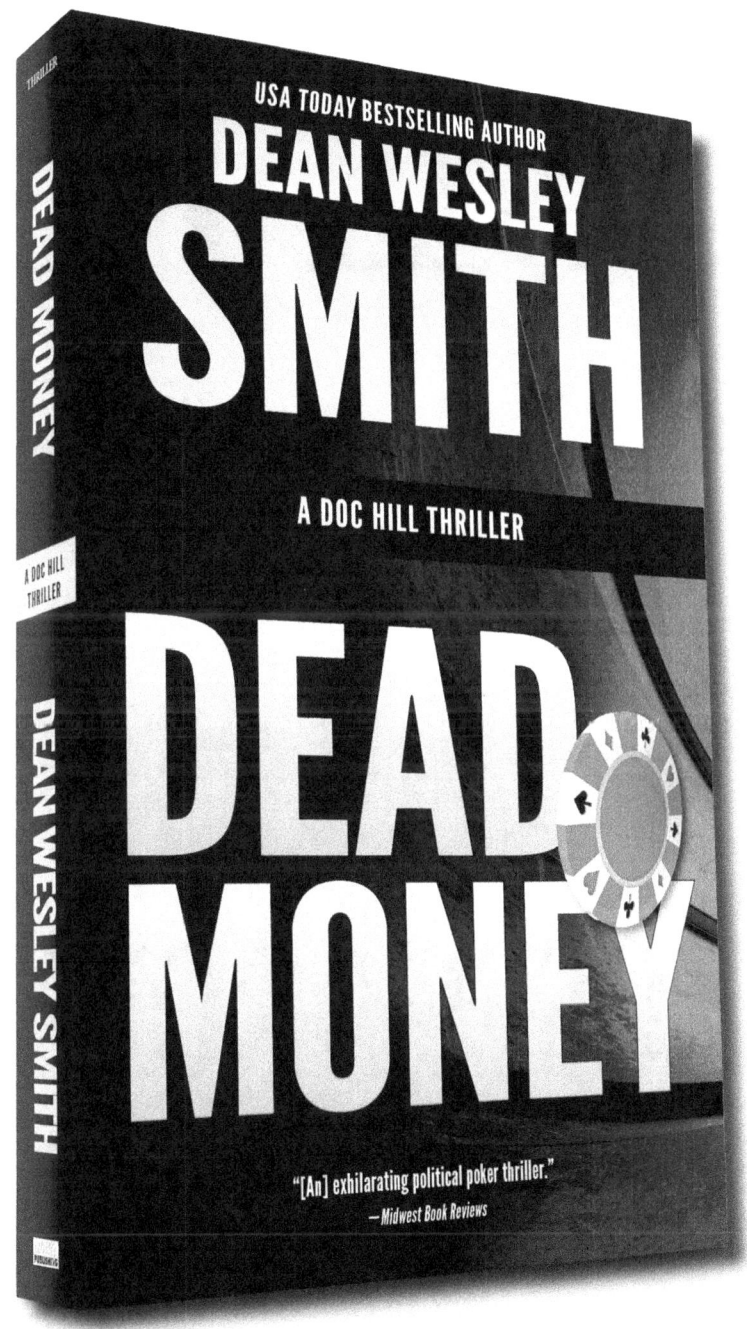

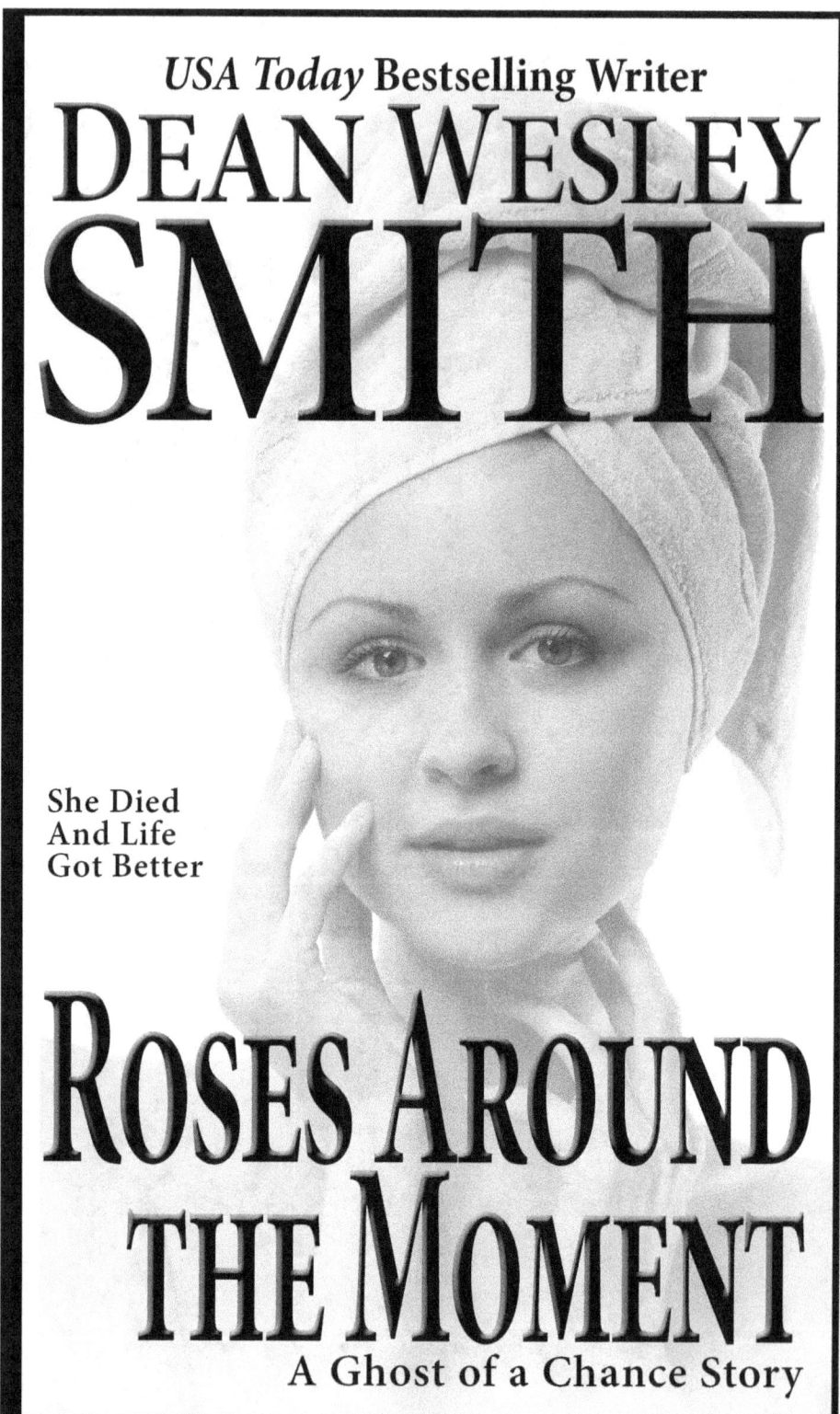

USA *Today* Bestselling Writer

DEAN WESLEY SMITH

She Died
And Life
Got Better

ROSES AROUND THE MOMENT

A Ghost of a Chance Story

Eve Bryson died so fast that she felt fine, standing on a twisting mountain road in the rain, not realizing her body lay broken in her Miata down a slope.

Then hunk-of-a-man Deputy Cascade steps into her life, arriving on the scene to investigate her death.

Wet, cold, hungry, and needing to pee, she finds herself dead and in lust. Then things really start to happen.

Eve died. And life got better.

ROSES AROUND THE MOMENT
A Ghost of a Chance Story

ONE

EVE BRYSON DIED so fast, she didn't even realize she was dead for a few minutes.

The rain was pounding down hard, one of those storms that felt more like standing under a cold shower. She had on only a light cotton summer dress, sandals, and panties. No bra, so this rain was sticking her dress to her like a second skin. Not pleasant in the slightest.

Around her the heavy pine forest seemed frighteningly dark, even though the sun was hours from setting. She could hear nothing but the pounding rain against her head, matting her long brown hair into a mess down her back.

She wasn't even sure how she had ended up in the rain. A moment before she had been driving toward a dinner date at a local brewpub in downtown Portland with three friends from college.

In the years since college, the four of them had managed to get together every month or so and she loved those evenings. It took her mind off her worthless husband and even more worthless job she couldn't figure out how to get out of.

She had thought she would love high-tech work after coming out of college with her masters in engineering. But she hated it, hated the people more than anything else. Their goal wasn't to create new things, use their brains for good. All they did was try to figure out how to get ahead in the corporate game.

And just like her job, she thought marrying Simpson Smith right out of college was a good idea as well. It didn't matter that he was taking a break from finishing his degree. They had had great sex, lots of fun traveling, and planning for a future. She thought she had found a soul mate.

Maybe a soul mate for her single sock. But that might be giving Simpson more credit than he deserved.

It seemed good ol' Simp to his friends never understood that working was required to get ahead. She had no idea what he did all day while she was working, but it certainly wasn't anything to bring in money. She had a hunch he just looked at porn and played online games. She had gotten tired of asking about six months ago.

The marriage was that dead.

So for two years now she had supported him and that was going to end very, very soon. All of the rebel things she had found charming with him in college now just annoyed her beyond belief.

And all of her friends didn't like him either right from the start. That should have been a clue to her, but when a girl was in the first blush of love and sexual satisfaction, thinking with the logical brain wasn't that possible.

So she had made two mistakes right out of college. In six months, she would be out of both mistakes.

She shivered from the pounding cold rain and looked around. What had happened?

The two-lane winding road through the trees was empty. Water ran down one side, it was raining so hard.

Then she saw her wonderful little classic blue Miata off the road and down an embankment. Then she remembered. She had been thinking about how Simpson had complained that she wouldn't cook his dinner before she left. She had gotten so angry, she had been driving far too fast down the twisting area through the trees from their house in the hills to the main street below.

Far too fast for a pounding June rain.

She had slid into one corner, managed to get straightened out, and then didn't make the next corner. The last thing she remembered was the Miata heading over the bank and for a large pine tree.

She must have bumped her head. She didn't remember climbing up here to the road.

She quickly felt her forehead, looking for any sign of blood in the rain pounding at her.

Nothing.

The Miata's lights were still on and she went to the edge of the road to look down at it. It was pretty smashed up, but it wasn't that far off the road and the next person to come by would certainly see it and her.

She felt really sad she had totaled her Miata. She had bought it right out of college as well and it was the only fun thing left in her life after two years. Now it looked like she would be starting over completely.

The rain kept pounding at her and she could feel she was starting to really get chilled. It had been a seventy-degree day today. How could she be this cold?

A blue pickup, brand new from the looks of it, came around the corner, saw the lights from her car and quickly braked and pulled over onto the gravel shoulder of the road, putting on its flashing red warning lights.

The driver was a guy about forty. Maybe older. She could never tell with men in that range.

He pulled on a rain jacket with a hood as he climbed out and went to the edge of the road to look at her poor car.

She put one arm across her chest to cover what was showing through her wet dress and said to the guy, "I sure made a mess of it, didn't I?"

He said nothing, but instead quickly scrambled down the bank. When he got to the Miata, he looked inside, then shook his head and at a fast climb came back up the bank and started toward his truck.

"Why are you ignoring me?" Eve asked.

She reached for the guy as he went past and her hand went right through his arm.

And as it did, she could feel and read his mind.

All he was thinking was to get help out here quickly. And that he doubted the woman in the car was alive. Her neck was badly twisted in a way that necks didn't twist.

She watched him move to the truck and climb in and use his cell phone to call for help.

Then in the pounding rain, she moved over to the edge of the bank and once again looked at her car.

She could see now that she was still inside.

She was dead.

And she was just about as cold and wet as she could ever remember being. And she was getting hungry.

She was dead.

She was a ghost.

How the hell could she be hungry?

TWO

EVE MANAGED TO find a tree on the inside of the road to give herself some shelter from the rain, but by the time the first cop arrived, she was shivering so bad, she doubted she could even walk. Was it possible to die twice, once from a car crash, another from freezing to death?

One of the county sheriffs left his car running when he climbed out in his rain slicker. So she went over to his car and tried to open the backseat car door, but her hand went right through it.

"Shit!" she shouted into the rain. "Just shit."

She needed to do something, so she closed her eyes and just pretended she was going to climb into the back seat. She wouldn't have been surprised if she had ended up sitting on the concrete, but she actually ended up in the back seat of the car.

Success. She could go through a door, but not fall through a seat. Who knew?

And thankfully, he had the heater running on defrost to keep the windows clear, so it was warm in the car.

He had a towel beside his seat and she grabbed it, coming away with what felt like a towel in her hands, but the original towel remained in position. The one in her hand looked identical.

She didn't care. Ghost towel or not, it was a towel.

Since she was a ghost, she figured no one could see her, so she stripped off her soaked dress and underwear and used the towel to dry off. Then she finally used the towel to wrap up her wet hair on the top of her head.

She twisted the water out of her underwear and slid them under her butt to protect herself a little from the cold seat. Then she twisted as much water out of her dress that she could and draped it over the front passenger seat to dry.

She was finally starting to warm up. She was naked and sitting in the back of a cop car. Under any other circumstances than being dead, this might have caused nightmares.

It still might. The evening was just getting started.

Suddenly the cop climbed back into his car. He was holding her wallet and as she watched, he pulled out her driver's license and shook his head. "Too damn young."

"Thanks," she said from the back seat.

He pushed his raincoat hood off the back of his head and she gasped. Sheriff man was about her age and a looker, with short brown hair, a square chin, and from what she saw in the rearview mirror, bright green eyes.

And she instantly noticed he wasn't wearing a ring.

She stared at him for a moment as he called in her personal information and then sat waiting for even more information to come up on his computer screen.

She really wanted to know more about this guy. Maybe if she touched him,

she could read his mind like she had done with the guy who found her wreck.

She reached forward and put her hand on his shoulder.

Only her hand went inside him and she instantly felt the sadness he was feeling at her death.

"Holy shit, someone who actually cares," she said aloud.

He glanced around, making her pull back and cover herself.

Then he shook his head and went back to studying the information coming through the screen.

"Can I make someone hear me if I am touching them? How cool would that be?"

He didn't turn around at that, so she reached forward and once again put her hand inside his shoulder.

This time she let herself try to find out who he was before saying anything.

His name was Deputy McCall Cascade. Everyone just called him Cascade.

He was exactly her age a twenty-six, liked his job except for events like this. He liked helping people and he didn't have a girlfriend.

But there was even more. He really worked as a superhero in the law enforcement area under a woman who was a low-level god in law enforcement by the name of Reanna. She reported to some gods above her, but he had never met any of them.

She had no idea what the superhero thinking was. Some sort of game or something. He was new at it, only being recruited by the gods of law enforcement two years before right after he got out of college and joined the force.

"Mr. Perfect," she said aloud with her hand still in his shoulder.

She could instantly tell he had heard that.

He shook his head, put up his raincoat hood and climbed back out into the rain as another sheriff's car arrived followed by an ambulance.

She watched for the next thirty minutes as they got her body out of the car and up into the ambulance.

She had no idea what was going on. She had never believed in ghosts or an afterlife or anything. But clearly she was living, at least for the moment, some sort of afterlife.

And she was hungry and pretty soon would need to pee. You would think a ghost wouldn't have to deal with all the real world stuff. Rules of ghostieness were sure different from any thing she had ever read.

Twenty minutes later, with her purse in his hand with her wallet back inside it, all tucked into a plastic bag with a label on it, he climbed back into the patrol car and again lowered the hood on his raincoat.

Her breath caught, if she had been breathing, which she was pretty certain she had been. He had gotten even more handsome, if that was possible.

He put her purse on the passenger seat, then waited until the ambulance in front of him pulled away and he pulled out to follow it. It seems he had gotten the duty of staying with her body.

If he could actually see her in the back seat, sitting nude on her still damp panties, wouldn't he be surprised?

Actually, she was the one sitting here that was surprised.

She had expected a great night with friends.

She hadn't expected to die.

But she supposed no one expected to die.

She actually wasn't that upset about it for some reason. But she really needed to pee.

THREE

EVE HAD NO idea why the ambulance took her body to a hospital. She was clearly dead and they weren't even bothering to run with lights. So as they pulled into a hospital loading area, she touched Deputy Cascade again.

The answer she was looking for came easily. Because she died alone and under suspicious circumstances, they had to do an autopsy. And it seemed in this area, the hospital morgue was where that was done.

"You won't find anything in my blood stream except anger and a lot of regret."

She could see in his mind that he heard her. He wasn't certain what he was hearing, but he clearly heard what she had said.

He picked up her purse and she grabbed her dress. They were parked under a canopy so she wouldn't get wet. She closed her eyes and pretended to open the door and step out of the back seat of the car.

The evening air had a chill to it and she quickly slipped her still-damp dress over her head. That sent shivers down her spine. But it was better than walking around a hospital completely naked.

She still had his towel wrapped on her head. So if there were other ghosts, she was going to make a great first impression.

Cascade was striding toward the big double doors, following the gurney with her body on it.

She ran and caught up to him, going through the wide door beside him. Inside the dim hallway smelled of antiseptic and roses, of all things.

The gurney with her body on it sort of clicked going down the smooth tile floor and she walked beside Cascade. In this part of the hospital, there sure weren't a lot of people.

But as her body turned to the right toward a service elevator, Cascade turned left and went through two swinging doors and out into a much more active and brighter area of the hospital.

Nurses and doctors were moving around, along with patients and guests. Cascade seemed to know where he was going with her purse, so she just tagged along, trying to stay out of everyone's way, since none of them could see her.

And she almost succeeded in that task except for one man who came around a corner carrying a dozen roses. He had a dark look to his eyes and wore jeans, a T-shirt, and tennis shoes.

She went right through him before she really saw him.

And as she did, she saw why he was here.

His name was Jack Nevada and he was headed for a room she and Cascade had passed down the hall. Hidden in the roses he had a syringe that he was going to inject in a woman by the name of Stephanie to kill her. It would look like a natural death.

He was a paid killer, hired by Stephanie's husband.

"Holy shit!"

Eve froze in the hallway, watching Jack Nevada stroll toward his murder victim.

"What the hell! What the hell! What the hell!"

No one heard her.

What could she do? She was a ghost. She couldn't shout or even try to stop the guy.

She glanced back in the other direction. Deputy Cascade, gun and all, had stopped at the nurse's station and was smiling at a young nurse in front of him.

Eve had to tell him, somehow.

She ran toward Cascade, her sandals slapping on the tile. She tried to stop before she got to him, but instead slid and went right inside him.

He stood up straight as she did.

"Hi, handsome," she said. "Eve Bryson here inside you in ghost form. We got a problem that you need to solve real quick!"

He nodded to the nurse and stepped back, which made Eve smile. Even under stress of hearing voices, he could stay cool. This guy really was a superhero.

"I am, actually," he said out loud.

Some guy in a white smock looked at him and frowned.

"No need to talk in your out-loud voice," she said. "I can hear everything you are thinking."

She felt him panic and she laughed.

"Yes, even the fact that you thought I was hot. Thank you, by the way."

He took a deep breath.

"So what do you need?" he thought at her.

She described the guy she had touched and what room he was headed toward and what he was about to do."

"Shit!" he said, again out loud. "Are you sure?"

"One hundred percent," she said to him. "And if you want to save that woman's life you had better get this handsome hunk of a body moving."

He touched the counter in front of the nurse. "Security to room 1003. Stat!"

He turned and started toward the room, using his mike attached to his collar to call for backup of real police.

When he reached the room, he drew his gun.

She sent him calming thoughts.

"Thanks," he said.

Then he went inside, gun drawn, leaving the door standing open for backup to come in behind him.

The killer had put the roses down near the window and had a syringe in his right hand. He was working with the woman's IV and in another fifteen seconds would have injected her.

The woman under the blanket was a very large woman. And the room smelled like she had had an accident in the sheets.

"Step back and drop the syringe and put your hands in the air!" Cascade said.

Cascade's power and authority in his voice gave Eve little goose bumps. He could order her around like that any time he wanted.

"Trying to work here," he said in his silent voice.

"Sorry," she said, laughing. "Forgot where I was."

The man with the syringe looked shocked at the deputy and gun facing him.

The man took a step back.

"No worry," she said to Cascade. "He's not armed with anything but the needle."

"I said drop the needle and put your hands on your head."

The guy finally realized he had no options, so he dropped the syringe with a light click on the tile, then raised his hands.

At that moment two hospital security men came through the door.

"Needle on the floor," Cascade said to the security. "He was about to inject this woman with it. Hired kill I'm betting."

Cascade handed one of the security men his handcuffs. "Secure his hands behind his back."

The security man did and Cascade had the would-be killer sit on the floor with his back against a wall.

Then one of the security men used a tissue to pick up the syringe.

At that point, two police officers came through the door and the shit-smelling room got real crowded real quick.

"You're going to be busy," Eve said to Cascade. "I'm going to leave you for a bit."

"You coming back?" he asked in his inside voice.

"I think so," she said. "But I'm still new at this ghost stuff."

"So where are you going?"

"You don't know?" she asked.

"Not a clue."

"I've really got to pee."

"Ghosts pee?" he asked.

"I'm going to find out for the first time very, very shortly," she said.

And with that she stepped out of his body and worked her way out of the room to find a woman's restroom. She doubted the hospital had ghost restrooms. But who knew.

FOUR

IT TOOK DEPUTY Cascade two hours to fill out the paperwork on her body and on the arrest at the hospital. He said he had caught a glimpse of the syringe in the roses when he passed the man walking in, decided it could be nothing but bad.

Eve had suggested that story, since he pretty much couldn't tell anyone he had a ghost inside him helping him.

She had raided a candy machine for a few snacks by just sticking her hand through the glass and pulling out the ghost equivalent of a candy bar. The two bars helped a little to hold back the hunger, but she was going to need a real meal pretty soon.

Cascade then had to spend another thirty minutes at his desk at the police station filling out more paperwork before he could get off work. Wow did cops have a lot of paperwork or what? She had no idea.

So as he finally stood and started for his patrol car, she got back inside him.

"How you doing?"

"I was wondering if you were still here."

"Been watching the entire time," she said. "I figured if I was inside your body, I would just be a distraction to all the stuff you needed to get done."

"More than likely yes," he said.

And she could tell he appreciated that.

"Dinner at Shari's," she said.

"Ghosts eat?"

"I need to because I'm ravished."

So fifteen minutes later they were in Shari's restaurant. She sat across the booth from him so she could see him, but she put her feet up so that they were in his lap, so she could be inside his head and he could hear her.

She told him how she was sitting.

"Kind of forward, don't you think?" he said, smiling.

Damn from across the table, she loved that smile.

"Thank you," he said, hearing her thought about his smile.

Then as the waitress came up, he ordered his regular French dip and fries and a glass of iced tea.

"I'm going to go get something," she said. "Back in a moment."

She wandered into the kitchen and there, sitting under the light ready to take

out, was a wonderful chicken fried steak meal. It smelled heavenly.

She picked up the plate, feeling the heat on her fingers.

The real plate just stayed there under the light. It seemed food had a ghost component as well.

She took the plate back out to the table, put her foot against his leg and said, "I have chicken fried steak. So pardon me if you get moaning sensations as I eat. I'm that hungry."

She took a couple of bites, then realized while she was gone, he had called for his boss on the superhero side.

Just as Eve realized that, a striking black-haired woman in a police uniform came up to the table. She had to stand a good six feet tall and her uniform looked like it had actually been starched.

The woman nodded in Eve's direction and then had Cascade scoot over.

"This is Reanna," Cascade thought at her.

"Figured as much," Eve said between bites.

This had to be the absolute best tasting chicken fried steak she had ever had. Ever.

"I understand you just died this afternoon," Reanna said out loud to Eve. "Sorry for your loss, but glad you could help Deputy Cascade."

"Tell her it was my pleasure," Eve said out loud. "Ask her if she wants me to touch her so she can hear me."

"I can see and hear you just fine," Reanna said.

Then Reanna waved a hand in the direction of Cascade.

He blinked and then said to Eve, "Wow you are more beautiful alive than dead."

"Thanks," Eve said, "I think."

At that moment she realized her dress was still damp, more than likely her nipples were still showing, and she still had her hair wrapped up on top of her head in his car towel. "I got a little wet out there at the crash site."

Then she ignored the feelings of attraction she was getting from Cascade through their touch and looked at Reanna. "If I'm a ghost, how can you see me? And how can Cascade now see me?"

"You are a ghost agent," Reanna said, her voice firm and compact, just as she looked. "You will be recruited to join the Ghost of a Chance Agency and trained by them."

"You lost me with ghost agent thingie," Eve said.

"When a person dies," Reanna said, "almost everyone just goes on into the next life, whatever that is. But for a few thousand around the world, they are asked to stay on as ghost agents and try to help people, as you two did by saving that woman's life this evening."

Eve nodded. "That did feel good."

"I have contacted the head of the Ghost of a Chance agency," Reanna said, "and they will be sending some other agents to help you train and explain everything to you."

Eve nodded, but her disappointment matched what she was feeling from Cascade.

"However," Reanna said, "after your collaboration this afternoon with Officer Cascade, I have also asked if you could be assigned to my department and you and Officer Cascade work together to solve cases."

Reanna turned to Cascade. "Would that be all right with you?"

"I would be honored," he said.

Eve could feel his excitement at the idea. And she had to admit that hanging around with Mister Handsome Superhero sounded like a great time to her.

"Would you be interested in such an assignment?" Reanna asked Eve. "You both would be a very special team, the only ghost and live superhero working together. It has never been tried. You might work with Poker Boy and his team at times as well as reporting to me. He was very interested in meeting you both once you were up to speed."

She instantly felt Cascade's excitement. It seemed this superhero named Poker Boy and his team often were called on to save the entire world.

So she had a chance to go from a worthless husband and a dead job to being someone who could help save people and work with superheroes and gods.

Not counting staying with the hunk of a man sitting across from her.

How could she say no to that.

"I would be honored," she said out loud.

Reanna smiled and nodded.

Cascade's excitement at her answer sent tingles to places she hadn't felt tingles in a very long time.

Damn, this being dead was going to be a blast.

Who knew?

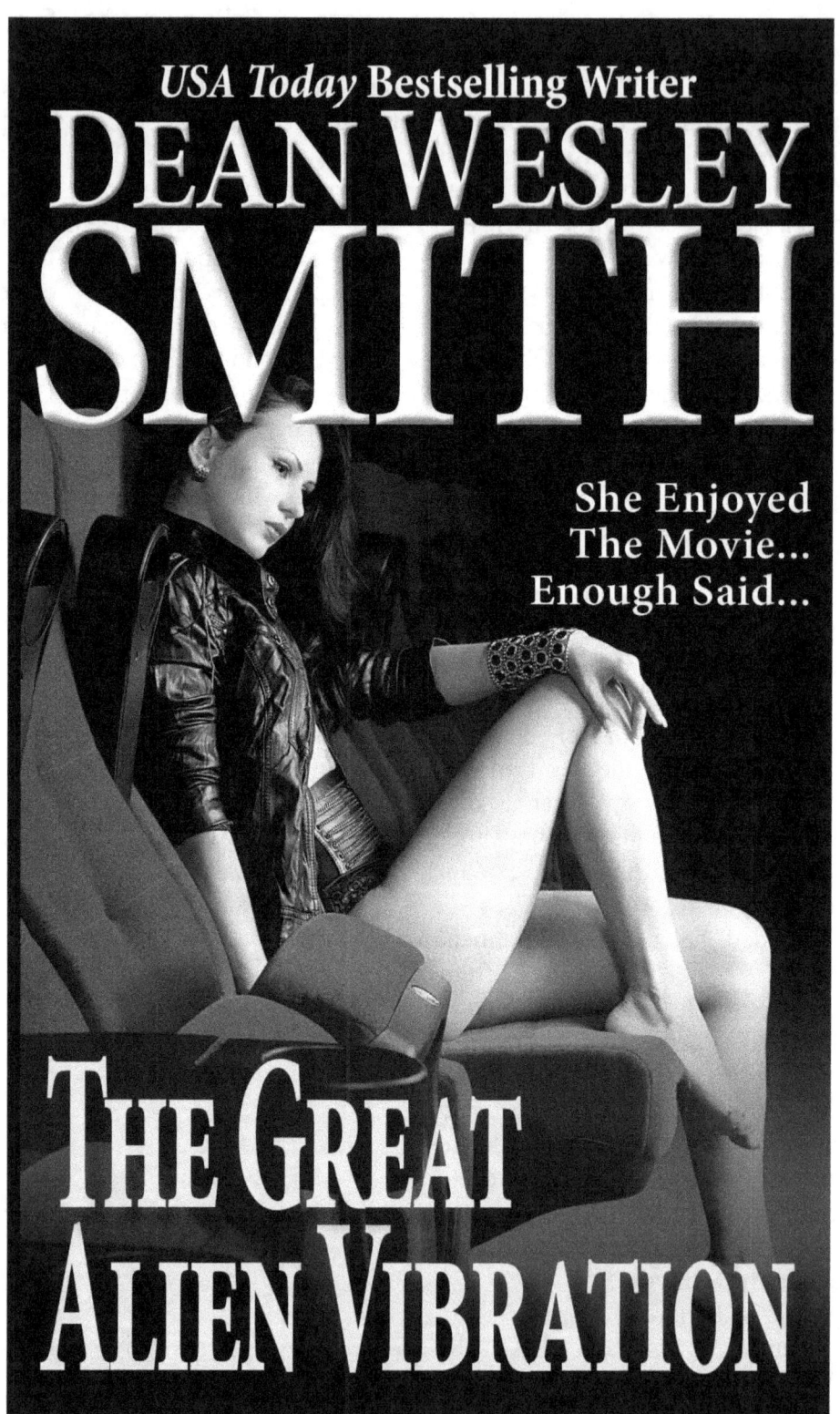

USA *Today* Bestselling Writer

DEAN WESLEY SMITH

She Enjoyed
The Movie...
Enough Said...

THE GREAT ALIEN VIBRATION

As first dates go, a failure for him, a total success for her.

As first alien contacts go, he will walk funny for a few days

Jimmy Loche asks Stephanie Peters to a special test of a new movie done with brand new technology.

A first date that never reaches a second date.

Put it this way, she enjoyed the movie. Enough said...

THE GREAT ALIEN VIBRATION

AS FIRST DATES go, it had been a failure for him, a total success for her.

As first alien contacts go, he would walk funny for a few days.

Jimmy Loche had first met Stephanie Peters at work. Actually, at first he only saw her from a distance. But he considered that meeting-without-talking sometimes a much safer form of interaction for him.

He found her amazingly attractive. Short brown hair, large oval glasses that accented her green eyes, and a figure not well hidden by her white lab coat she always wore while working.

She most likely stood about two inches taller than he did, but at five-foot-five, he had grown used to being around taller women and didn't much mind it at all. Especially if they talked to him. Always a key to his not minding the height difference.

She was a bio-tech chemist; he worked in the engineering side of the same company. The company they both worked for was cutting-edge development and research into devices that would be needed in space. The company had numbers of clients, including NASA and five different private firms.

On the third time that he noticed Stephanie, he smiled at her and she smiled back. That had made his day.

They kept smiling at each other at various points of the day over the next few weeks, usually around either arriving at work through the massive stone lobby or at lunch in the plant-filled white and tan company cafeteria.

At work he usually wore jeans, an open collared dress shirt, and tennis shoes. And they both always carried iPads. He started tipping his iPad to her to say hello across any distance and she would smile and nod back.

Starting the second week of tipping, she tipped her iPad back and things moved forward from there.

Two weeks later, they had talked a few times, she had seen he was shorter than her and hadn't seemed to mind or even notice. And they had discovered they were both major movie fans.

Through a friend of a friend in another cutting-edge company, Jimmy managed to score seats in a private first screening of a new and very secret feature film that used new technology in theaters.

His friend told him that he would be the only man in the small test theater, since the show was a test-run to see how women liked it.

Jimmy had no problem with that.

In hindsight, he should have had a problem with that. He should have just asked Stephanie to see the new Marvel movie. But no, he had to feel like someone special and get her into a first-run test of a brand new movie with brand new technology in the theater.

She had agreed to go with him, of course. It was special and very secret. They didn't even know the name of the movie.

But that evening, when they met in front of their company headquarters, it was the first time he had seen her without her lab coat. And she looked even better in jeans, a white blouse, and tennis shoes. They had decided to just go in their normal casual clothes so he remained in what he had worn to work that day, only with a clean shirt.

It seemed that casual to both of them was the Jimmy level, which boded well for the night ahead.

They walked, talking all the way to a local chain restaurant for a fun meal, then did the ten minute walk from there to the small theater in the back of a local university science building.

It seemed she liked to walk as much as he did, and considering he had an old Ford with far too many fast-food meal remains on the backseat floor, it was good she liked to walk. He hated cleaning that car.

There was no popcorn or anything at the theater, and only a man taking their tickets and indicating where they should sit. From the looks of it, there sure wouldn't be trailers for new coming attractions either.

Over dinner, he and Stephanie had laughed and both figured that even if the movie was the worst thing ever, it was a fun first date. He had liked the sound of the word "first" being used in such a fashion to modify date.

Clearly she liked him. And he clearly liked her.

So they ended up in the back row of the theater. There were about thirty large chairs in all up a steep-stair-step theater, with only sixteen people spread out in the thirty chairs.

Almost everyone had come in pairs. He saw no woman sitting alone. And as he had been warned, he was the only man in the room.

"These are comfortable," Stephanie said, indicating the chair.

She was right, they were comfortable and very modern. The padding seemed to almost form around him like one of those expensive beds did around people on television. He only had an apartment near the company headquarters and he had bought his mattress used at a flea market. It was soft all right, but not in a good way.

The seats had wide armrests and when he sat back, his head was supported like a really fancy car seat.

Then, as the movie started, the lights went dim. But not dim enough that he couldn't see the others in the theater below him.

The title of the movie was "Alien Vibration" and it had nothing else after the title except the words "Test Number One."

And today's date.

Jimmy was amazed. His friend was right, this really was the very first showing of a new movie. This might turn out to be the best first date ever in his meager list of first dates.

At twenty-six, he just hadn't had that many first dates, and not for the lack of trying. Too much time instead working to get that doctorate in engineering to date. That was the excuse he gave himself.

"This is fun," Stephanie said, leaning over and whispering softly to him.

"It is," he whispered back.

That was a first. No woman on a date with him had ever told him something they were doing was fun.

Then the movie started and for Stephanie and the other women in the theater, the fun really started.

For him, not so much.

The movie began with three well-muscled men working out, talking in deep voices, and joking around to show they had a sense of humor. One was white, one black, the other some sort of Asian mix.

Then the movie followed them to the showers. That's when Jimmy started to get worried about this new movie.

Thankfully, it was nothing graphic, no actual body parts were shown, but camera angles allowed all of the audience to see a lot more of those three men than Jimmy wanted to see.

Especially their butts.

Jimmy hadn't seen another man's butt since gym class in freshman year in high school.

He wasn't happy about seeing them now.

He glanced at Stephanie. She didn't seem to be minding at all.

And it was at that point that Jimmy noticed the seats were moving slightly, sometimes in timing with one of the guy's on the screen hip movements.

As the men dressed in a very well-filmed fashion, and then left the gym, Jimmy was expecting them to become aliens or something, considering the title "Alien Vibrations."

But it didn't work that way.

The story-line jumped among the three men, one to the other, as they went through rather mundane days, then met again in a clean back room of some club.

The seat was getting annoying at that point with its movement, but Jimmy noticed that Stephanie was following the show with her mouth slightly open. And she was pressed back into the chair.

The three men went into a dressing room of the club and again stripped off their clothes, showing perfect bodies while not showing their more-than-likely important body part.

But close.

Very close at times.

One camera angle was so close to a body part reveal that a few of the women in the audience gasped and then sighed as it didn't happen.

Beside him, Stephanie just sat, focused completely on the movie.

Completely.

And one hand was between her legs as if it was cold, but Jimmy had a hunch that hand was far from cold.

And the damn seat just kept vibrating. As the three men finished dressing in skimpy underwear, then clearly rip-away costumes, Jimmy finally clued to what the job these men had entailed.

Then the camera angle went from the dressing room, following the first man out and onto a stage.

There was no one in the audience.

No one.

It was clear this guy was going to put on a show just for the women in this theater.

And when he looked into the camera as the music built and ripped off his pants, Stephanie let out a gasp and shuddered beside him.

He was about to ask her if she was all right, but then he realized he had a hunch what had just happened, since the cushion of the chair he was in was moving in motion with the guy's hips on the screen.

Perfectly timed motion, actually.

It wasn't doing anything for him, but it was clearly doing something really great for Stephanie.

And from the sounds of the gasps and sobs and sighs in the small theater, it was having an effect on the other women in the place as well.

And then the guy on the screen was down to his tiny, tiny shorts that showed nothing tiny underneath the shorts.

The guy's hips and the chairs kept moving in exactly the same pattern and then, as the music built and built and the guy's hips and the chair under Jimmy moved faster and faster, the guy suddenly stopped and thrust his slightly-hidden part right into the camera.

And as he did, something in the seat poked upward, making Jimmy jump.

It made Stephanie grunt and then pant, "Yes! Yes! Yes!"

And then the next guy came out onto the stage as the camera left the first guy. The second guy was fully dressed and he started the old hip movement and the chair picked up on the hip movement.

And the entire music started to build again, this time a little faster than the first guy.

More urgent.

Pounding music with a vibration that also carried into the chair under Jimmy.

And again the part of the dances ended with the mostly-naked guy on the screen thrusting his far-too-large and barely-covered private part at the camera as something in the seat again poked upward.

The guy thrust again.

The seat hit Jimmy in the butt again.

But this time Jimmy had been ready and had lifted his butt off the chair enough to not get the brunt of it right in his ass.

Beside him Stephanie was just panting "Yes! Yes! Yes!"

Over and over and over like the worst corporate flunky in existence.

Jimmy glanced at his watch.

Can't Get Enough of Poker Boy?
These stories and more are available at your favorite booksellers.

This had been going on now for almost forty minutes, and now the third guy's movement on the screen was controlling the seats and the music was building faster and faster.

And the seats went faster and faster.

And the vibrations intensified.

And the camera panned over the man's huge, but covered, part more and more times and each time something under Jimmy poked upward.

Finally, the camera went in tight on the guy's body part, something in the seat poked up even more, and all hell broke loose in the theater.

More than likely it wasn't hell for anyone but him. But women were panting, crying, sobbing.

Beside him Stephanie was just shuddering and not even trying to control the fact that she had the hiccups. Her head was down, her eyes closed, and she was sweating.

In fact, her entire blouse was wet from sweat and he could see her white bra through it.

The film had stopped, but the lights had not come back up yet, which allowed all the women in the place to slowly pull themselves back together.

Jimmy sat there watching it all, shocked.

This had all been alien to him completely. He had never even gotten to first base with a woman and was scared to death to click on any porn sight on the internet for fear of viruses in his computers and someone finding out.

Yet he was fairly certain he had just watched an entire theater of women have multiple orgasms.

After two minutes, the lights came up slightly.

Stephanie had managed to pull herself back together with one final sigh.

No one had really moved or stood up yet.

Finally, on the screen, words appeared. "Thanks for Coming."

The lights came up farther and the women snickered and laughed and that broke the tension.

"Well, that was fun," Stephanie said, turning to him. "You up for a pizza?"

"I would love one," he said.

They were the first out of the small theater and neither of them talked at all about what had happened, or why her blouse was soaked through, or anything. But they had great conversations about a lot of other stuff.

Then, when he walked her back to her car at the office, she beamed at him.

"That had to be the best first date a girl could ever ask for," she said.

She kissed him on the forehead, thanked him again, and turned for her car.

He knew right then and there that there would never be a second date.

And he was relieved.

No chance in the world could he measure up to those three men on the screen. Not in height, not in strength, and certainly not in the hidden-body-part area of things.

That theater had been state-of-the-art, cutting-edge technology that seemed to work just fine for everyone but him.

For him, it had been alien contact completely, especially with whatever was under that seat.

He had no doubt his ass was going to be sore for days.

Now Available
from all your favorite booksellers in trade paper and electronic editions.

DEAD HAND

A COLD POKER GANG MYSTERY

DEAN WESLEY SMITH

USA TODAY BESTSELLING AUTHOR

More than two hundred couples get married in Las Vegas every day. And some people just go missing right before their planned wedding.

Some show up later. Some are never found.

The Cold Poker Gang decides to look into an old cold case of a woman who went missing right before her wedding. What they dig up shocks the entire city to the core. And exposes the dirty side of an industry beyond the roses and cake and white dresses.

Another twisted mystery from USA Today bestselling author Dean Wesley Smith.

DEAD HAND
A Cold Poker Gang Novel

Part One
A WEDDING DRESS

PROLOGUE

May 17th, 2010
Las Vegas, Nevada

TRUDY PATTERSON RAN her hand along the lace edge of her white wedding dress as it hung in her suite's bedroom. The dress was so beautiful, with a full skirt and short train, and it fit her perfectly, almost magically, especially over her shoulders.

She had hung it out in the open just to be able to stare at it the last few days and enjoy the wonderful future it promised. Amazing how a simple dress could mean so much.

Outside Trudy's top floor suite, the sun was shining and the day was promising to be warm. She had some errands to run, then she would pick up Tommy, the love of her life, at the airport and they would have dinner. So when she got back from the errands, she needed to put the dress away so he wouldn't see it. That would be bad luck.

She didn't really believe in that sort of thing, but when it came to getting married, she was going to take no chances.

But for the moment, she liked having the wonderful dress and all it offered for a future out in the open.

The dress had been her grandmother's on her father's side. Her grandmother would have been proud to see Trudy wearing it, but her grandmother had died a year before Trudy met Tommy in their last years of college.

Tommy's parents and family and friends would arrive tomorrow from Los Angeles and Trudy's parents and sister would fly in the following day.

In three days, Trudy would walk down the aisle in that dress in a beautiful chapel in the rocks just outside of town and marry Tommy. They had been living together now in Denver for three years and both of them had always wanted to get married in Las Vegas. Now, it was finally going to happen, just as they had both dreamed and planned.

She had been here for almost a week, arranging all the details for the rehearsal dinner, the wedding, the justice of the peace, the flowers, everything. Her mother had offered to get time off work

and come and help her, but Trudy had wanted to do it alone. She felt that would make it even more special.

Her hand brushed the dress again, then she checked herself in the bathroom mirror to make sure her long brown hair was still tied back and her shorts weren't riding up on her and her light blue blouse was buttoned correctly.

All fine. Just three last quick errands, not more than a few hours, and she would come back, shower, and change to meet Tommy.

She took her rental car keys, her small brown purse, and a bottle of water and headed out of the suite's door.

The hotel's security cameras followed her to the valet parking, where she got in her blue 2010 Ford Taurus rental car, buckled her seat belt, and pulled into traffic without a problem.

She was never seen alive again.

Five days after she was scheduled to be married and her frantic family and fiancé shouted at everyone they could shout at to get help, Trudy Patterson's body was found in a white wedding dress, holding a bouquet of red, wilted flowers, sitting in her rental car, parked at the top of a slight ridge looking out over Las Vegas.

Because she had been sitting in the hot car with the windows up for three days before being found, cause of death was never determined.

And with her fiancé and family all having complete alibis, there were no suspects.

None.

Within months, her case went cold and her grandmother's wedding dress, the one that had hung in the suite, not the one she wore in death, was put back in a box for storage.

ONE

October 18th, 2016
Las Vegas, Nevada

RETIRED LAS VEGAS Detective Debra Pickett locked her silver Jeep Grand Cherokee SUV on the second floor of the Golden Nugget parking garage and then, out of years of habit, checked everything around her as she started for the sky bridge.

She walked with a long stride for her five-four size. Not quick, like would be expected, just long, which allowed her to cover more ground. At sixty-one years old, she kept her hair short and dyed her natural brown, the color it had been before it started turning gray.

Her color of gray had been faded and ugly, not silver like her mother's had been. So keeping it brown was her only choice.

Many a person over the years had underestimated her thin, wiry stature and paid a price by often ending up face down on the pavement. She had a reputation around the station of being too tough to mess with and she liked that. She had played it up at times to her advantage.

Around her, the four-story concrete parking garage was mostly quiet. A young couple headed for their car on the far side, her heels clicking on the pavement and her far-too-short mini-skirt hiking up even as she tried to keep it down. A black Ford with another couple cruised upward along the ramp looking for a place to park, its engine surprisingly silent.

At ten in the evening, the air was starting to have a slight bite to it. She loved this time of the year in Las Vegas. Comfortable days, cool nights. Perfect.

She was dressed in her normal jeans, a light-colored tan blouse, and a light-tan cloth jacket. She had her badge in her back pocket and her gun in her large purse. She normally liked to carry the gun in a holster under a jacket, but wearing a gun while playing cards at Lott and Julia's place just felt odd.

The noise from the bands over on the Fremont Street Experience was faint in the garage. It was still too early for most people to be leaving the casino and Fremont Street and too late for many new arrivals.

Pickett lived only a few blocks away to the east at the Ogden Condos, but since parking here was easier than the walk along the Fremont Street Experience this time of the night, she figured there was no point in parking at home.

For the last six months, after the Cold Poker Gang poker games at Lott and Julia's home, Pickett and her partner, Robin Sprague, had come here for a late dinner. It had become a tradition for them and they both liked the time to unwind and talk about the cold case they were working on.

During the week between games they often spent every day tracking down leads. Robin was an expert with computers, so she took that end while Pickett took the lead on the real-world stuff.

Besides, the footwork took more time and since Pickett was single and Robin married, Pickett didn't mind picking up some of that slack at all. Least she could do for her best friend who had actually managed to hold a marriage and a police career together at the same time.

That was a feat not duplicated by many.

Last week they had cleared a tough old missing person's case from the 1970s and both felt great about that. Even that old of a case gave families some closure.

And the Cold Poker Gang last week had given them a round of applause, a tradition she liked when someone closed a case. Having other detectives she admired and respected applaud her work never got old.

At this point, there were fourteen retired detectives in the Cold Poker Gang, but only about ten showed up on any given Tuesday. She and Robin had decided they wouldn't miss a night, they loved it that much.

And they loved working the cold cases. Before they retired, they never seemed to have enough time for many cold cases. That's why the Las Vegas Police Chief had given the Cold Poker Gang special status to work on cold cases. They could all still carry their guns and their badges. They just didn't get paid.

Having an unpaid group of experienced detectives volunteering to work cold cases freed up the on-duty detectives to do the more pressing work and allowed Las Vegas to now have one of the top-rated levels of closing cold cases in the entire country.

Besides that, no member of the gang had to do any paperwork. Pickett considered that the best of both worlds. She could work at her own pace, do the job she still loved, and not have to do paperwork.

She had retired and gone to police heaven, as far as she was concerned.

This week, Retired Detective Andor Williams, the Cold Poker Gang's official contact with the Chief of Police, had given her and Robin a cold murder from 2010 as their next focus case.

And Andor had suggested that Retired Detective Ben "Sarge" Carson join them on the case.

That had surprised her. Neither Pickett or Robin had met Sarge before tonight, but Pickett remembered seeing him around the main police headquarters at times over the years. And she had heard how good he was, often working alone to solve cases.

Sarge had been stationed out of the university area headquarters, out the Strip toward the airport, and she and Robin had worked out of the Sunnerlin Station to the west of downtown.

It seemed that Sarge had been an early member of the Cold Poker Gang and had been pulled away by some family crisis for a couple years, but as of tonight he was back.

Pickett had been surprised at how handsome Sarge was. He had thick, gray hair, a square jaw that looked like it had never been punched, and was solid and very much in-shape. He looked to be about her age, but she couldn't tell for sure.

Plus he had a smile that seemed natural and hit his hazel eyes every time.

And he had smiled at her when he shook her hand. For a moment she hadn't wanted to let his hand go. She hadn't felt that way about a man since long before her cheating bastard of a husband moved with his thirty-year-old secretary to Los Angeles ten years ago in a mid-life crisis that could be described as only a laughing cliché.

The bastard had paid the price. She had gotten her wonderful three-bedroom penthouse condo in The Ogden and more than enough money to not have to work again.

So the sudden attraction to Sarge sort of flustered Pickett. He had been playing on another table. When the games broke at ten as they always did, Pickett noticed he had more chips than he started with. So he was a poker player to watch out for. She liked that.

So now he was going to join her and Robin here at the Golden Nugget for dinner to talk about their new case.

It seemed that for one case, for the first time in years, she and Robin would have a third member on their team.

And Pickett decided she didn't mind at all, if he just kept smiling and looking handsome.

TWO

October 18th, 2016
Las Vegas, Nevada

RETIRED DETECTIVE BEN "Sarge" Carson headed across the street from the first floor of the Golden Nugget parking garage and in through the main doors by the Starbucks. He was whistling softly to himself and walking lighter than he had in years. It felt great to be back working again.

He liked the Golden Nugget more than he wanted to admit and had made it a four-times-a-week habit of coming here for the buffet at breakfast. It was an easy walk from his condo, which also helped him get out and get a little exercise as well.

The buffet had great food, reasonable prices, and friendly people. And that breakfast routine had given him some structure in his days. For the last two years, structure was what he had missed the most.

He would get up in the morning and wonder what to do with his day.

He had spent some time traveling, a long cruise, and two trips a year to New York City to see his daughter, Steph, who worked there for a magazine.

But since Andrea had divorced him five years ago and moved to Chicago with a guy she had met from work, finding some sort of structure had been an everyday project.

Sarge had retired from the force just after Andrea left and for a short time worked casino security at the MGM Grand. Also, during that year he had been a member of the Cold Poker Gang.

But even on that he couldn't keep his mind focused. There was just something about a woman he trusted and loved and lived with for over thirty years suddenly just saying she was leaving and moving in with another man.

In hindsight, he could see all the signs. He had worked more and more, stayed away from home more and more, because it just wasn't pleasant to be home once Steph had gone off to college.

And Andrea had worked more and more and they barely saw each other the last few years. He knew, in his heart, the marriage was over. He just hadn't wanted to admit it.

He admired Andrea for taking the step to clear things out. He wasn't angry at her and actually liked the guy she moved with to Chicago. She wasn't the problem.

He was the problem. He just couldn't figure out what to do with his life at sixty-two years of age. So he had sold their family home, given half of the proceeds to Andrea, then bought a penthouse condo in the Ogden using just a tiny, tiny bit of his inheritance money from his father who had died the year before. Sarge loved the condo, but still needed a great deal more in his life.

Tonight, being back with the detectives of the Cold Poker Gang and talking solving crimes had felt wonderful. He knew he had found at least a part of what he had been looking for.

As Lott had said to him when they talked about Sarge rejoining the Cold Poker Gang, "It gives life a purpose."

Sarge could feel that clearly tonight.

And then Andor had suggested he join up with Pickett and Sprague, the two best women detectives ever to work the Las Vegas streets. Sarge had been surprised at that, but when Sarge heard what the case was, he had almost hugged Andor.

Andor had known Sarge was coming back, so he had pulled a cold case that Andor knew Sarge had a personal connection with.

The "Wedding Dress Murder" as it had been called, had been Sarge's case originally. And not solving that poor girl's murder had bothered him more than he wanted to admit over the years.

Now, with two of the best detectives the city had to offer, just recently retired, he was finally going to have the time to run at the "Wedding Dress Murder" as it should have been.

And that just had him whistling and smiling.

It was time to get back to work, time to do what he had loved once again.

THREE

October 18th, 2016
Las Vegas, Nevada

WHEN PICKETT GOT to the restaurant, Robin was already sitting at their favorite booth in the back of the twenty-four hour café on the main floor of the hotel. The restaurant, in the last remodel, had gone from being open with hundreds of tables to being smaller, but much nicer.

Now the booth was cloth-covered brown tones with nice wood tabletop and plants between the booths giving a feeling of privacy. The restaurant staff were always friendly, and at ten in the evening they had switched over to their late-night menu which was mostly sandwiches, desserts, a few steaks, and breakfasts of all kinds. All of it good.

Usually Robin sat on one side of the booth with her back to a kitchen door and Pickett sat on the other, but tonight Robin had scooted around to the back of the booth to give Sarge one side when he arrived.

Retired Detective Robin Sprague was about as tough a cop as there was, and Pickett had zero doubt Robin was a lot smarter than she was.

Robin was square and solid, with arms and shoulders of a swimmer even at sixty. She often spent time swimming as exercise and had competed in some senior's events. She kept her gray hair cut short and often wore a wide-billed base-ball cap to keep the sun off her face.

Pickett burned easily in the sun, while Robin seldom seemed to use suntan lotion and just seemed to tan evenly as the summer went on. They had been partners for over twenty years since both were promoted to detective at the same time.

Robin had one kid, now back east working in Washington. And her husband, Will, still ran one of Las Vegas's top security firms. He managed to keep safe some of the most powerful and famous people on the planet every day.

Besides that, he was one of the nicest men Pickett had ever had the pleasure to meet. After Pickett's divorce, Robin and Will had almost adopted her, asking her over for all kinds of things to keep her mind occupied.

Wonderful friends that didn't come any better.

"So what do you think of working with Sarge?" Robin asked as Pickett slid into her normal side of the booth and took a sip from the glass of ice water already there.

"I think it's going to be fun, actually," Pickett said. And she did think that.

"Because he's a hunk?" Robin asked, smiling.

Pickett knew that smile and that evil grin from her partner.

Pickett laughed. "There's that. But if I remember right, he's married."

"Nope," Robin said, still holding that evil grin. "Divorced right before he retired five years ago."

Now that sat Pickett back in her seat. She had been instantly attracted to Sarge tonight. And he was available.

"Seriously?" Pickett asked.

"You can ask him yourself," Robin said, indicating the entrance to the restaurant.

Sarge had just come in and spotted them in the back. Pickett watched him weave through the tables, his solid form moving with an ease that you didn't often see in someone at his age. He seemed completely in control of himself and his movements.

Pickett could feel her stomach clamp up at watching him. Damn, he had to be the most handsome man in downtown Las Vegas. How the hell was it possible she was even attracted to him? She had figured that part of her life was done. It certainly had been shut off for a lot of years.

And Sarge was smiling as he reached the table and nodded. "Detectives."

Robin indicated that he should join them and he did. The wonderful smile never left his face.

"You win tonight?" Robin asked as Sarge sat down.

All Pickett could do was just stare at him, so she was glad her partner picked up the slack for the moment.

"Being able to work with you two is a win in my book," Sarge said.

"Now that's smooth," Pickett said, smiling.

"Oh, I like him already," Robin said, laughing.

"Yup, me too," Pickett said.

And then Sarge looked up into her eyes and she damn near forgot to breathe. His hazel eyes just held her and she decided right at that moment all she really wanted to do was just stare into his eyes.

He seemed frozen for a moment as well, then laughed and said, "And I won forty bucks as well."

And that broke the ice and the intense moment and Pickett actually managed to take a drink of water without her hands shaking. She was very proud of that fact.

FOUR

October 18th, 2016
Las Vegas, Nevada

SARGE WAS STUNNED at how attracted he felt instantly to Pickett. Her brown eyes had held his gaze and she seemed to see everything about him. He hadn't had a reaction like that in memory toward a woman. Nothing that was that kind of instant and strong.

Now he hoped he didn't make a fool of himself working with them. She was considered the best woman detective who ever wore a badge in Las Vegas. Maybe one of the best detectives ever, period. And her partner Robin was almost as good. He was way outclassed with this partnership.

They gave their drink orders to a kind woman with tinted blue hair and tattoos on both arms and then Sarge decided he needed to get things clear as quickly as possible.

"I bet you are wondering why Andor suggested I work with you two on this new case."

"It did seem surprising," Pickett said, nodding.

Damn, her voice was thick and rich and had a wonderful throaty sound to it. He loved that.

"Andor did it as a favor to me because I was coming back to the gang," Sarge said. "The Wedding Dress Murder was my case originally. Driven me nuts for years. Haunted me, actually."

Robin laughed and sat back, shaking her head. Pickett just kept smiling, a smile that reached her eyes and Sarge wouldn't mind seeing a lot more of that.

"Wow, do we know that feeling," Robin said.

Pickett nodded. "I still have nightmares about a couple of our cold cases. But Andor doesn't want us to tackle them yet."

"I trust Andor and Lott and Julia," Sarge said. "That's why when he gave you two the new case tonight, he suggested I might be able to help. I think he figured I wouldn't get anywhere with it alone and you two could crack it."

"You didn't know he was going to give that case to us?" Robin asked.

"Not a clue," Sarge said. "Surprised and pleased me. I thought about giving Andor a hug, but figured I would never live that down."

Both detectives broke into laughter and Sarge could feel the tension easing.

"Damn," Robin said, "I would give anything to see you hug Andor."

"We solve this case and you might get your wish," Sarge said.

"Oh, that is so a deal," Pickett said, laughing.

At that moment the waitress came back with their drinks and they all ordered.

Sarge went with a straight cheeseburger while Pickett had a Denver Omelet and Robin had a club sandwich that she said she would take home half to her husband.

Sarge decided he needed to figure out how he was going to fit in with a long-term working team.

"So, how do the two of you work together?" Sarge asked. "And how can I help and stay out of the way at the same time?"

Pickett smiled at him with that question. Clearly she appreciated it.

"I'm the computer geek and I have a husband," Robin said. "So I often let Pickett do the field work and I do the tracking online."

"And I like the field work," Pickett said. "More than I want to admit at times."

"I do too," Sarge said. "Banging on doors and face-to-face questions can sometimes work wonders."

"So looks like you join Pickett," Robin said. "You got a problem with that, partner?"

Sarge watched as Pickett smiled back at her partner, then turned to Sarge with the same smile that reached her wonderful brown eyes. "No problem at all."

"Perfect," Robin said.

Sarge nodded. "Perfect by me as well. Just don't let me slow you down."

Pickett nodded. "Oh trust me, I won't."

He had a hunch that was the truest statement he had heard in a long, long time. He was really, really starting to like this woman and he didn't even know her.

FIVE

October 18th, 2016
Las Vegas, Nevada

"NOTEBOOK," PICKETT SAID to Robin, signaling that they were going to get to work.

Robin brought up onto the table from beside her a blue spiral-bound notebook and the file folder for the case.

Pickett was excited about this new case and actually excited to get to work with Sarge. And to get to know him better. Two cops out pounding the pavement

together definitely got to know each other fairly quickly.

And he had sure said all the right things so far, telling them up front why he was with them and also asking about their methods to see how he would fit in. Both of those had impressed her.

"We use a notebook when we are talking to try to think out our plans and leads," Robin said.

"Amazing how that helps us be organized," Pickett said.

Sarge smiled and pulled a small notebook out of his back pocket and flipped it open. "Can't agree more. If I don't write a thought down these days, it pretends to never have existed and goes and hides."

Pickett laughed. "Damn, do I know that feeling."

"So what can you tell us about this case?" Robin asked.

"Damn near nothing that's not in the file there," Sarge said, shaking his head. "And it's a thin file I'm afraid."

Pickett could see that really, really bothered him. He actually cared about cases like she did. Another thing she liked about him already.

"The victim's name was Trudy Patterson," Sarge said without looking at the file that Robin had opened. "She was twenty-five and from Denver."

He took a sip of water and then went on.

"She was in Vegas by herself for three days planning a wedding and on May 17th, 2010, she left her suite in the MGM Grand to run a few errands and was never seen alive again."

"Did you find her?" Pickett asked.

Sarge nodded. "Five days later her body was found in her rental car sitting on a bluff overlooking Vegas to the west. She was wearing a wedding dress, but not the one she planned on wearing for her wedding."

"I don't see a cause of death," Robin said, glancing at the file.

"Impossible to determine," Sarge said. "We ruled out all the normal causes such as blunt force trauma and obvious wounds. She had been sitting in the closed-up car, in the heat, dead for days. It wasn't a pretty sight. But there didn't seem to be any obvious injuries to her or any sign of sexual activity, from what could be figured out from the decomposing body. In fact, it's not even officially a murder."

Pickett knew for certain now this was a case that had haunted Sarge. He hadn't even glanced at the file and yet remembered all the details after six years. She had a couple cases that ate at her like that as well.

"Family all clear?" Robin asked, still glancing at the file.

"Completely," Sarge said. "They were the ones that insisted to me, sometimes at the top of their voices, that this wasn't just a woman who got cold feet and ran away from a wedding. That something horrid had happened to her."

"But you checked all of them anyway?" Pickett asked, smiling at Sarge.

He smiled back. "I would have found a flea on one of them if it was there. Nothing. They all loved her and she seemed to have no other enemies at all."

"Wedding dress?" Pickett asked, staring at Sarge. He must have gone down that road as well.

"She was about to be married and we found her in a wedding dress," Sarge said. "So I chased that down as much as I could. The dress she was found in was a standard one that could be bought in a hundred stores and nothing in her planning seemed to connect in any way to anyone of interest. And nothing in her financial records showed that she bought the dress she was wearing when we found her."

"But that's where we start digging," Robin said, writing in her notebook.

"Agreed," Sarge said. "I kept feeling I was missing something in her wedding planning, but could never put my finger on it."

Pickett watched as Sarge seemed to vanish into his own thoughts for a moment, his handsome face very serious.

"So why did this case become the one that haunted you?" Pickett asked.

"I have a daughter named Steph who lives in New York," Sarge said. "Steph was talking about getting married and was only two years younger than Trudy Patterson at the time of the murder."

Pickett sat back, nodding.

"So how did the wedding go?" Robin asked.

"Thankfully, they eloped to Hawaii," Sarge said.

Pickett laughed and then leaned forward. "With a little financial help from Dad I bet?"

He just lit up smiling and shaking his head. "I must plead the fifth on that."

Pickett laughed and at that moment the food came and let Sarge off the hook.

SIX

October 18th, 2016
Las Vegas, Nevada

AS THEY ATE and talked about different things, Sarge found himself relaxing more and more with Pickett and Robin. Both were smart, funny, and focused.

It was about halfway through the meal that the conversation turned back to the case at hand. He decided he needed to give them the questions that had puzzled him from the start.

"So my biggest question about this case has always been why the dress?" Sarge said. "Did the killer, if she was actually killed, know she was going to be married and did the killer find her through something she did in the marriage preparation?"

Robin nodded and wrote all that down.

"No traction on those questions I assume?" Pickett asked.

"Nothing," Pickett said. "And right up until I retired I was still trying to retrace some of Trudy's movements in the three days ahead of her disappearance and murder. Nothing. I have my notebook full of all that at home. I would have brought it, but didn't realize I would be working on this case tonight."

Pickett smiled. "Glad we are."

"So am I," Sarge said, smiling back at her.

For a moment they stared at each other. Sarge felt as if Pickett was looking into his every secret. And he honestly didn't mind.

"Why did it take her so long to be found?" Robin asked, breaking the moment between him and Pickett. "Makes no sense if she was sitting up there in the car for days. I'm familiar with that bluff area and it gets a lot of traffic because of the view."

"She was strapped in and upright in the car in the driver's seat," Sarge said, remembering clearly the image of Trudy's body in that hot, hot car. "So we think no one thought anything was wrong. It wasn't until a couple on foot walked past the car that they noticed she was dead and called it in and we connected the car to the missing person's case."

"Similar cases?" Pickett asked.

"I had a couple people try to dig up what they could," Sarge said, "but I honestly don't think we covered that very well."

"That's going to change," Robin said, writing in the notebook.

Sarge looked at her and then at Pickett, who was smiling.

"Robin's husband is Will Sprague," Pickett said.

"Oh," Sarge said. He knew of Will Sprague, the head of Sprague Securities, the best security agency in the city. He ran an entire force of retired Special Forces men and women to protect the rich and famous. He did everything aboveboard and worked closely with the police at times for major events.

Plus Sarge knew that Sprague had more money than almost anyone in this city, and that was going some.

"We have an entire office suite full of the best computer people on the planet," Robin said. "If this case hooks up at all to any other, we'll find the connection."

Sarge laughed. "I sure got with the right team here."

"We like solving cases," Pickett said.

"Damn right we do," Robin said. "So a couple more questions I'm not seeing here in the report. Was Trudy fully dressed under the wedding dress?"

"No," Sarge said. "And no sign of the clothes she was wearing when she left the hotel either."

"It says here she had on a wedding ring," Robin said.

"She did?" Pickett asked, leaning forward.

"She did," Sarge said, nodding. "And her family insisted they had never seen the ring before. All it had was a number two-seventy-three etched inside."

The two women looked at each other and Sarge watched the clear communication of years of being partners.

"What are you thinking?" he asked.

"The killer married Trudy," Pickett said. "Before killing her."

Robin nodded.

Sarge sat back. He had always wondered if it was something like that, but having Pickett and Robin both jump instantly to that conclusion confirmed his suspicions.

He turned to Robin. "That's the link to other cases you want to search for."

"Damn, you're right," Robin said, writing in her notebook.

Sarge glanced at Pickett who was smiling at him.

And he liked that smile more than he wanted to admit, even to himself.

Part Two
THE TRAIL EXPLODES

SEVEN

October 19th, 2016
Las Vegas, Nevada

PICKETT WAS SURPRISED at how comfortable the Golden Nugget Buffet was, and how wonderful it smelled at ten in the morning. Eggs, bacon, with a background smell of waffles and maple syrup. She got instantly hungry just getting near the place.

Sarge said he ate here four mornings a week and just approaching the place gave her an idea why. The buffet was up an escalator away from the casino and then surrounded by planters with tall green plants under the high ceiling.

The far wall was all windows that looked out over the large main-floor pool and shark tank below. Those windows really made the entire place feel almost like sitting on a balcony instead of in a dark casino.

Everything was oak and brown-toned cloth and there were more than enough tables to hold a fairly large crowd. At this point, there weren't more than thirty people scattered around the restaurant and Sarge sat at a table off to one side, reading the morning newspaper.

He had a cup of coffee in front of him, but no food.

She read the same paper, but always on her iPad in the mornings. She smiled at how handsome he looked sitting there, clearly absorbed in the reading.

As she neared the front desk, he glanced up and waved to her over the planter that she should just come in. She did, going past the cash register and a smiling woman hostess who just nodded to her.

He stood as she approached, the smile reaching his eyes.

Again, she was struck at how really, really handsome he was and how attracted to him she had become in just one day. And he had manners. She couldn't remember the last time a person had stood for her when she approached a table.

"You didn't need to buy me breakfast," she said, smiling at him as she sat down and he sat back down as well. "But thank you."

He laughed. "I didn't. But maybe I should take the credit."

"Do I need to go pay?" She glanced back at the cashiers who didn't seem to even notice she was sitting down.

"Nope," he said, holding up what looked like a ticket to a show on the Strip. "I eat here so often, they keep giving me two-for-one coupons, but until today I never had a chance to use one."

"Glad I could be of service," she said, laughing.

"Then let's eat," he said, standing.

Ten minutes later they were back at the table. Both had personally-made ham-and-cheese omelets and she had some fruit and a small slice of a waffle. He had gone for a slice of ham and two strips of bacon with his omelet.

"I can see why you like this place," she said. "Lots of choices of food, comfortable place with lots of light, and friendly people."

"I have a hunch I would eat here seven mornings a week if I let myself," he said, shaking his head.

"And what would be wrong with that?" she asked, biting in to the fantastic omelet and savoring the taste.

"Just never imagined myself in my early sixties being in a rut like this," he said.

"Honestly," she said, smiling at the slight look of worry in his eyes. "I like morning routines. With all the craziness of being a cop during the day, my only sane time was mornings."

"Yeah," he said, nodding. "That I agree with. Just feels wrong doing it alone I guess."

Pickett understood that as well. She wanted to get to know this man better and she was known for being blunt, so no time to fade on that now.

"So divorced, huh?" Picket asked. "Do you have more than one daughter?"

"Just the one," Sarge said, the grin returning to his face as he said that. "She's amazing."

"Tough divorce?" Pickett asked.

Sarge shook his head as he kept eating. "Actually, no. Andrea and I had drifted apart as this job tends to do to people. She met a nice guy and decided she wanted to start over just as I retired. I like the guy she met and she and I are still friends. They live in Chicago."

Pickett actually sat back with that. Sarge just kept eating and she could tell there was no emotional energy at all talking about his ex-wife. He really did still get along with her.

Pickett was really, really liking this man more and more.

"So how about you?" Sarge said, glancing up and noticing that she had stopped eating and was staring at him.

"Wonderful daughter living in Washington, DC," Pickett said. "My husband had a midlife crisis and went off to LA with a twenty-some-year-old and a new red sports car. I got enough money to live comfortably the rest of my life and a wonderful condo in the Ogden, all paid off."

"Wow," Sarge said, staring at her. He seemed surprised about something for a moment. Then he said, "Seems you are over it because I heard no anger there at all."

Pickett shrugged. "Only time I got angry was at him being so stupid. I don't do well with stupidity in general, but especially from him. So I made him pay to get rid of me and it hasn't bothered me much since."

Sarge laughed and kept staring at her, smiling.

"I got egg on my nose or something?" Pickett asked, after a moment, pretending

to wipe off her face. She loved it when he looked at her like that.

"Nope," he said. "just admiring someone who I have a lot in common with. Me and stupidity are not friends either."

"Oh, God," Pickett said, going back to eating. "Heaven help a poor fool who runs into us together."

"Doubt heaven would help him," Sarge said, laughing.

Pickett laughed as well. Damn, how was this man even possible?

But it seemed he was.

EIGHT

October 19th, 2016
Las Vegas, Nevada

SARGE COULDN'T REMEMBER the last time he had enjoyed a breakfast as much as this one with Pickett. Not only was she the best-looking woman he had met, but she was funny, and smart, and a fantastic detective.

And she liked the Golden Nugget Buffet.

He wasn't honestly sure which of those things scared him more about her. But he was going to just enjoy the time with her as he had it and see what happened.

After breakfast, she had pulled out a notebook and he had taken his small notebook out of his back pocket with his notes about the case, and they set to work.

"I haven't heard from Robin yet about any of the searches she is doing," Pickett said. "So got any ideas as to where we start?"

Sarge liked the sounds of the "we" part of that. He had been fighting this case so long on his own, it felt fantastic to have top help with it.

"I had an idea about six months ago I haven't been able to do anything about yet," Sarge said. "How about we detail out what a woman like Trudy would need to do to prepare for a wedding here in Las Vegas, then eliminate the stops she already made to figure out what her errands might have been the day she disappeared?"

Pickett brightened up with that. "I like that a lot. Somewhere on one of those last errands is where things went bad for her."

"Exactly," Sarge said. "But who do we know that would be able to detail out a Las Vegas wedding like that? My daughter eloped."

Pickett smiled. "Robin and I have a friend who could do that easily. So let's put together the details we know that Trudy did before she disappeared, then head there."

"Your friend wouldn't happen to be Elvis?" Sarge asked, poking at her.

"Nope," Pickett said, smiling at Sarge. "Elvis's wife. Didn't you know, Elvis is dead?"

Sarge just laughed and shook his head. Then they spent the next thirty minutes putting together every detail that was known about Trudy's three days in Las Vegas and what parts of her wedding details she had already taken care of.

Then, with to-go cups full of fresh coffee offered by a friendly waitress, they headed out to Pickett's car, a blue Grand Cherokee SUV parked on the second level of the parking garage.

Sarge buckled into the passenger seat and tried to remember the last time he had ridden with someone to go anywhere. With him and Andrea, he had always driven.

And with the rotating partners he had over the years, he had always been the main driver. It felt very, very weird to be in the passenger seat, that was for sure.

But Pickett got them out of the garage easily and merging into traffic without a problem. She drove one-handed, with a confidence of a long-time driver who just knew where to look and when. After a few blocks, he relaxed completely. More than likely she was a better driver than he was.

Was there anything at all wrong with this woman?

The chapel they were headed to was on the Stratosphere end of the Strip, closest to downtown, so the drive only took about five minutes. Pickett pulled the SUV into a small parking lot behind a building with a giant Elvis holding a wedding ring on the front. Damn, she hadn't been kidding. They really were going to an Elvis chapel.

The business looked like it had seen better days and needed a coat of paint, at least. A gutter was hanging loose off of one side and some graffiti scarred up another wall. Sarge just couldn't imagine anyone wanting to get married in such a shabby place. But it was Las Vegas, so anything was possible.

The sun was starting to get warm already and Pickett pulled out a baseball cap from the back seat and made sure the wide bill shaded her face.

"I burn instantly," she said, shaking her head.

Sarge laughed. "You ought to see the hat I wear in the summer. The brim is so wide all the way around, my daughter told me I look like a villain from a spaghetti western."

Pickett laughed as they opened the large front door of the building. The door had a stained-glass window in the middle that hadn't been cleaned in months, at least.

The inside was cool and dark and smelled slightly moldy. A background smell of old cigarettes covered everything. To Sarge the place felt more like a run-down mortuary than a wedding chapel. There were some overstuffed couches around a waiting room with dark-wood paneling and cheap end tables covered in ashtrays. Two of the ashtrays were still full of cigarette butts.

Sarge had no desire at all to sit on the couches. God-only-knew what was on them, considering he could see patterns of stains in places waiting-room couches should not be stained.

There were no signs, no pricing, no images of Elvis anywhere in the room. Just a plain room with dark wood paneling and ugly maroon couches. This really had to be the worst wedding chapel he had ever been in.

A heavy-set woman came out of the back door. She had on a pink print dress that looked faded and a beehive hairdo that seemed to defy gravity.

Her hair was a bright silver and her face had what looked like built-up layers of make-up. Her eyes had so much dark make-up around them, she looked like a distant relative of a raccoon.

"Detective Pickett," the woman said, her voice hoarse like a person who smoked far, far too many cigarettes. "What a welcome surprise on a dull morning."

"Business bad?" Pickett asked.

The woman shrugged and the hair towering on her head didn't even shake. "Got five weddings this week I'm working on around town, but that's slow."

Pickett turned to Sarge. "This is Detective Carson," Pickett said. "Detective, this is Madeline Stein, just

Stein to all her friends. She's the best wedding planner in the city."

"Nice meeting you," Sarge said, nodding to the woman who nodded back at him and seemed pleased at Pickett's description of her, but not surprised.

"So we have an old cold case we're working on," Pickett said. "We had a woman back in the spring of 2010 go missing right near the end of planning her wedding."

The woman nodded, the tower of silver hair staying firm on her head, and Pickett went on. Sarge was going to let her lead on this one all the way.

"We have traced most of everything the woman did before she disappeared. But we are wondering what she would have left to do."

Stein smiled. "To see who the woman planning her wedding was going to visit when she vanished to give you some leads, huh?"

"Exactly," Pickett said.

"You got a list of what she already had done?"

Sarge handed Stein the list. "This is what we know she did and in the order she did it."

Stein scanned down the list quickly, nodding. Then she looked up and asked, "Do you know if her dress needed a fitting?"

"Already done before she came into town," Sarge said.

Stein nodded again and once again the tower of hair didn't seem to even shake, let alone threaten to fall off her head. The thing had to be wired up there somehow. No hair could hold that shape without a lot of help.

"The woman was a good planner," Stein said. "She did everything exactly right and in the right order. Right out of my book, actually."

Sarge was surprised at that mention of a book, but said nothing.

"So if she was following your book," Pickett asked. "What last-minute things did she need to do?"

"Could be a number of things," Stein said.

Sarge took out his notebook as Stein started to list things Trudy Patterson might have done that final day.

"If she was alone in town, she might have been taking care of the groom's tux."

"She was alone," Pickett said.

"She would have checked on the flowers she ordered," Stein said. "She would have had a final appointment with the wedding chapel and she might have wanted to set up limos for the guests arriving at the airport."

Stein handed the list back to Sarge and turned to Pickett. "Was this woman ever found?"

"Five days later," Pickett said, "In her car."

"Wearing a wedding dress with nothing under it and a ring no one had seen before with a number on the ring," Stein said.

Sarge damn near staggered backwards. How in the world did this woman know that?

Pickett seemed rocked as well. "Stein, how did you know all that?"

"Did the girl give a description of her rapist?" Stein asked.

"She was dead," Pickett said.

"Sat for days in a hot car," Sarge said.

"Oh, the poor girl," Stein said, shaking her head. "Never heard of any of them dying before."

"Them?" Pickett and Sarge said both at the same time.

"Sure," Stein said. "I can give you a list of the ones I remember. But I'm sure they all filed rape reports, or at least most of them. The bastard doing that cost all of us planners and chapels around town a lot of business over the years and you folks could never get a lead on him. When the bride gets raped right before a wedding, the wedding always gets called off."

Pickett and Sarge just looked at each other. Sarge felt like he was in shock.

Stein laughed a throaty, deep laugh. "You two are surprised, I can tell."

"We are," Pickett said. "We are homicide detectives, so we didn't follow much else."

"And this case never linked to any rape cases," Sarge said.

"I think the detectives who came by here a few times called the guy the Bride Rapist."

"Any cases lately?" Pickett asked.

"I've heard of one or two," Stein said, nodding. "Might want to check with some of the bigger chapels and with your own folks."

Sarge just couldn't believe what he was hearing. His one case, his nightmare case, had just gotten a lot, lot bigger.

And even more nightmarish.

NINE

October 19th, 2016
Las Vegas, Nevada

PICKETT DIDN'T SAY anything after they thanked Stein for her time and headed toward her car. The heat of the morning was picking up and the parking lot pavement made it worse.

As she unlocked her car and climbed in, she called Robin, then turned on the car to get it cooled down.

Sarge climbed into the passenger seat and closed the door as Robin came on the line and Pickett switched the phone to speaker so they could both listen.

"Sarge and I discovered something huge," Pickett said before Robin could say anything but "Hi, partner."

It took Pickett about three minutes to explain what they had just discovered from Stein, including the stops Trudy might have taken the morning she vanished.

When Pickett finished, Robin was silent for a long moment. The only sounds were the air-conditioning and the traffic on the nearby Strip.

Finally Robin said, "Jesus, the poor girl."

"I'm betting we're not dealing with a purposeful murder," Pickett said.

Beside her, Sarge was nodding.

"She was raped right before her wedding," Robin said, "so in shock she went up to that ridge and just sat and passed out and died from the heat."

"Exactly," Pickett said.

"That just makes me sick," Robin said. "But we still take this bastard down for her death."

"Agreed," Sarge said.

Pickett couldn't agree more. Her stomach was twisted up like she was staring at a freshly-opened grave. She hated that more than anything, and this felt exactly like that.

Again the silence was broken only by the air-conditioning hum and the street noise. It seemed like a very heavy silence.

Sarge just stared at his notebook.

"So you want us to go get the files from the sexual crimes unit on all of the cases?" Pickett asked.

Two Cold Poker Gang Novels
Available at your favorite booksellers.

"I can do that easily from here," Robin said. "I'm going to get one or two of our computer people on this, searching for patterns, anything that might give this sicko away."

"We'll follow up on the leads that Stein gave us that Trudy might have done that last morning," Pickett said. "Let us know at once if a pattern starts to emerge so we can focus down."

"Got it," Robin said.

And she hung up.

Pickett clicked off the phone and turned to face the handsome detective beside her. His expression was one of determination.

"Suggestions on which thing Trudy did that we tackle first?" Pickett asked.

Sarge nodded and looked at her, his hazel eyes intent. "Since there are so many, and all of the cases are around weddings of some sort, I'm thinking that narrows it down to the flowers or the tuxes or the chapel."

Pickett nodded. "Tuxes. That kind of shop would also have access to wedding dresses."

"Good place to start," Sarge said, nodding.

He flipped open his notebook and went through it quickly until he reached a page about halfway through. "August's Tux Place."

Picket was impressed that he had taken that detailed of notes.

"I went in there," Sarge said, "but they claimed to have never seen her that day."

"Of course they did," Pickett said.

Then she realized there was a huge bit of data they didn't have. They were so used to working homicides where the victims couldn't talk, it just dawned on her that there were survivors. From what Stein had said, a lot of them.

"We need the information from the survivors first," Pickett said. "See what they remember."

"Of course," Sarge said, shaking his head.

Pickett smiled. A homicide detective seldom had survivors to talk with.

Pickett called Robin back and asked her to quickly scan a bunch of the reports to see how the rape victims were taken. That alone would narrow their focus.

"Give me three minutes," Robin said and again hung up.

Pickett glanced over at Sarge, who was staring at his notebook.

"Anything there that make sense with this new information?"

Sarge nodded. "No real clear cause of death. Now that makes sense. And why she was on that ridge makes sense now as well. So many questions suddenly answered as a ton more questions pop up."

Pickett looked at the handsome detective. Then she said, "Why do I have the suspicion this is bigger than even a serial rapist?"

"I was thinking the same thing," Sarge said, glancing at her. "Not a clue why, however. But my gut is twisted on this one, which tells me we're missing a lot of this."

Pickett knew that feeling as well. And as detectives, you learned to trust that gut. Sometimes your subconscious could see things your waking mind couldn't see. Someone had once explained to her that was what "gut sense" meant. She just knew she had learned to trust hers.

At that moment Robin called back and Pickett clicked on the phone.

"No help," Robin said.

"How can there be no help?" Pickett asked. "That makes no sense at all."

"That's what has stumped the detectives working these cases," Robin said. "The women have no memory at all on the day they were taken."

"Any record of some of them being hypnotized to bring up lost memories?" Sarge asked.

"Six of them that I can tell tried that," Robin said. "I'm still digging, but what the pattern is that the women seem to remember is leaving for an errand on their own, then waking up as they are being married to a tall man wearing a plastic face in some sort of wedding chapel. They are drugged and can't speak or even talk. Then they are taken to a nearby bedroom and raped, then the next thing they remember, they are in their cars."

"Drugs," Sarge said a moment before Pickett could.

"That's the theory on this," Robin said, "but no drugs were found in the women's systems in any fashion. No DNA traces, nothing."

"So we have someone who knows chemicals and drugs," Pickett said.

"You said they were married?" Sarge asked Robin. "Someone else there?"

"Yes," Robin said. "A third person was always involved in the ceremony wearing an Elvis mask and dressed like Elvis."

Sarge glanced over at the Elvis chapel at the same time Pickett did.

Then Pickett decided she needed to quickly ask Robin one more question to make sure Stein was cleared.

"Any description of the groom or the Elvis person besides the masks?"

"Both extremely thin," Robin said after a moment. "And a lot of the victims have a memory of a smell of roses."

Pickett just shook her head. This was beyond strange and ugly.

Then Sarge twisted it one more twist.

"Robin, would it be possible for your people to review missing persons' cases where a near-future bride went missing. I know I dealt with a lot of them and always thought it was just the bride getting cold feet."

Pickett looked at Sarge who was frowning and intent. "You think the women who were set free are only the tip of this?"

"I have a hunch," Sarge said. "And Robin, if not too much problem, add in the men who vanished right before getting married as well."

"Crap, just crap," Robin said. "I'll get more people on this. Back with you two as soon as I can."

And Robin hung up.

"God, I hope you are wrong on this hunch," Pickett said.

"So do I," Sarge said.

He turned and looked at her intently. "But you don't think I am, do you?"

"No," Pickett said.

And she hated that more than she wanted to admit.

TEN

October 19th, 2016
Las Vegas, Nevada

SARGE GLANCED AT Pickett, then back at the Elvis chapel. "Is Stein some sort of marriage expert?"

"Wrote the major book on how to get married in Las Vegas," Pickett said.

"What's with this old chapel?" Sarge asked.

"It's not used anymore," Pickett said. "Stein's husband, Bernie, was the Elvis here who married people and kept the building up. He died of a heart attack about twelve years ago and Stein wrote her book and then started freelancing for other chapels and numbers of the casinos."

"How much do you trust her?"

"She helped Robin and me on more cases than I want to count," Pickett said. "So a lot. She knows weddings and a lot about the darker sides of this city. She and Bernie lived and worked here through the mob days."

Sarge nodded. They were going to have to trust someone at some point and if Pickett thought Stein good, they might as well trust her for the moment.

"I think we need more information about Elvis chapels," Sarge said, "why they came about, and if Stein has an estimate of how many marriages are performed in Las Vegas every year."

"Robin can get us the license information easily from the Clark County clerk," Pickett said. "But how many actually happen would be another number completely. Stein might have a guess on that."

Sarge nodded and then climbed out into the heat. The day still wasn't that warm and chances are would end up being one of those really wonderful fall days that Vegas had a lot of. Not too hot, not cold at night. Spring and fall here were the best times, and over the years Sarge had really come to appreciate the nice days.

Sarge held the large front door for Pickett and she nodded to him and gave him that wonderful smile he was coming to really enjoy as they entered the lobby.

Stein appeared almost at once, her white beehive hair still towering over her like a magic act. This time she smelled more of smoke, as if she had just crushed out a cigarette. Sarge stared at her hair for a moment trying to figure out, without success, what held the thing up. Maybe it really was magic.

"Saw you two still sitting out there on the security cam," Stein said. "Figured you would be back. What can I help you with?"

Pickett gave Stein a quick summary of some of the information, including the rape victims remembering being married by a tall man in an Elvis mask.

Stein just shook her head at that. Sarge could tell that upset her, but didn't surprise her.

"So how did this Elvis marrying people come about?" Sarge asked. "Always wondered, never knew."

"Elvis and Pricilla got married here in the old Alladin Hotel in 1967," Stein said. "That started it all and it became a thing to attract tourists who wanted to get married, just like drive-through weddings and underwater weddings and all of that."

Sarge nodded. Vegas was the home of the Elvis impersonators, so it made sense from that side as well.

"So how many marriages actually happen in Vegas every year?" Pickett asked.

Stein shrugged. "Not a clue, actually. Every casino, hotel, and small place like this one can perform them. To be able to perform a legal marriage all it takes is a simple license from the state that anyone can get for a small fee."

"Isn't there more?" Pickett asked, sounding surprised.

Sarge was surprised at that as well.

Stein shrugged. "Not much. Each couple needs to get a license from Clark County, and I think there are over eighty thousand or so of those a year normally. You can file for that online and just pick it up with proper ID when you get here. Very easy and cheap. But not sure how many of those marriages actually happened and were legally filed after they did."

Pickett nodded. "Robin should be able to find that number if we need it."

"I heard one place claim," Stein said, "that on average there were over three hundred weddings every day here. But the math on that doesn't work out compared to the licenses. I would estimate about two hundred a day is closer to the number."

Sarge just shook his head. Two-hundred weddings a day. No wonder the industry around weddings was so huge in this city.

"So how regular do either the bride or the groom get cold feet and vanish?" Pickett asked.

Sarge was impressed she had managed to stay on topic. He was still lost in the number of weddings.

"All the time," Stein said, shaking her head. "All the time."

"So much so that it's normal?" Sarge asked.

"Completely normal," Stein said. "Maybe one out of four weddings don't make it to the final kiss."

"Oh, god," Pickett said.

Sarge felt his gut clinch.

"Why?" Stein asked, looking worried and puzzled.

"We think our rapist might be doing more than raping women," Pickett said. "Just our gut sense."

Stein's face got even whiter, if that was possible under her layers of makeup, and she bent forward.

And once again, her hair remained solid and in place.

ELEVEN

October 19th, 2016
Las Vegas, Nevada

PICKETT LED SARGE out to her Jeep and they both climbed in and she got the air-conditioning going again. She just felt stunned at how large this had become. It was no wonder the detectives investigating the rapes hadn't gotten anywhere.

"So now where?" Sarge asked. "I honestly have no idea where to even jab a stick into a mess this big."

Pickett laughed and nodded. "I have no idea either."

"So until we hear from Robin and all her computer geeks," Sarge said, "let's try August's Tux Shop. Nothing to lose at this point."

"Don't let Robin hear you call her computer people geeks," Pickett said, laughing as she backed the car around to head back out onto the Strip.

"What does she call them?" Sarge asked.

"Elves," Pickett said, grinning at Sarge before pulling into traffic. "But she's the only one allowed to and only with me."

"Got it," Sarge said, laughing.

Pickett drove, really enjoying how having Sarge beside her made her relax. She usually got all wound up in a case about this point and stressed, but his humor and just solid presence beside her made her stay level and focused. And that felt damn good.

She was really, really starting to be attracted to this man and she hadn't even known him for a full day yet. She wasn't sure how that was possible, but she sure wasn't going to slow it down. She could see no point in that in the slightest.

And even better, he seemed attracted to her. And at times they almost seemed to think the same.

It took her about ten minutes to get them into the parking lot of August's Tux Shop just off the Strip. It was a clean, modern, single-story building with windows across the front full of different forms of tuxedos. Under the name of the store it said, "Established 1967."

"Wow, almost fifty years in business," Pickett said as they climbed out and headed through the warm afternoon air toward the front door. "That's downright ancient for this town."

"Family business," Sarge said, "if I remember right. Let me lead on this one. I have an idea."

"Be my guest," Pickett said, smiling at him as he once again held the door open for her. A girl could get used to that kind of treatment.

Inside the place was cool and bright, with racks of tuxedos along three walls and a lot of them on mannequins in different poses.

A man about their age came forward, smiling. "Can I be of service?"

The man had dark blue eyes and a smile that didn't reach his eyes. He was perfectly dressed in dark slacks and a tan shirt and matching tie. His gray hair was combed back, also perfectly.

"Detectives Carson and Pickett," Sarge said. "Would it be possible to ask you or one of the owners a few questions?"

Now the smile actually reached the man's eyes as he said, "I'm August LaPine, the owner. Be glad to answer what I can."

LaPine shook both of their hands in a formal manner and then led them to a counter in the back. LaPine went around the counter and then again smiled.

The counter was a display for all sorts of things like cufflinks and tie clasps and behind the counter were two desks, both neat, yet clearly used with new computers on both. This most certainly looked like a solid, well-run business.

"We're working on the Trudy Patterson case from 2010," Sarge said as Pickett watched LaPine.

The man showed no signs of awareness of the name in the slightest.

"Trudy was in town for her wedding and disappeared and was found dead about five days later. One of her stops that day was supposed to be here to check on the tuxes for her future husband and his friends."

"Oh, the poor girl. What day was that?" LaPine asked.

"May 17th, 2010," Sarge said.

LaPine indicated they should wait a moment and he went to one desk and sat down and started working on a computer. A moment later LaPine nodded, hit a print button, waited for a moment for a paper to print, and then came back to the counter.

Pickett was impressed at how willing he was to help and how clearly organized his records were. But all the smiles and help seemed slightly fake and that bothered Sarge a little. Not sure why, but he made a note of it.

LaPine slid the paper around for the detectives to see. "She did reserve and pay half-down for the tuxedos. She never picked them up, so as per contract we kept her deposit. I have a note that a Detective Carson stopped by a week later to ask about her."

"I did," Sarge said, nodding. "So I was wondering, if it wouldn't be too much trouble, approximately how many no-shows like her do you have in a month?"

"A great deal," LaPine said, shaking his head, clearly seeming to be sad about the fact. "It's why we must ask for half down."

"Do you ever hear why some don't show?" Sarge asked. "Do they ever call in?"

"A few do," LaPine said, nodding. "If they give us enough notice, even though we don't have to, we refund their deposit. But most don't bother."

Pickett was impressed at where this was going. Not sure how it was going to help, but Sarge clearly had something on his mind.

"Say if you did a hundred reservations for tuxedos for weddings," Sarge said, "approximately how many wouldn't show without calling?"

"Ten or so," LaPine said. "Nature of the wedding business in Las Vegas I'm afraid."

"And you keep track of all the no-shows?" Sarge asked.

"We do," LaPine said, nodding.

"Thank you for your time," Sarge said, surprising Pickett as he stuck out his hand to shake LaPine's hand. "We're just doing some basic research to try to understand the wedding business in this town."

"Glad to be of service, detectives," LaPine said, bowing slightly as he shook Pickett's hand again.

With that, Sarge turned and headed for the front door and Pickett stayed with him.

When they reached the car and climbed in, Pickett turned to Sarge. "Want to explain what that was all about?"

Sarge smiled at her as she got the car started and the air-conditioning going.

"We need some more data. And as I remembered, that store is, and always has been, very organized."

"But we have no grounds to get a warrant for their files," Pickett said. Then the

moment she said that, she laughed. "You know a guy who knows a guy, don't you?"

"We're only going to use the information for deep background," Sarge said, smiling at her. "LaPine will never know it's been borrowed. I'm just trying to figure out a way to narrow this mess down some."

Pickett just sat there smiling at the handsome man beside her.

"Lunch?" Sarge said.

"My stomach was thinking the same thing," Pickett said. "Bellagio Café is good and we're right out here."

"Perfect," Sarge said. "Want to have Robin join us?"

"We'll call her when we get there and see," Pickett said. She didn't say that waiting to call Robin until then would give her more time alone with Sarge and she wanted to get to know him better.

"Sounds great," Sarge said.

"Scares me how we think alike at times," Pickett said, finally moving and getting the car headed back toward the street.

"I kind of like it," Sarge said, smiling at her.

"Yeah, actually," Pickett said, "So do I."

And then she couldn't believe she had actually said that.

TWELVE

October 19th, 2016
Las Vegas, Nevada

THE BELLAGIO CAFÉ had an atmosphere Sarge really liked. Brown tones of oak and cloth, with lots of plants between the booths to give each booth a sense of privacy.

The sounds of the casino were muted and even the sound of others talking didn't seem to get very loud.

He often came here for lunch or dinner when out this far along the Strip. Almost always alone. His condo was far, far closer to the Golden Nugget than here, but this was his second favorite place.

One of the big reasons was that not only was it comfortable, but the food was good and the selection amazing at any time of the day or night.

He knew that Julia and Lott and Andor also came out here a great deal, but he didn't see them today, which he was glad about, actually. He really wanted to just spend a little time with Pickett to get to know her better.

Sarge waited until they got seated in a back booth before calling his friend Mike Dans while Pickett called Robin.

Mike and his girlfriend, Heather Voight often worked with Julia and Lott on cases as well. Sarge had met Mike on a robbery case about ten years before and liked him. Mike was a former Special Forces guy who hadn't lost a step or a bit of muscle. He kept his hair short and had an infectious smile that hid a brilliant mind.

He also controlled a small army of Special Forces retired soldiers for all sorts of jobs, many off the books.

Mike had done Sarge favors at times over the years and Sarge had done a few in return. Mike ran a security firm, only not a famous one like Robin's husband's firm, but a firm that stayed behind the scenes.

Mike and his people were also experts in all sorts of computer issues.

Mike sounded happy to hear from Sarge and was pleased to hear Sarge was back working again with the Cold Poker Gang.

Sarge quickly told Mike about the case they were working on, that it might be huge, and what he was thinking about the August Tux Shop records and how it might help them cross-reference a few details. And that no one would know and the records would only be used for deep background.

Mike seemed to have no issue with the favor and said he would e-mail Sarge the files that night.

As Sarge clicked off his phone, Pickett clicked off her phone as well.

"Robin will be here in thirty minutes," Pickett said. "She's bringing some information."

"My friend is getting us the August Tux Shop records tonight," Sarge said.

"Is this the same friend that works behind the scenes with Julia and Lott at times?" Pickett asked, smiling.

"One and the same," Sarge said.

"Got to meet this guy someday," Pickett said, shaking her head.

"I would think that with Robin and her husband's business," Sarge said, "you wouldn't need my friend."

"Oh, we need him," Pickett said, laughing. "For things like the reason you called him. Robin's people could never do that. Wouldn't dare."

"Then I'll be glad to introduce you when we get a chance," Sarge said, smiling.

They both ordered coffee and water and then Sarge decided he needed a snack while waiting for Robin, so he ordered them some chips and salsa.

After the waitress moved away, Sarge turned to face Pickett. She had scooted to the back of the booth to leave room for Robin. Sarge liked being that close to Pickett. It felt right and that should be worrying him, but it wasn't.

"So why did you retire?" Sarge asked. That seemed like the easiest question to start with to try to get to know her better.

Pickett smiled and stared at him with her wonderful brown eyes. "Honestly, both Robin and I were tired of the grind. Tired of the paperwork, and tired of being submerged in the cesspool of the lowlife of this city."

Sarge just nodded to that. "I know that feeling."

"After the ex ran off with his bimbo girlfriend," Pickett said, twisting her coffee cup in her hands, "I had enough money to do what I wanted, so figured I would do some traveling."

"Did you?" Sarge asked.

Pickett shrugged. "Don't much like hotel rooms considering all the crime scenes I saw in hotels here. And I would be away from Vegas for a few days and get bored and miss this stupid town."

Sarge laughed. "Wow, we really do think alike. I felt exactly the same way. Exactly."

"How much did you travel?" Pickett asked.

"The worst was a ten-day cruise," Sarge said. "All alone, bored out of my mind, and I couldn't eat enough or drink enough to change that, so I ended up reading a couple dozen novels. That I enjoyed."

"Robin and I were going to try that," Pickett said, shaking her head. "Came to our senses before it cost us too much."

Sarge decided to just plow on ahead. "Are you seeing anyone. None of my business, I know, but figured I would ask."

Pickett's brown eyes lit up and she smiled. "Nope. And you?"

"Nope," Sarge said. "Been thinking of getting a cat though."

Pickett actually laughed at that. "Can I help you pick it out? The shelters around here are always looking to find homes for some of the cats. I would love to help you rescue a few from the cages."

"You like cats?" Sarge said, actually surprised.

"Had one named Vice, but he died a couple of months before the ex left town with the bimbo. Haven't felt settled enough since to go for another."

"I love the name," Sarge said. "My wife and I had two named Come and Go. But they were her cats and she took them with her when she moved to Chicago. I missed the cats more than I missed her, which is kind of sad to say."

Pickett shook her head. "You know there is a horrid joke there about two cats named Come and Go leaving?"

"Oh, yeah," Sarge said. "And thanks for the restraint."

Picket laughed. Then said, "Feels empty at home, doesn't it?"

Sarge nodded. "And a goldfish just wouldn't do it."

Pickett laughed. "Then a cat it is."

"And I would love the help finding one."

"Deal," Pickett said.

At that moment their waitress came back with the chips and salsa and their coffees.

Sarge just smiled at Pickett as she dug into the chips. Damn he was starting to really be attracted to this woman.

He just hoped she felt the same. But only time was going to tell on that. Now at least he had help finding a cat or maybe two.

THIRTEEN

October 19th, 2016
Las Vegas, Nevada

ROBIN JOINED THEM just a few minutes after the chips and salsa arrived. Pickett was very much enjoying the conversation with Sarge. Not only was he handsome, he wasn't seeing anyone, and he liked cats.

And he made her laugh. She hadn't laughed much in a very long time, so that felt great.

He felt a little too perfect, but at this point, at her age, she wasn't going to question too much an almost-mister-perfect. She was just going to enjoy her time with him and see what happened.

But she had to admit, after less than a day of knowing him, she was hoping a lot would happen between them.

Robin sat down, putting a couple of folders off to one side and dug into the chips as Sarge told Robin about the list of names they were getting from the August Tux Shop.

Robin just shook her head. "I didn't hear that," she said, "but I'm glad we are getting the records. They should help some."

"That bad?" Pickett asked. She knew the sound of her partner's voice and Robin sounded discouraged right now.

"Massive numbers," Robin said, opening a manila folder in front of her.

Pickett glanced at Sarge, who looked suddenly very worried.

"We dug only back to Trudy Patterson's disappearance in 2010," Robin said. "In a quick search, we found in six years over six thousand missing person's cases filed, men and women that had something to do with a marriage. That's out of the five hundred or more missing persons cases filed every month."

"Oh, wow," Pickett said. That sounded like an impossible number.

"We were able to eliminate just about half of those we targeted because the person actually was just running away from the marriage, either before or after, and showed up at home or called in when they discovered a report had been filed about them."

"That leaves three thousand in six years," Sarge said. "All attached to marriages, right?"

Robin nodded. "We eliminated another five hundred because of drunk marriages and one party or the other woke up and ran."

"Walk of shame with a marriage attached," Sarge said. "The worst kind."

Both Pickett and Robin laughed. Pickett was really starting to enjoy Sarge's sense of humor. He had a way of cutting building tension and keeping them focused.

"We got rid of another thousand," Robin said, "because the couple was reported missing by family members, mostly parents of the bride."

"And they never showed up later?" Pickett asked.

"We never went any farther with those," Robin said. "And since missing person cases are never investigated unless there are suspicious circumstances, those had little information attached."

"So that leaves about fifteen hundred over six years," Sarge said.

Robin nodded. "Not quite one per week for the entire six years. All somehow attached to weddings. All now officially missing persons' cold cases."

"That many, huh?" Pickett asked. That number shocked her. She knew there were a lot of missing person cases in Vegas, but to hear it put that way was hard to grasp.

"I learned a ton about that side of our job today," Robin said. "The detectives that work missing persons are an amazing bunch in every precinct. And Las Vegas is the only city in the country at the moment to have a dedicated missing persons' cold case detective."

"You're kidding?" Pickett asked.

"Nope," Robin said. "We never met him. Started the job after we all retired. He works out of the main offices. And the missing person detectives around town use a lot of volunteers from the VIPS Program."

"What's that?" Sarge asked a half second before Pickett did.

"Volunteers in Police Service," Robin said. "We were really sheltered on the homicide side of things because volunteers were the last people we wanted messing around in a case. But with missing persons, quick action and lots of boots on the ground can often save lives."

"Wow," Sarge said, shaking his head. "Never knew."

Pickett shook her head as well.

"Lot of this is new, coming in about the time we three were calling it quits," Robin said. "There is now NCMA, the National Center for Missing Adults. We searched all their data bases as well this afternoon, plus a bunch more."

Pickett just looked at Sarge. For the first time in a while she was feeling in over her head on something, and from the look on Sarge's face, he wasn't feeling much different.

"So here is what my husband's people are doing," Robin said. "They are trying to file down that list by data-mining every database they can find around the world. Comparing everything from DNA to fingerprints to blood types and so on."

"Looking through morgue records as well?" Sarge asked.

"First place they are looking," Robin said. "Homicide cases, everything."

"So they might be able to get the number down to one per week since Trudy Patterson went missing and turned up dead," Sarge said.

Robin nodded. "If we're lucky."

Pickett stared at her partner, who was studying the file in front of her, then at Sarge, who seemed to be lost in thought.

"We also need to focus on the women who were falsely married, raped, and then let go," Pickett said.

Robin took a deep breath and Pickett didn't like that at all. Robin only did that when she had really bad news.

"About one per week," Robin said, "over the same time period, if you figure a certain normal percentage were never reported."

"Please tell me that number isn't certain," Sarge said.

Pickett just wanted to be sick.

"As close as we can figure it from the records," Robin said. "We figured that about a quarter of the cases would not be reported. Maybe more. That's why the August Tux Shop records will help us firm that up some."

Sarge sat back for a moment.

Robin went back to staring at the folder in front of her.

Pickett wanted to just toss this entire thing in and run away. Women abducted and raped right before getting married. The same number of women and men vanishing right before getting married. This was just too ugly to even try to wrap her mind around. As it was, she had no doubt she wouldn't be sleeping well over the next few nights. Something major was going on and regularly for a lot of years.

Sarge sat forward suddenly and looked at Robin. "Witnesses to the abductions? If these numbers are correct, we are having men and women abducted off Las Vegas streets at the pace of two per week. Someone has got to have seen something. Can we put the witness descriptions together to make a pattern?"

Robin shook her head. "So far we haven't found a single witness to an abduction in any of these cases."

"Nothing?" Pickett asked, now feeling even sicker.

"Nothing," Robin said. "The victims are just vanishing without a trace and the ones that come back from the rape have no memories."

"We'll," Sarge said, sitting back again and shaking his head. "That settles it."

Pickett looked at the handsome detective. "Settles what?"

"It's aliens," Sarge said. "Aliens in spaceships came and beamed them all up."

It took Pickett a moment to see the slight grin on Sarge's face before she and Robin both broke into laughter, breaking the tension of the moment.

But it was sad that the situation seemed so hopeless, alien abduction sounded plausible.

Part Three
THE PROBLEM GETS BIGGER

FOURTEEN

October 19th, 2016
Las Vegas, Nevada

SARGE AND PICKETT and Robin spent the rest of their lunch at the Bellagio Café working to figure out where to start into all this. And what they came back around to was focusing on Trudy Patterson's abduction and then death.

But at the same time, Robin would continue looking for patterns among the fifteen hundred that had gone missing around their own future wedding and stayed missing. And also look for patterns in the rape cases focused also on marriages.

Around them the normal world went on with the distant sounds of the casino and other lunch customers eating and laughing. Sarge bet most of the people near them would be appalled at what the three of them had been talking about so casually.

It was right at the end of lunch, when Robin was about to head back to her computer people, that Sarge had one more idea. He didn't much like the idea, but it seemed logical to at least add it in.

"We're dealing in three different areas of detective work," Sarge said. "Missing persons, sexual assault, and homicide. Right?"

Pickett looked at him with a puzzled look and nodded.

"So how many unsolved homicide cases do we have similar to Trudy Patterson's case that had a future wedding in the mix?"

Robin flipped back open her notebook that she had closed and started writing.

"Good thought," Pickett said, nodding.

"A little more in our wheelhouse, at least," Sarge said.

At that point Robin closed her book and scooted out of the booth. "I'm headed back to the computer elves. We got a lot of information to crunch to pull some patterns."

Sarge watched her go and then glanced at Pickett. "She always leave that suddenly?"

"Always," Pickett said, laughing, "when she's focused on a case."

"So any idea how we figure out how these women and men are being targeted?" Sarge asked, sipping on the last of his coffee. He had almost finished his club sandwich before finally pushing it away for the waitress to take. After that much food, coffee tasted wonderful.

"I had a thought after we talked with Stein," Pickett said. "These couples will have a bridal registry for gifts. That has an outside chance of being a link and I mentioned it to Robin."

"I wouldn't even begin to know how those work," Sarge said. "Are the gifts picked out and bought delivered to the chapel or hotel room or something? Or just brought by the people who bought them?"

"Yes," Pickett said, smiling.

Damn he was coming to really enjoy her smile. And she had the whitest teeth he had seen in a long time, especially for a detective who drank a lot of coffee.

"The problem with bridal registry is that not many do it these days," Pickett said, "and gifts are often just sent to their homes. So after I had that thought and talked with Robin, we have pretty much ruled it out."

Sarge smiled. "I do that all the time. Come up with an idea and then talk myself away from it. At least on this case that is considered progress."

"Agreed," Pickett said. "So we need to really figure out how these women and men are being targeted. There has to be one point all of them walk through."

Sarge instantly knew where that was. "County clerk is the only common thing they all do ahead of time."

Pickett nodded. "They must show proof of identity to pick up their license."

Sarge quickly picked up his phone and called Mike Dans.

"Still early," Mike said.

"This is another lead," Sarge said, smiling at Pickett who looked a little puzzled. "Would it be possible for you to check, very, very carefully, to see if a system database has been hacked?"

Pickett smiled and nodded, now understanding what he was doing.

"Sure," Mike said. "Which one are we talking about?"

"County clerk's office for marriage licenses," Sarge said. "At this point, until we get more data, it's the only place we know for sure every person touched who disappeared or was raped or murdered with a wedding in their future."

"Ahh," Mike said. "Damn good thinking. It shouldn't take too long to carefully see if there was a hack without setting off alarms. Back with you in ten minutes."

"Thanks," Sarge said, and clicked off his phone.

He turned to Pickett. "Figured we had better determine if there was a hack from the outside before digging into the county employees."

"A really, really good idea," Pickett said. "How long until he can figure it out?"

"Ten minutes," Sarge said.

"He's that fast?" Pickett asked, clearly shocked.

"He's that good," Sarge said, grinning. "He'll go in and leave no trace or set off any alarm a hacker might have installed."

"Damn," Pickett said. "We turn over enough rocks, we might actually find a slug."

"You believe that?" Sarge asked, smiling.

"Nope," Pickett said. "Not with this case. But a girl can hope."

"I like hope," Sarge said, laughing. "And some luck might be nice here as well."

Pickett's beautiful face suddenly became very serious. "I have another rock we really need to turn over."

Sarge looked at her and nodded for her to go on.

"If this is all tied together," Pickett said, "which it sure seems like it might be, I think we need to focus on what kind of person could be doing this."

Sarge sat back in the booth, thinking. Pickett was right. They hadn't given any thought at all to the type of person,

or group of people who could do these crimes. And do them so perfectly as to not have even one witness in six years.

"And why?" he said, looking at her. "If fifteen hundred people have vanished right before their weddings, where did they go?"

"And why release some and not others," Pickett asked.

"Assuming this is all tied together," Sarge said.

"Yeah, assuming that."

Sarge had no doubt that it all was tied together. And until now, no one had put the entire picture together before because of the vast size of the wedding industry in Las Vegas.

And that worried him more than he wanted to admit.

FIFTEEN

October 19th, 2016
Las Vegas, Nevada

PICKETT LET THE soothing sounds of the restaurant and casino wash over her as she sipped on her coffee and thought about the problem of profiling the person or people doing this.

She knew they were making an assumption that all of this was tied together, but it was the only assumption she felt comfortable with at this point.

It seemed unlikely that fifteen hundred people could go missing before weddings and never be found in such a short amount of time. Sure, thousands went missing all the time in Vegas, but they could account for most of those now over the last six years.

And they knew that the rapes were tied together because of the exact same circumstances of each one.

So it wasn't that far of a leap to tie the missing persons with the rapes. They just needed to figure out why some victims were handled differently.

"I might have someone who could help us with the profiling," Sarge said after a moment when they both sat sipping their coffee. "We'll check him out this afternoon, see if he'll help us, but I have another question that might help Robin do some connections."

Pickett stared into the handsome face of the detective sitting beside her in the booth. In less than one day she had become amazingly comfortable being beside him and talking with him.

And she flat loved looking into his hazel eyes. At this point his face was puzzled and very serious, which made him even more handsome.

Pickett managed to nod and look down at her coffee before she did something like a young school girl.

"Rental cars," Sarge said.

Pickett instantly looked back into his eyes. "What are you thinking?"

Sarge shrugged. "Wondering if there is a pattern with rental cars. They are hard to ditch and easy to track."

Pickett was stunned at the very idea. "Are you thinking that maybe if the victim was driving a rental car, they were raped and put back in their car, but if driving an owned car, they were taken?"

"Grasping at straws," he said, shaking his head. "Said out loud like that, it sounds even crazier than it sounded in my head."

"This might be more like a fire hose if you are right," Pickett said, grabbing her phone and calling Robin.

"Sarge has an idea," Pickett said before Robin could even say hello. "Can you check and see if only the rape victims had rental cars and the missing people had regular cars when they were taken?"

"Shit," Robin said. "Give me thirty minutes. My husband has given me two more people to help on the computers on this. He thinks we may be on to something huge here and wants his best helping us nail it down."

"Wonderful," Pickett said.

That made her feel even better about the assumption this was tied together if Will and Robin both had the same feeling.

Robin hung up and Picket clicked off her phone and smiled at Sarge. "Thirty minutes."

Sarge indicated to a passing waitress that they both needed fresh coffee. Then he said, "Now this is the kind of detective work I like. Sitting and drinking coffee and coming up with ideas while others do the work."

Pickett laughed and let the waitress fill her cup. She had no doubt this was about as far from standard detective work that Sarge got. But she had to admit, for the moment this did feel great.

Especially sitting beside him.

SIXTEEN

October 19th, 2016
Las Vegas, Nevada

MIKE CALLED SARGE back after a couple more minutes and about half-a-cup of coffee.

"It's hacked," Mike said without even a hello. "A good one, downloading full data twice a month in a flash grab. It had alarms all over it to go off and erase itself if found."

"Shit," Sarge said. "I was afraid of that. Traceable?"

"We're working on that," Mike said, "but chances are, from the level of the sophistication on this, it's going to a dark web location, not traceable and not in existence for more than a few seconds that this hack takes every couple of weeks."

"How long has it been going on?" Sarge asked. He didn't really want to know the answer, but he had to.

"Best we can figure, it started in early 2008."

Sarge felt his stomach just tighten into a knot. Over eight years this had been going on without anyone having a clue. How was that possible?

"Thanks, Mike. I owe you," Sarge said. "Now at least we know how these sickos are finding the victims."

"I'll keep my people on this and see if we can trace it and feed them old data on the next hack, which will be in ten days. You still need the data from the tux place?"

"Skip it," Sarge said. "I think we got enough."

"Figured," Mike said. "I'll be back to you when I got more."

Mike clicked off and Sarge slowly lowered his phone and put it on the table in front of him.

"That bad, huh?" Pickett asked.

Sarge glanced at her very worried face. Her eyes seemed to be almost slits and her mouth was tight and firm.

Sarge nodded. "Mike found a very sophisticated hack on the County Clerk's records for marriage certificates."

Pickett sat back, clearly stunned.

"The records are hacked twice a month and it has been going on since early 2008. He's trying to trace it, but doubt it will work. We got ten days until the next one and Mike's going to try to feed the hack false data at that point."

"We need to extend back the search two years ahead of Trudy Patterson," Pickett said, her voice hushed and soft. "That's a lot of people."

All Sarge could do was nod. His nightmare case had turned into a complete horror, not only for poor Trudy Patterson, but for a lot of other men and women.

Pickett quickly called Robin and told her what they had discovered and to extend the pattern searches back to 2008.

"We need to keep this to ourselves for the moment," Pickett said to Robin. "Swear your husband to secrecy even with top officials, because if this gets leaked, it might spook these sickos. We don't know who they are and we only have ten days until the next hack."

Pickett nodded for a moment, then said, "Will do."

After she clicked off her phone, Sarge asked, "Will do what?"

"Be careful," Pickett said. "This is a lot bigger than one cold case."

Sarge could only nod at that.

They sat, not talking, both thinking, as the happy, real world of the surface of Las Vegas went on around them. Dishes clicking, people laughing, the sounds of slot machines announcing a winner.

But there was so much more under the surface in this town.

So much happened the tourists here for a good time just didn't see. He always knew that as a detective, but something about the size, scale, and focus on the happy moments of a wedding really made him even more disgusted at his own city.

But as long as the tourists didn't know or care, things were fine.

And that was just better for everyone concerned.

SEVENTEEN

October 19th, 2016
Las Vegas, Nevada

PICKETT WAS NOW certain that all the disappearances and rapes were tied together. And she was betting there were very few homicides besides Trudy Patterson's death attached. She just had that feeling.

So now they had options. None of them good, but they had options.

"So let's say over the last six years," Pickett said to Sarge, "since Trudy Patterson was taken, about two thousand others were taken and fifteen hundred of them disappeared completely while five hundred of the women were raped and released. How is something like that possible in a town with a million security cameras?"

Sarge turned to face her, nodding. "We have in the file security footage of Trudy Patterson leaving the parking garage of her hotel but nothing after that."

"When did rental car companies start putting in tracking devices for their cars?"

"Worth figuring out," Sarge said. "If we know these cases are linked, we should be able to find patterns in how the people were abducted."

"Exactly what I was thinking," Pickett said. "In this case numbers work on our side. I am sure that Robin and Will and their people are already on that part of things."

"So how about we tackle the why?" Sarge asked.

"Why would a group of people kidnap that many people?" Pickett asked. "First thing that springs to mind is the sex slave trade. The victims are being sold overseas."

She hated the idea, but it was the most logical from where they were sitting. But the wedding part made no sense at all with that.

Sarge looked at her. "You think it is the sex slave trade?"

"I hope not," Pickett said.

"Either way," Sarge said, nodding, "You think any of these missing are still alive?"

"I can't imagine how or why?" Pickett said. And she couldn't. After this many years, it would be logical that if the missing were kept alive, one or two would get away and return, even from sex slave trafficking. It did happen.

"So we go on the theory we have a real sicko serial rapist and killer," Sarge said. "Let's go see if we can get some profiling help on this while Robin does her magic."

Pickett nodded as Sarge stood from the booth and tossed enough money on the bill to cover it and a good tip.

"Next time my turn to buy," Pickett said.

He smiled. "Deal. But I didn't tell you I have enough money to last me far longer than I'm going to live. Family inheritance four years ago. Father died, I was the only child and he was disgustingly rich."

Now she understood why he had quit the Cold Poker Gang the first time. He had been dealing with that.

"That rich, huh?" Pickett said.

"Triple disgustingly, actually," Sarge said, laughing.

At that he indicated they should head out of the restaurant and deeper into the casino. Even with the wide aisles, the number of people and families kept them both weaving in and out of tourists.

The Bellagio poker room was a beautiful room off to one side of a slot machine area. It was decorated in ornate oak wood and rich furnishings and from what she could tell a good dozen tables were full of players.

Sarge indicated she should stay outside for a moment and he went inside and up a few steps in the back to a slightly higher level to a game going on inside a glassed-in room off the back. Pickett bet that was a high-stakes game. The Bellagio was known for that.

She watched as Sarge stood outside the room for a moment until a man inside smiled and stood and headed to the door. The man was about thirty and tall and rugged and had a tan that surprised Pickett even for the sun of Las Vegas. He wore a dress shirt with the sleeves rolled up and jeans and tennis shoes. She recognized him from somewhere, but she couldn't remember where.

Sarge and the man came across the poker room and out to where she stood to one side of the flow of tourists. Around her the sounds of the slot machines filled the air, but not so much as to make it impossible to hold a decent conversation.

"Detective Pickett," Sarge said, "I'd like you to meet Doc Hill."

Pickett shook Doc's hand, nodding. "Annie's boyfriend, Lott's daughter. Right?"

Doc smiled a smile that could melt ice from a hundred yards. "Guilty as charged."

"Wonderful to meet you," Pickett said. She was now also remembering that she had seen Doc's picture on a number of magazines over the last few years. And that he was amazingly rich and helped out Lott and Julia and Andor with cases all the time, sort of in the same way that Will helped out her and Robin with cases.

"So what can I do for you, detectives?" Doc asked.

"We're working on a really ugly case that is seeming to explode in size around us," Sarge said. "And we're looking for some profiling help on who might be pulling the strings. Thinking maybe Mac might help, but I don't know him well enough to ask."

Doc nodded and glanced around at the room behind him. Pickett had no idea who Sarge was talking about, but Doc seemed to think the idea made sense.

"I'll get him," Doc said. "Looks like he could use a break."

Doc turned and headed back into the poker room.

"Mac used to be an FBI profiler," Sarge said, "one of the best in the business, before going to play poker full time. He can read a person sitting across from him with the best players in the business and has gotten rich using his skills on other poker players."

Pickett nodded. That sounded like the best hope they had at the moment to even start to get inside this case.

She watched as Doc knelt down beside a guy with a gray cap clearly covering a bald head.

The guy listened to Doc for a moment, then said something to the table and stood with Doc. Both of them turned toward the door to the room.

Mac couldn't have been any taller than five-five and was a distance beyond two hundred pounds. Pickett guessed him to be in his early forties. He had on dark dress slacks and a white long-sleeved shirt with the cuffs buttoned.

Doc introduced them, then said, "I'm going to get back."

"Thanks, Doc," Sarge said.

"Thanks for the break," Mac said to them after Doc left. "I was grinding and getting hungry, not a good state to be in while playing poker with the likes of the sharks at that table."

"Doc said you looked like you could use a break," Pickett said, smiling.

"That guy scares me sometimes," Mac said, shaking his head.

"Cheeseburger and fries for a half hour of your time?" Sarge asked, smiling.

Mac smiled at Pickett and winked. "Detectives, you toss in a milkshake and you can have thirty-five minutes."

"Deal," Sarge said, laughing.

And back they went toward the Bellagio Café.

Pickett had no doubt she was going to spend far more time than she normally did in the café before this case was all over.

EIGHTEEN

October 19th, 2016
Las Vegas, Nevada

THEY GOT SETTLED back in the same booth Sarge and Pickett had just left. It had been cleaned off and Mac took Robin's spot.

Sarge wasn't sure what he was going to ask Mac, but figured this was worth a shot.

Pickett got out a notebook and Sarge took his small notebook out of his pocket as the waitress took their drink orders and the order for Mac's meal.

Sarge ordered himself and Pickett a basket of fries to share since it seemed wrong to not eat while Mac did.

"You do know," Mac said after the waitress left, "that anything I can tell you here about your case is just going to be off-the-cuff opinion. To do what I used to do right would take a lot of detail work and time and more information than you are going to be able to give me."

Sarge and Pickett both nodded.

"Actually," Sarge said, "even an opinion will put us farther along than we are."

"That bad, huh?" Mac asked.

"Worse," Pickett said.

"So lay it out for me," Mac said.

He pulled out a small notebook from his back pocket and a pen from his shirt pocket and opened to a blank page.

Sarge glanced at Pickett and she nodded that he tell Mac the case.

In five minutes, Sarge told Mac about Trudy Patterson and how that started all this, the information about the rapes, the fact that the wedding license information was hacked twice a month with a very sophisticated hack, and that somehow over 1,500 people had vanished completely from Las Vegas without a trace right before the weddings over the last six to eight years.

Mac wrote down notes, shaking his head at times. Finally, when Sarge was done, Mac looked up. Sarge could see the man's eyes were haunted.

"That bad, huh?" Sarge asked.

"As bad as you think it is," Mac said. "The wedding is the key. You are on the right track there, I have no doubt."

"We just can't find a damn door any key fits yet," Pickett said.

"Weddings are a marker of a new beginning," Mac said. "Crossing into a new life. That symbolism is powerful, if not real for the perps here."

Sarge sat back. "Starting over?"

Mac nodded. "Starting over. And to the perps something is flawed with the women who are raped and released. Something about them doesn't fit what the perps are looking for so they use them for something else."

"We were thinking they might have had rental cars and the others didn't," Sarge said.

Mac shook his head. "It's something far more personal than that. I would run the details about the women who were raped, see if any one thing comes up that makes them similar in some fashion and unacceptable."

Sarge looked at Pickett who was frowning. "We need to have Mike search the women's medical records."

"Mike Dans?" Mac asked.

Sarge nodded.

"Mike would do it right," Mac said. "Good idea. But also interview a few of them, look through their records, rape kits, things like that to see if you can find a pattern."

Sarge looked at Pickett who was writing in her notebook and nodding. That was going to be a lot more work for Robin, but Sarge had a hunch she and her husband's team could handle it, if they weren't already doing it.

At that moment their food came and Mac dug into his cheeseburger.

Sarge sort of pretended to take a fry, but he wasn't hungry in the slightest, even though they smelled great.

Pickett put down her pen and grabbed the salt shaker. "Mind?" she asked.

"Please," Sarge said and Pickett salted the fries about as much as Sarge would have.

"So any opinions from what little we know what these sickos are like?" Pickett asked Mac.

"Controlling," Mac said between bites. "Of that there is no doubt. Very careful, very meticulous, very sexual focused."

"Slave trade?" Sarge asked.

Mac shook his head. "I doubt it with the marriage connection. I dealt with my share of those who kidnapped for the sex trades and this doesn't have that feel."

Sarge wasn't sure if he was relieved or disappointed.

"Marriage often has a religious element to it," Mac said. "So chances are these people are religious which is why they are marrying the victims of the rapes before the sexual act."

Sarge and Pickett both nodded and Pickett wrote it down in her notebook. All of what Mac was saying made sense so far.

"If I could make one more bet on this," Mac said. "I would bet the people involved have a lot of money and are possibly community leaders. Going on this long without even a crack in the pattern is a sign of money, intelligence, and connections. So be careful who you talk to."

And with that, Mac finally said something that just scared hell out of Sarge.

And Sarge had a hunch Mac was right.

NINETEEN

October 19th, 2016
Las Vegas, Nevada

PICKETT AND SARGE walked Mac back to the poker room and thanked him again.

"Keep me in the loop if I can help," Mac said.

Pickett promised him they would, and then she and Sarge headed back for her car.

She had no idea what they were going to do next. Not an idea, but clearly they both felt they needed to be moving doing something.

Robin and Will were both still working at all the data, trying to pull any pattern that would help them pry open a door with this thing. And that was going to take a little more time, if not all night and into tomorrow to even dent the vast size and scope of all this.

Pickett walked beside Sarge in silence out the door and across the parking lot.

The day was warming, but not hot. It actually felt good to Pickett.

Sarge was clearly in as much thought about all this as she was, and the silence didn't feel uncomfortable at all. In fact, it felt as if they had been partners for years already.

She liked that.

And she really liked having Sarge at her side. It felt right and very comfortable. And she still hadn't known him for a full day yet.

As they got in and she got the SUV running and the climate controls set, she turned to him before putting on her seat belt. "Any ideas?"

"A couple," he said, nodding, looking straight ahead and clearly thinking.

She waited a moment until he was ready to put the ideas into words. Robin waited for her in the same way.

After just a few seconds, Sarge turned slightly in his seat to face her. "I'm thinking there are two areas here where we might catch a break. First are the victims' cars. That's been haunting me."

"Rental cars are tracked all the time these days," Pickett said, nodding. "And some newer model cars as well."

Sarge nodded.

That same thing had been bothering her as well, but she honestly had no idea how they could get to the data if it wasn't already in the files for each case. And she couldn't imagine the rape detectives not following up on that with each victim. So Robin and Will would have some answers in that area, she hoped.

"So how do these people hide the cars from tracking?" Sarge said. "Or do they? Think Robin and Will might know that?"

"I would think that would be a major area she and Will and her computer elves are digging into," Pickett said. "But if not, you might be able to get Mike Dans and his people really digging behind the scenes."

Sarge nodded, again staring straight ahead.

"But what about your second idea?" Pickett asked.

Sarge again turned and looked at her. "This doesn't feel like kidnapping for selling sex slaves overseas. But I can't seem to let go of the fact that both men and women have vanished. Why both? That shouts to me sex trade of some sort."

Pickett sat back, thinking. He was right.

But for what reason were both men and women taken?

"If this was any kind of sex trade," Sarge said, going on, "wouldn't there have been some reports of sightings of the missing people at some point."

"Maybe there have been," Pickett said. "I would hope those would have gotten to the files. We can check with Robin after they get more of this together."

"So you and Robin have any contacts that would know the sex trade in this city?" Sarge asked.

Pickett laughed. "Actually, we do."

Sarge looked at her and then smiled. "Don't tell me it's the former wife of Elvis with hair that won't fall down?"

"Then I won't tell you that," Pickett said, laughing. "But Stein knows a ton about everything to do with weddings and the underground scene of hookers and walkers and sexual fetishes."

"Hand-in-hand with weddings?" Sarge asked.

"It's huge business in this town to help with bachelor and bachelorette parties," Pickett said as she started up the car. "Bigger money than the weddings, actually."

"Of course," Sarge said, shaking his head and laughing as he buckled his seat belt. "Just not one of those connections I would make naturally."

Pickett laughed. "Didn't want to think about that part with your daughter, did you?"

"Have I told you how happy I was that she eloped to Hawaii?"

"You mentioned that," Pickett said, smiling at the handsome man in the seat beside her.

TWENTY

October 19th, 2016
Las Vegas, Nevada

SARGE SAT COMFORTABLY beside Pickett as she worked her Jeep SUV through traffic like an expert. He couldn't remember being so comfortable riding with someone before.

They were headed back to Stein's old wedding chapel. Sarge didn't consider himself a prude and after an entire career on the Las Vegas police force, he had seen most everything. But he had a hunch he just might learn a few new things this afternoon and the idea didn't excite him in the slightest.

About two blocks from the chapel, Robin called and Pickett put it on speaker.

"Sarge and I are headed to talk with Stein again," Pickett said. "What do you have?"

"A bunch of stuff starting to shape into patterns," Robin said.

Sarge sat forward, feeling a flush of excitement for the first time in this case.

"Hang on a sec," Pickett said. She swung across two lanes of traffic and into an empty parking lot and parked.

"I'm stopped," Pickett said. "Fire away."

"We've been going back and digging out information from the rental car companies on the rape victims who had them," Robin said. "The tracking all shuts off or is blocked in the same general area, a circle about ten blocks in diameter just off the Strip and to the west of the University."

"And turns back on?" Pickett asked a moment before Sarge could.

"When the car leaves the circle," Robin said.

"Blocking frequency," Sarge said. "That's a lot of territory inside that circle."

"Works with rape victims with modern cars and OnStar as well," Robin said.

"What's at the center of that circle?" Pickett asked. "Anything to do with weddings?"

"The August Tux Shop," Robin said.

"Shit, shit, shit," Sarge said. He wanted to punch something, including that bastard who owned the place.

"Not all victims and missing persons got near the tux shop," Robin said.

"I'm betting you discover with enough digging," Pickett said, "that the owner or owners of the tux shop also own other bridal and tux shops around town."

"You got it in one," Robin said. "But all cars vanish into that circle around the August Tux Shop. The missing people's cars never reappear."

"They don't?" Sarge asked. "There a garage near there?"

"Nothing at all close by," Robin said.

Sarge just shook his head. How in the world did fifteen hundred or more modern cars go missing in this new world?

"Well," Pickett said, "that's a ton more than we had before."

Sarge could only agree with that. This felt like a major step forward, all because of good computer work.

"We're still digging," Robin said. "Very, very carefully. The information on the hack on the clerk records really clamped a lid on our security and slowed us down a bunch."

"For the better," Pickett said.

"I agree," Sarge said. "Robin, on the missing persons cases, have there been sightings reported?"

"A couple dozen in the records is all," Robin said. "All in sex tapes that might have been done before the person vanished for all the detectives knew."

"Overseas type of stuff?" Pickett asked.

"No," Robin said. "All peeping tom voyeur crap. Hidden cameras. Faces not shown or blurred, but the people reporting them didn't want to say where they supposedly saw the person. You know the type. A friend of a friend saw this but there is no record and no one would admit to going to one of the porn sites."

Sarge looked at Robin who was looking puzzled.

"All the reports were like that?" Sarge asked.

"All the ones we have found so far that the detectives put into files," Robin said.

Sarge had a very large hunch that was a key, but damned if he knew how they could even begin to trace that. The underground porn world was huge and very secretive in the fetish areas. He knew that much.

"Keep looking in on that, would you?" Pickett said. "We'll ask Stein about it in a few minutes."

Robin laughed. "Anyone know about that kind of shit it would be Stein, the queen of the porn wedding photographers. Let me know if you learn anything."

And then Robin clicked off.

"Porn wedding photographers?" Sarge asked Pickett as she got the car going again.

"This is Vegas," Robin said, laughing. "An amazing number of newlyweds want their first night recorded as well. Maybe show their kids or something when the couple gets fat and old."

Sarge just sat there looking at the traffic around him. He had been right. By the time this case was over, he was going to learn stuff he didn't really want to know.

Too much stuff.

Part Four
NOTHING IS AT IT SEEMS

TWENTY-ONE

October 19th, 2016
Las Vegas, Nevada

PICKETT THANKED SARGE for holding open the large front door to Stein's chapel. Over the years, since Stein's husband had died, nothing had changed at all in here, except for the fact that once in a while someone emptied the ashtrays on the coffee tables. But it still smelled of old cigarettes and a faint smell of lilacs.

Stein came out of the back room, smiling as she always did. Her hair hadn't changed at all in years and Pickett couldn't imagine the work it took to keep that massive beehive on her head and in place. Either that or the beehive was fake, but Pickett and Robin over the years could never spot any sign of that. And they had both looked.

And neither of them had had the courage to ask.

"Detectives," Stein said. "Back so soon."

"Third time's the charm," Sarge said, smiling at Stein who just sort of beamed at the handsome detective.

"We're digging up more and more dirt," Pickett said. "Can you keep what we are about to talk about among the three of us?"

"Sure can," Stein said, and indicated that they should follow her.

She led them through a second room that clearly had been the wedding chapel at one point, but had now fallen into dust-covered relics. Clearly no customer came back this way and Pickett had never been in this area either in all the years of knowing Stein.

Stein led them into the back into a large office that was clean and well-organized. She indicated chairs and then closed the door behind them. A number of monitors showed that the entire building was under surveillance and Stein could see everything going on around the building from her office.

"I record everything in this building except what goes on in this office," Stein said, indicating the monitors as she closed the door and moved around behind her desk.

"Clients wanting to skip on agreements, huh?"

"That," Stein said, nodding, "and asking for things illegal that I don't provide. I don't mind a few kinks in the wedding planning, but I draw the line at illegal."

Pickett nodded and she could see out of the corner of her eye that Sarge was nodding as well.

"You're going to ask me to keep some secrets," Stein said. "I need you to keep one as well."

"No problem," Pickett said.

"Thanks," Stein said. "This damn thing is killing me today for some reason. Just couldn't get it to settle into place this morning."

With that she reached up and using both hands she pulled off all the hair on her head and set the beehive and the hair that looked like it had been on her scalp on the corner of her desk like a trophy.

Stein was impressed that it didn't move or fall over or even jiggle like a bowl of jelly.

Stein was completely bald and it actually looked good on her. She looked twenty years younger and far more alive, which surprised Pickett. She never would have recognized Stein on the street without the hair.

Stein then quickly took off the three pieces of tape that were stuck to her scalp and sighed. "That's better."

Sarge laughed and said, "I was wondering how you managed that miracle."

"As with most things in Vegas," Stein said, smiling at Sarge, "things are not always what they appear."

Pickett laughed as Sarge just shook his head and smiled.

"So what's going on?" Stein asked, leaning forward. "You two closing in on the Wedding Rapist?"

"Not closing in," Pickett said, "but finally getting a little traction. What can you tell us about the August Tux Shop?"

Pickett thought Stein was going to spit as she sat back. "Other than to avoid them at all costs, not much. They overcharge for

everything and make all sorts of reasons to not do refunds when another place would."

"Anything else?" Sarge asked, making a note in his notebook.

"Family that owns the place is stupidly rich," Stein said. "And they didn't get it from overcharging for tuxes. Not sure where the money came from. Might be worth checking into, but careful, that family is just flat nasty."

Pickett nodded and waited a moment until Sarge finished writing in his small notebook, then she asked Stein the next question. "We've had a few reports about some missing persons who went missing right before their weddings who turned up in porn videos."

Stein shrugged. "No surprise. People seem to think others will find their humping attractive."

"These were all voyeur videos," Pickett said.

Stein actually showed surprise at that. "Are there enough of them to show a pattern?"

"Working on that," Pickett said. "Anything you can help us on that?"

Stein shook her head. "Filming someone without their permission in a private place is very, very damn illegal. Some of the grooms want me to do that on their wedding night and when I try to get the bride's permission, the wedding usually is suddenly called off."

Pickett laughed. "I wonder why?"

Stein just shook her head. "I've heard of a number of houses down near campus where college kids for free room and board and a little cash every month agree to be filmed twenty-four-seven."

Pickett nodded and she could see Sarge nodding beside her.

"Any money in that sort of thing?" Sarge asked.

"Porn is a billion dollar business," Stein said. "A lot of the money goes unreported. There is something out there catering to all kinds."

"Wedding porn?" Sarge asked.

Stein nodded. "Lots of young couples are here for free, making a nice killing and getting a free trip and wedding because they agreed with some company or another to be filmed on their wedding night. Of course, they have to film some of the wedding and she has to keep the dress on for a while in bed and it has to last a certain amount of time. I stay away from the couples doing it for the money."

"Never see their faces?" Sarge asked, glancing at Pickett, then back at Stein.

"Nah, never," Stein said. "Even the ones just into it for their own viewing pleasure don't want their faces in the mix."

Pickett sat back and again watched as Sarge wrote. But she had a hunch they might have just figured out why some women were married and then raped.

It was a hell of a lot cheaper to get actors that way than paying for a vacation and wedding.

TWENTY-TWO

October 19th, 2016
Las Vegas, Nevada

SARGE LISTENED TWENTY minutes later as they sat in Pickett's car and she filled Robin in on what they had discovered. And their theory on why the rapes had happened.

Sarge didn't much like the theory, but at the moment it fit both a reason why and also what Max had said about the type of people doing these crimes being focused on sex.

"We'll see if we can find a money trail leading into that tux shop business," Robin said.

Sarge doubted that would be possible with the porn industry, but it was worth the shot. At this point, any lead was worth a shot.

So when Pickett hung up and turned to him, he just shook his head. "So we add in more suppositions."

Some Classic Dean Wesley Smith Stories
Available at your favorite booksellers.

Pickett nodded. "And no real suspects on any of this."

"Besides the family behind the tux shop," Sarge said.

"Besides them," Pickett said, nodding. "More than we had I suppose."

They both sat quietly for a moment, then Sarge asked the question that had been bothering him from before going in to see Stein.

"We are working on where the people are going, but where are the cars going to?"

Pickett looked at him with those wonderful brown eyes. "You think something more is happening besides taking out the tracking and moving them?"

"Seems that there were police reports on many of those cars fairly quickly after the kidnappings," Sarge said, trying to make sense of what was bothering him. "It would be risky to move the cars if the person was disappearing for good."

"But that would mean about fifteen hundred or more cars over the years," Pickett said. "Where would you put them? There are no warehouses or shops at all in that blank tracking area."

"There is nowhere to put them," Sarge said, still not getting what his mind was trying to get to. "So they had to be moved. Maybe by truck, maybe after being painted and such."

"Or chopped up and sold for parts," Pickett said.

Sarge nodded, but he didn't feel that was right either. A shop or warehouse of that size could be seen in that area and there just wasn't one.

Again they sat there in silence. It was a comfortable silence, something Sarge really enjoyed, actually. He just hadn't felt this comfortable with another person in a very long time.

"Any ideas on where to go next?" Pickett asked.

"Not a one," Sarge said.

"So how about I drop you back at your car," Pickett said. "I'd like to get some running in and clear my head some. I like running every afternoon in the exercise room in my building."

Sarge laughed. "Actually, I was thinking I could use a nap to try to clear my head a little as well, so sounds good."

"Don't you love this retirement stuff?" Pickett asked, smiling, as she got the car moving and headed back onto Las Vegas Boulevard. "Naps and exercise when we want."

"Beats the hell out of the paperwork," Sarge said, laughing.

"Got that right," Pickett said.

TWENTY-THREE

October 19th, 2016
Las Vegas, Nevada

PICKETT DROPPED SARGE back at the Golden Nugget parking garage and then headed back to her condo in the Ogden.

She was surprised at how instantly she missed having Sarge beside her. She hadn't felt that way about anyone for a very long time, and she had only known Sarge for just a day. Yet she felt completely comfortable beside him and liked having him around a lot more than she wanted to admit.

And besides all that, she found him amazingly handsome. She wasn't sure how all that combined could be possible.

She spent forty-five minutes putting in some miles on the treadmill and then took a quick shower. It didn't help her come up with any new ideas, but it made her feel better.

Two hours later, she was back at the Golden Nugget, this time in the steak house with the big fish tank in the center. Sarge was already there and Robin had called and said she would be twenty minutes late. Picket had to admit she didn't mind the alone time with Sarge at all.

Sarge looked even more handsome than earlier. He had on a light suit jacket with an open-collar blue shirt under it. His thick, gray hair was combed back and shaped his square face perfectly. She now felt glad she had decided to dress up a little.

Sarge had said he was buying dinner tonight. He said he had been looking for an excuse to try out the steak house here, but could never make himself go in alone.

Pickett had gladly agreed to help out with his test run of a new restaurant. The place had cloth tablecloths, cloth napkins, three empty glasses in front of each place, and a bunch of silverware including one fork turned sideways across the top of her clearly expensive plate. She never felt that comfortable in these sorts of high-end restaurants, but she had a hunch Sarge would ease that discomfort a lot.

He stood as she approached their table and pulled out her chair. She just shook her head. "Always a gentleman, huh?"

He laughed as they sat down. "I'm sure many people would call me far worse names than that."

"Why detective," she said, smiling at him. "Are you telling me you have made enemies over the years?"

He smiled and laughed. "Maybe a few. But they tend to be locked up or a long ways from a place like this."

They chatted for a few moments, then Sarge got a serious look on his handsome face. "I had an idea after I woke up."

"On the case of something else?"

"Case," he said.

She nodded. "Want to wait for Robin?"

He shook his head and looked slightly worried. "I would rather run it past you first and have you shoot it down than both of you laugh at me at this point. Fragile male ego and all that."

She laughed and indicated that he go ahead. She had no doubt his ego was far from fragile, but it made her feel great that he was already trusting her enough to talk with her about things he might not mention in front of others.

"I have an idea where the cars might be going," Sarge said. "I think they are going into the tunnels."

It took her a moment to realize just what he was talking about. Then it dawned on her and she nodded and sat back, thinking. Around them the sounds of laughter and conversations seemed to fade slightly.

When Las Vegas first started growing, flash floods tended to wipe out areas of it regularly, including roads and some buildings, so the city in conjunction with the county, built a vast network of concrete storm drains, called "the tunnels" by locals under the desert to take the run-off.

The tunnels were like a vast spider web under Las Vegas and for decades and decades they just were added on to seemingly without much pattern or thought as Las Vegas expanded.

The tunnels varied from around thirty feet across and ten feet tall to the size of mine shafts four feet wide and eight feet tall. All had concrete on all four sides. She had been down into the tunnels near the entrances a few times on murder scenes, but had had no desire to go farther into the pitch darkness of the hundreds and hundreds of miles of concrete.

Now the tunnels were known as shelter for the homeless from both the heat and the cold. No one knew how many, but the estimates ranged from five hundred people to far higher in numbers.

Full families lived down there in makeshift houses, often up on wooden pallets to get above the small amounts of water that sometimes ran through the concrete tunnels.

Pickett figured the tunnels were at least better than being on the streets or in a car in the wind and cold and hot sun of the seasons.

But not much.

She looked up at Sarge, who seemed to be thinking a long ways away from their table at the moment.

"Did you check to see if the tunnels ran under or near that August Tux Shop area?"

He came back into his eyes and nodded. "That area of the tunnels is so deep and so far away from most of the tunnel entrances, very few people have been in there, at least that I could find reference to before dinner."

"Wouldn't city and county maintenance people check the tunnels regularly?" Pickett asked.

"I'm sure they do every year or so, but if something was dug off to one side of the tunnels and then hidden, they would never see it," he said.

"You think they might be driving the cars out?" Pickett asked.

She doubted they were, considering that all the large tunnel entrances were heavily monitored. Cars coming out of the tunnels without going in would surely be noticed eventually.

Sarge shook his head. "I don't think so. I'm betting they are all still down there somewhere. It would take nothing to dig hidden rooms off to the sides of some of the deep tunnels in that area, let the water slowly take out the sand and dirt on the occasional storm."

"Wow," she said, laughing and shaking her head. "That must have been a hell of a nap."

He smiled. "I've always said I do my best thinking while asleep."

She laughed and at that moment Robin walked up and sat down. "Do I get to hear the joke?"

"Not a joke," Pickett said, looking intently at her partner. "Sarge may have figured out where all the cars have been going."

Robin stopped and stared at Pickett, her cloth napkin halfway unfolded.

"The tunnels," Pickett said. "They've been hiding them all off the tunnels."

All Robin could do was just blink, the perfect response.

TWENTY-FOUR

October 19th, 2016
Las Vegas, Nevada

SARGE COULDN'T REMEMBER a fancy dinner that he had enjoyed as much as this one. Even his crazy idea about the cars being in the storm drains hadn't ruined it.

And Pickett looked fantastic in a light blue jacket, a white blouse and pearl earrings that seemed to set off her beautiful brown hair and wide smile. He was really glad he had decided to put on a jacket as well. He would have felt really out of place beside her. She just looked wonderful and he had no memory of being this attracted to a woman in a very long time.

They had talked about the case, about their lives, about Will's business, about Sarge's time as a security guard after he first retired, and so much more. And, of course, they had all talked glowingly about their kids. After all, that's what parents their age did.

And from the sounds of it, they all had fantastic kids. Clearly they had all been lucky, especially raising kids while being a detective. Nothing ever easy about that.

As they all three declined the dessert menu and went for coffee instead, Robin brought the case back up again.

"We're getting even more reports in various places about the missing being seen in voyeur videos. Mostly just living in some house somewhere that is filmed twenty-four-seven in every room."

Sarge sat back with that. He just couldn't wrap his mind around why someone, or some group, would do this to so many people. But with the vast amount of money to be made from porn, maybe that was the core of everything here, from the wedding rapes to men and women being taken.

Stranger things had happened over his years as a detective, but not at this scale they were facing here.

"Any way to trace any of the film stuff?"

"No chance," Robin said, shaking her head. "And the money into the August Tux Shop family seems to be a bust as well at the moment, but we are still digging very, very carefully."

"You want me to get Mike and his people looking deeper?" Sarge asked.

Robin shook her head. "At the moment we're all right. But we might need that at some point. Will and his people just won't cross a few lines, but they have no problem letting others cross those lines for them."

Sarge nodded. He was clearly going to enjoy meeting Will at some point.

"So how about after the coffee we walk over to my place," Pickett said, "and get on a big screen computer and see if we can make sense of the old maps of the tunnels."

Robin nodded and reached for her phone. "I'll have Will e-mail you all the links and data about the tunnels in that August Tux Shop area, including how big they are and how often they are checked."

Sarge liked the idea and liked how they were both taking his tunnel idea seriously. And the more he thought about it, the more he liked the idea as well. It was crazy enough to make sense.

"Can you get him to send the information as to how far underground those car sensing devices would work?" Pickett asked.

Sarge nodded to that as well.

Then, for the next fifteen minutes, the three sipped their coffee, maybe the best-tasting coffee Sarge could remember, and talked about cats. And how Pickett was going to help him find a cat or two when this was all over. And how Robin thought it was about time Pickett got another cat or two as well.

Sarge liked that conversation because it meant that Pickett planned on spending time with him even after they stopped working on this case. And he liked that more than he wanted to think about.

TWENTY-FIVE

October 19th, 2016
Las Vegas, Nevada

PICKETT FELT INSTANTLY worried as she and Robin and Sarge got off the elevator at the top of the Ogden and moved to her door. There were only two other doors off this lobby and she had never met any of the other residents of the other two condos. She didn't even know who they were and had never bothered to ask. They seemed to be very quiet people.

She now just hoped her place was clean and she hadn't left underwear or something draped over a chair. She couldn't remember the last time anyone had been in her condo. More than likely it was right after she moved in when she made dinner for Robin and Will.

Luckily, she hired a cleaning service every week to take off the rough edges. Even retired, she hated cleaning things. She seemed to always think of better things to do.

As she unlocked her door and led them into the tiled entranceway, she felt as if she was seeing the place through Sarge's eyes. Her brown wood floors, tan and brown soft cloth furniture, and dark oak bookcases filled to overflowing gave the place a comfortable and lived-in feel.

She made herself take a deep breath and headed for the kitchen after slipping out of her shoes She never wore shoes around her apartment. Shoes were for going out.

"Coffee, water, or Diet Coke is all I got at the moment."

"Water," Robin said.

"Same," Sarge said. "And wow is this a nice place. Comfortable."

He had moved to the big windows looking along the Strip. The view was spectacular and one of the reasons Pickett had bought the place. But it pleased her that Sarge thought it comfortable as well.

"Thanks," she said, pulling out three bottles of water from her fridge.

"Where are you hiding the computer?" Robin said as Pickett handed her a bottle.

"Office through that door there," Pickett said, pointing to a closed door beside the kitchen. She wasn't sure why she always kept that door closed, but she did. Sort of like an unofficial boundary between work and the comfort of her home.

"How big is this place?" Sarge asked as she handed him a bottle and then they turned to follow Robin into the office.

"Three bedroom, two bath, about twenty-six hundred square feet," Pickett said as Robin dropped into Pickett's black leather office chair and got the big Mac computer started up.

"Wow!" Sarge said.

"You ought to see the deck," Pickett said, smiling at him. "I spend a lot of evenings and early mornings out on that deck just staring out over this stupid city I love so much."

"With a view like this," he said, pointing at the big windows behind them, "it would be a crime to not stare at it."

Robin took only a moment to get the map of the storm tunnels under Vegas opened. She did a few quick strokes and a circle appeared in one area off the strip.

"Where the cars vanish from tracking," she said, pointing at the circle.

Pickett was surprised at how large that area actually was and she and Sarge stood behind Robin in front of the computer.

"Only two tunnels run under this area," Robin said. "One is a really old one and it's down about a hundred feet and the second is a newer one from thirty years ago. Both are too far for any kind of ground penetrating radar."

"Can you isolate just those two tunnels on the map and show the entrances on either end?" Sarge asked.

Robin nodded and a moment later it was clear that the older tunnel merged into the newer tunnel on both ends. And it was smaller.

"Any bet that old tunnel is blocked off on both ends, with only small holes to allow the water to run out," Sarge said.

"No bet," Pickett said.

She just kept staring at the screen. Could it really be possible that the old tunnel running close to the August Tux Shop was where all those people had disappeared into?

And if so, why?

And could any of them still be alive down there? That idea just made her stomach tighten into a knot.

This entire thing was a nightmare.

TWENTY-SIX

October 19th, 2016
Las Vegas, Nevada

SARGE HAD KNOWN from the first night that Pickett lived in the Ogden, but he had never expected her to be his neighbor.

On the penthouse floor.

Her view faced the Strip, but he was pretty sure she didn't know that his penthouse next door was two stories tall and had an almost three-hundred-and-sixty-degree view of the entire area on the upper level.

He couldn't believe that in the years they had both lived here they had never run into each other in an elevator or either of the lobbies or in the parking garage. He was sure he would have recognized her and remembered if he had.

And he was a little worried about what she was going to think when she discovered he lived next door. His living in the Ogden had just never come up in conversation over the last two days. He wasn't sure how he would feel considering his interest in her. He had a hunch he would like that she was close, but he was going to have to tell her soon or there would be other problems.

But there was no doubt that as ex-cops, they both lived pretty darned good. He loved how she had decorated her place. His looked similar, with brown tones and lots of books. And he loved how she got comfortable in front of them when she came in.

For about fifteen minutes Robin explored every angle about the tunnels they could think of. He liked standing next to Pickett watching Robin work on details from the tunnels. It felt right to be beside Pickett.

The old tunnel had been dug out of solid sandstone and was about ten paces wide and eight feet high. And it hadn't been inspected since the city had closed it up in 1996.

Finally, there was no more to get from the computer so they all headed back out into the living room and sat down.

Robin sat in a large brown chair facing a large brown and tan cloth couch. Pickett sat on the couch near one end, clearly her favorite spot and Sarge sat on the other end. A large coffee table filled the space between the chair and the couch. It was covered with a few books, one without a dust jacket that was clearly in the process of being read. Sarge couldn't see the title, but he was very curious.

"So what next?" Pickett asked.

"We keep digging," Robin said. "I would like to know what we might be running into down in those tunnels before we ever go down there or send anyone else down there."

Sarge could only nod to that. "We are working on just guesses at this point anyway."

"Let's tick off what we do know," Pickett said. "We know first off that a lot of people about to get married have gone missing over the last number of years."

Sarge again nodded, as did Robin.

"We know," Pickett said, "that their cars vanish into an area and never come out again, at least in any fashion that has been traced."

"Center of the area is the August Tux Shop," Robin said. "Which is the tie to the weddings."

"Circumstantial," Sarge said, "but the only central tie to all of the men and women disappearing that we have at the moment."

Pickett and Robin both nodded.

"And we have unsubstantiated reports that some of the vanished people have been seen in voyeur porn videos," Pickett said.

"But we have no way to check that or any money trail yet," Robin said.

"And we know for a fact that someone has hacked the marriage license records in the county," Pickett said.

Sarge had to admit they didn't have anything that pointed to anyone at all except in very general terms. They really needed to find some sort of hard evidence or this was all going to grind to a dead halt again, as all these cases had done before.

They sat in silence for a moment, then Pickett said, "Something Mac said when we talked to him is haunting me."

Sarge watched her and Robin turned to face her as well.

"Mac said this has something to do with marriage," Pickett said. "He thinks that's one of the keys."

Sarge sat back, shaking his head. "Mac was right. It does have to do with marriages. Every detail of it, actually. But not in a standard way."

"Not in a church, happily-ever-after way?" Robin asked.

Sarge shook his head. "Not at all. Weddings in this city are a major attraction to draw all types from all over the country. Right?"

Both other detectives nodded, so Sarge smiled and went on.

"Porn is a major industry as well, including wedding night porn and voyeur porn, right?"

Again both nodded.

"So our creeps set up a way to get prospective, good-looking clients to come to them, to this city. That would be the August Tux Shop and the other wedding stores they own."

"And they know their clients are coming," Robin said, "from the hacks in the marriage license data base, so they have each person's personal information before they walk through the doors."

"So you are saying that this does have to do with marriage," Pickett said, "but just as a way to find porn actors to work for free."

"Exactly," Sarge said. He knew in his gut he was right on this. For the first time some of this was making a sick sort of sense.

"So this is a sex trade problem," Robin said. "But I'm betting not a one of these victims have ever left this country."

"You think they are in the tunnels?" Pickett asked.

"I would bet most anything on it," Sarge said. "The ones that are still alive."

"So now what do we do?" Robin asked. "Not a bit of this is strong enough to get a warrant."

"You and Will and your people keep digging," Pickett said. "Carefully."

Then Pickett turned to Sarge and smiled. "We're the field team. You up for getting some help and putting together an experienced expedition into those storm drains to see what we can see? Maybe interview some homeless people down there for what they have seen?"

"I hate the idea," Sarge said. And he did. Completely. But he also knew that Pickett was right.

He smiled at her. "But I don't think we have a choice at this point. We have to find out if this crazy idea is right or not."

"For the record," Robin said, "I hate this idea as well. But I also see no choice."

"I'll call Mike Dans tomorrow morning," Sarge said. "See if we can hire him and his team to help us."

"With him along," Robin said, "I hate the idea a little less."

"Speak for yourself," Pickett said, smiling at her partner.

Sarge just laughed. And considering the stupidity of the idea they were discussing, that felt good.

"Now I could use a drink," Robin said.

"I've got what some people say is a really good white wine at my place," Sarge said. "You two up for a glass of wine before we call it a night?"

"How far do you live from here?" Robin asked.

Pickett was looking puzzled as well.

"Not far," Sarge said smiling. He pointed to Pickett's bare feet. "In fact, you won't even have to put your shoes back on."

TWENTY-SEVEN

October 19th, 2016
Las Vegas, Nevada

PICKETT WAS STUNNED as Sarge led them out her front door, made sure she had her key, then instead of going to the elevator, turned to the left and put a key into the door right next to hers.

"We're neighbors?" she asked, feeling completely stunned. He had said he was rich, but she had no idea he was as rich as she was.

Maybe richer.

"I didn't know either until tonight," he said. "You said you had a condo here, but I didn't expect us to both be on the same floor."

"So you two have never run into each other in the elevators or lobby or anywhere?" Robin asked.

"And never once thought to ask who my neighbors were," Sarge said.

"I didn't either," Pickett said, laughing as Sarge led them into his penthouse condo.

"Two great detectives," Robin said, shaking her head. "You might want to find out who is in that third condo on this floor just to make sure it isn't our August Tux Shop owner."

"Oh, real good plan there," Pickett said, laughing. "Wouldn't that be funny if it was him?"

Both Sarge and Robin said at the exact same time, "No."

Pickett was amazed at how comfortable she felt in Sarge's condo. In fact, it felt a lot like her place. He had decorated everything in brown tones as well, and had one full wall of oak bookcases filled completely with hardbacks on the wall that separated his place from hers. His living room windows looked to the north and east and she could imagine the beauty of the sunrises.

The ceilings over his living room were higher than hers and the windows taller, but the kitchen to the right of the main room seemed similar.

"Wow, two stories?" Robin said.

Pickett turned to see what Robin meant and saw the wide, almost grand-looking staircase leading up to a level above.

"Always wondered who had that top floor in this place," Pickett said.

"Are you really this rich?" Robin asked, staring at the place and making Sarge look slightly uncomfortable.

"Massive family inheritance the year after I quit the force," Sarge said. "Dead broke like all detectives before that. Figured a really nice place to live would be a good way to spend a little of the inheritance money and this place was open because of the recession."

"Can we see the upstairs?" Pickett asked.

Sarge smiled and said, "Be my guests."

He led the way up the staircase to a massive room at the top that had most of a complete view of all of Las Vegas and the valley and mountains around the city. His view was the same as hers, and with everything else around the valley included as well, seen clearly through the tall windows.

To Pickett it felt as if they had stepped up on the roof of the building, only the roof was covered and enclosed and had soft couches and furniture filling a central area. There were no other rooms blocking the view in any direction, so clearly all the bathrooms and bedrooms were on the main level below.

It was clear that Sarge spent a lot of time up here, judging by the pile of books and papers on the large coffee table in the middle of the room.

"Wow," Robin said moving to the middle of the room and slowly turning to take in everything. "Just wow."

Pickett glanced at Sarge. "This is just amazing."

"Sold me on the place when I saw it," he said. "And even in the summer in the day, the windows have a special tint that blocks the sun for the most part and the air conditioning can keep up with the rest. And on nice evenings such as this one, I can sit out on the deck.

He went to the side facing the Strip and slid open a wide glass door and stepped outside.

The cool night air felt wonderful to Pickett as she stepped out beside him, staring at the bright lights of the massive casinos. The deck seemed to run along the entire side of the upper floor and around to the right.

"There can't be many views like this in all of Las Vegas," Robin said.

"Costs a lot," Sarge said. "Sometimes I'm actually embarrassed to spend even the condo fees and utilities each month, considering they are more than my entire mortgage payment used to be on my old home."

"But we can't take it with us, can we?" Pickett said, laughing.

"Exactly," Sarge said, smiling. "I got my daughter set up so that if something

happens to me, she is even richer than I ended up. So nothing else to do but spend some of this on a wonderful place to live. And a lot of good meals."

"Well," Robin said, "if you two don't mind, I'm going to head for home and talk with Will about maybe moving to a place with a view. Maybe that third condo up here will come open."

Pickett laughed. "You can't fool me, partner. You're going home to work and see how the research is going."

Robin smiled as she headed down the stairs. "Well, that too."

TWENTY-EIGHT

October 19th, 2016
Las Vegas, Nevada

SARGE WASN'T SURE what to do next, considering that he was now alone with a beautiful woman in his place, something that had never happened before. It made him feel young and completely stupid, something he remembered feeling all the time when he actually had been young.

They both stared at the view from the balcony for a moment, then Sarge asked the question he needed to ask first. "Does it bother you that I am your neighbor?"

Pickett laughed and shook her head, looking up at him. "Not in the slightest. I kind of like it, to be honest. Does it bother you I live right down there?"

She pointed down at her deck under his.

He laughed, realizing that he liked having her that close. "Not in the slightest either.

So how about that glass of wine I offered. Clearly Robin wasn't into drinking."

"She's married," Pickett said, smiling. "She's forgotten how to have a good time."

"And we've remembered?" Sarge asked.

"Planning to remember," Pickett said. "And yes, I would love that glass of wine."

He liked the sounds of that a lot and all worry about them being neighbors just vanished. In fact, it looked like it might be a real advantage.

"You want to wait here or take a peek into my wine cellar?" Sarge asked.

"You have another level to this place?"

"Well," Sarge said, "from here we do have to go downstairs to get to the wine."

"This I've got to see," Pickett said, laughing.

Sarge let her lead off the patio and he slid the door closed and then followed her down the stairs as she just kept staring around.

"This place is amazingly comfortable," she said when she reached the bottom of the stairs, staring first at the kitchen, then around at the living room.

He loved to hear her say that. Pleased him more than he wanted to admit and again he realized he was back being a kid, worried about how a girl would think of something he did.

At his age, that actually felt nice, not at all like the panic he had felt when young.

"So is your place," he said. "I was surprised how similar our tastes were and I love that you had a lot of books scattered around."

"I liked the same thing about your place," she said.

He turned and led her down a wide hallway going away from the kitchen and toward the bedrooms. He had had the bookshelves along the wall of the hallway custom built just for fun. They were full completely of books he had read and others he planned on reading at some point.

About halfway down the hallway he stopped and made sure she was watching, then pulled out a book from the second shelf from the top. There was a click and the wall moved inward revealing an oak table and beyond the table a glass wall showing a large room of wine on racks beyond.

This had been a fourth bedroom when he bought the place, but it had just sat empty before he remodeled.

"You've got to be kidding me," she said, laughing and clapping her hands.

Her laugh sounded like a kid in a candy store and that just made him smile more than he already was smiling.

"Always wanted a secret room behind a bookcase," he said, feeling very proud of his wine room as they stepped inside. "I needed to build a climate-controlled room for a decent wine collection anyway, so why not go all the way. Having too much money can create things like this."

She laughed. "I flat love it."

"There's more," he said.

He turned and pushed a button and another wall to the right of the door slid back revealing a major computer terminal and half-dozen large screens.

He had a bunch of the research he had done on the desk beside the terminal and some printouts of the area and a large printout of the tunnels.

"This functions as a security system for the condo as well as a major computer set-up for research," he said. "Mike Dans' people set this up for me when I first moved in here."

"Wow, just wow," she said.

She looked up at him, staring with those wonderful brown eyes of hers at him. Then she said, "Thank you for showing me this. Makes me feel like a kid again."

"Thanks for letting me show it to you," he said. "I feel the same way."

With that, he turned and opened up the glass door into the climate-controlled part of the room and picked a special white wine, something he had been saving for a special moment.

This sure seemed like a special moment to him.

Very special.

TWENTY-NINE

October 19th, 2016
Las Vegas, Nevada

PICKETT DID AS Sarge instructed and went into the living room near the kitchen while he opened the wine. She sat down on the couch facing the windows. She couldn't believe how comfortable she felt with him and how wonderful his place was.

She felt just as comfortable here as she did in her own condo. And being right next door was a wonderful benefit no matter what they decided to do with a relationship. She had a hunch that Sarge could be a very, very close friend.

And she had to admit, she was hoping for more than friendship. A lot more, but she had to remind herself that she had only known Sarge for less than two days.

It felt now like she had known him her entire life.

Strange, very strange, but it didn't scare her in the slightest. In fact, she was going to enjoy the feeling. And it seemed like he was as well.

He had been like a young boy showing her his nifty hidden room. She had loved that look on his face of pride and happiness that she had liked it as well.

And she hadn't been making it up that she had liked the room and the computer set-up. She in fact loved it.

And she really loved that upper floor with the most amazing view of all the lights of the Las Vegas valley. On a clear fall night like tonight, that had just been stunning.

He came out of the kitchen and handed her a tall crystal wine glass.

"Can I ask what you are thinking?"

She smiled at him as he sat down beside her and put his feet up on the coffee table, clearly completely relaxed with her. She liked that more than she wanted to admit to herself.

"Honestly," she said, "thinking about how much I love your place and your nifty upstairs and even wilder secret room."

He smiled. "Thank you. That means a lot to me. You are the first person I have shown it to."

She frowned and turned to him. "Not even your daughter?"

He shrugged. "Nope. She and her husband don't drink and they stay in hotels when in town for more privacy, so the only time they are here is when they allow me to cook for them. Never occurred to me that they would even appreciate it."

"Thank you," she said, holding up her wine glass to toast him. "For sharing with me."

He clinked his glass lightly against hers and then she took a sip, startled at how wonderful the wine was.

"Wow, this is something," she said.

"It is, isn't it?" Sarge said, taking a second sip and smiling. "Lott suggested I try it, so I bought a bottle for a special occasion. I think I might need to buy a few more bottles, don't you?"

"Without a doubt," she said, taking another sip of the wonderful smooth wine.

She couldn't believe how pleased she was that he thought this was a special occasion. It felt that way to her, since this was the first time in memory that she had been in a man's apartment, alone. A man she was interested in as well.

"So what are you thinking?" she asked after a moment.

"Honestly wondering where this is headed with us," he said.

She was surprised that he had been so direct, but not really. In the short time she had known him, that clearly was his way of dealing with things. Direct, honest, and straightforward.

She set her glass down on the coffee table, then took his glass from his hands and set it beside hers.

Then she turned to face him and look into his slightly worried eyes.

"I think it should go this way," she said.

She leaned up and kissed him.

It took him a moment to kiss her back, then he did, wrapping his wonderful arms around her and pulling her up close.

She was lost in the kiss. Better than any kiss she had ever remembered.

Better than her first kisses in high school.

After a moment he broke the kiss and leaned back and looked into her eyes.

He was smiling, more than likely as hard as she was.

"That was really wonderful," he said, his voice slightly husky.

"I agree, detective," she said. "But I think we need more research on this topic, don't you."

He laughed and nodded and this time he kissed her, pulling her up and against him.

And it felt heavenly to be against him.

And right.

Perfectly right.

Part Five
UNDER LAS VEGAS

THIRTY

October 20th, 2016
Las Vegas, Nevada

SARGE COULDN'T BELIEVE that the evening had ended up in his large bed and the morning had started off with the two of them taking a shower together and soaping each other's backs.

He felt young again and seeing Pickett's beautiful naked body under the streaming water sure helped that feeling, so much so that they ended up taking a second shower after going back to bed.

He had thought that part of his life long past, and she had said the same thing. But it had been great.

Then in one of his bathrobes, carrying her clothes, she had gone back to her place to dress and he had knocked on her door fifteen minutes later.

She came out smiling. And gave him a kiss.

That was wonderful. A beautiful woman kissing him in the morning. Didn't get better as far as he was concerned.

Then they had walked together the five blocks to the Golden Nugget for breakfast.

To Sarge it all felt completely natural and when he mentioned that to her on the walk, she had laughed and agreed. "I wouldn't mind getting used to this," she had said. "Is that too forward too fast?"

He had laughed and mentioned that after what they had done last night and then again this morning, that seemed pretty slow.

She had agreed to that.

After they both had finished off their breakfasts and read the morning paper, her on her tablet and he with the actual paper, they turned their attention back to the case.

"So are we going into the tunnels?" Pickett asked.

Sarge hated the idea, but could see no other way around it. "Call Robin and see if she has any updates that will stop such lunacy. If not, I'll call Mike."

Pickett nodded and after a moment was talking with Robin on speaker phone. There was no one at any table close enough to overhear, luckily.

Robin and her computer geeks were making progress, and it all seemed to lead to the porn industry and the tunnels. No trace of any of the cars driven by a missing person had ever been found, not even a part. So the cars were clearly just being stored and there was more than enough room down in the old tunnels to do that, or to carve out new rooms.

"We have nowhere near enough evidence to get a search warrant on any of the August Tux Shop properties," Robin said. "So we can't look for any entrance from the surface."

"So we look for the evidence from below," Sarge said, nodding. "In the public areas. I'm going to call Mike Dans and hire him and his people to go with us down there."

"I'm coming as well," Robin said.

"Nope," Pickett said. "We need you right where you are at and I'm sure Mike can set up monitoring equipment so you and Will and his people can trace our movements."

"But…" Robin started to argue but Pickett cut her off.

"Partner, you know I am right," Pickett said. "So get as much information on that old tunnel as you can while we set this up with Mike."

"All right," Robin said. "Not happy."

"Not happy to be going into a tunnel either," Pickett said, smiling and winking at Sarge.

"Call me when you are set up," Robin said and clicked off.

"She gets that way," Pickett said, smiling. "But she knows I'm right. That's what annoys her."

Sarge got on the phone to Mike Dans and told him what they had found, what their suspicions were.

"You are going to need a team to go down in there," Mike said.

"That's why I called," Sarge said, glad that Mike was ahead of him a little. "I want to hire you and your team to go with me and Detective Pickett."

"No need to pay," Mike said.

"I'm paying," Sarge said. "I have more money than I know what to do with and I want you running this operation. So I want your best team that money can buy on this."

"Afraid what we are going to find?" Mike asked.

"Deathly afraid," Sarge said. "Besides, those damn storm drains scare hell out of me."

"Yeah," me too," Mike said. "Send me all your data and what you think is actually going on and where. I'll meet you at noon at the Bellagio Café so we can go over details. We'll go in right after dark."

"Thanks, Mike," Sarge said.

He clicked off the phone and looked into the worried eyes of the woman he was falling for.

"We've got a professional team," Sarge said.

"Which takes this idea up just a notch above totally nuts," Pickett said.

Sarge could only nod at that.

And try not to think about getting lost in cold, dark, concrete tunnels.

THIRTY-ONE

October 20th, 2016
Las Vegas, Nevada

PICKETT FLAT HATED the idea of going down into those storm drains. The tunnels were one of the better kept secrets of Las Vegas. Tourists never knew they existed, and the homeless used them for shelter. And as far as she knew, the homeless very seldom went very far in from the entrances.

And there were a lot of entrances all over the city. Some of the major ones were outside the main freeways, but a lot of the smaller entrances were in basements of parking garages.

Las Vegas had built two separate drainage systems, often running side-by-side underground. One system took away wastewater from homes and casinos and hotels while the second system only drained away surface water. But the second system had tunnels far larger than the normal sewers to handle the rare flash floods.

And the storm drain system got a lot less attention since it was seldom used for any storms. Even when it rained, the storm drains seldom had more than a few inches running through them.

When a large storm was headed toward Vegas back in her last years on the force, the charity organizations mounted a vast rescue operation to get the homeless out of the tunnels before the flood hit. No one knows exactly how many they didn't rescue, but those tunnels had mostly filled with that storm. If anyone had been down there, they wouldn't have stood a chance.

Now she and Sarge were going down into that storm drain system, something she had never had to do as a full detective. Seemed like being retired didn't have all the benefits it was cracked up to have.

Pickett had Robin send Mike all their data and theories and all the data on where the cars disappear and told her about the meeting at lunch.

Then after breakfast Pickett and Sarge decided they were going to need to buy some supplies, since neither of them had the clothes or supplies for what they were going to attempt later in the day. So for the first time in a very long time, she went shopping with a man.

She had to admit, she liked it and he had her laughing most of the hour it took them.

They both ended up with boots that were water repellant, heavy gloves, and powerful flashlights. They would wait to talk with Mike at lunch about what more they would need.

They dropped their new supplies back at their condos, then headed for lunch at the Bellagio, getting there about twenty minutes before Mike and settling into the same booth they had spent so much time in the day before.

Around them the casino noises were muffled by the thick green plants and the sounds of others eating and talking in the restaurant. Even the same waitress as yesterday waited on them, greeting them like old friends.

"Starting to feel like home," Sarge had said, laughing.

"Maybe on big cases we could reserve it," Pickett said.

She hoped that in the rest of their careers they wouldn't have a case this big again.

Robin was going to join them for the planning meeting so she could coordinate everything with Will and her computer people. And she really wanted to meet Mike Dans. But she hadn't arrived yet either, so Pickett decided to ask what Sarge was thinking about the plan. She actually had managed to not give it much thought.

"Trying not to," Sarge said. "I'm hoping that Mike knows someone that is an expert on the tunnels who he can trust and help us plan how we go in."

"Afraid of being monitored?"

"That and a lot more," Sarge said, nodding. "If this operation is as large as it seems

to be, they will have every possible entrance to that area of the tunnels monitored. And more than likely guards and other traps for anyone getting too near the area."

Pickett sat back, slightly stunned. The idea of a firefight in the tunnels had never crossed her mind, but it sure made sense. And then something else sent a chill down her spine.

"If those people are alive down there," she said, "or some of them, we have to go in with the element of surprise."

Sarge nodded. "That's why I want to wait for both Mike and Robin on this and just try not to think about it. They are going to know how to block security cams and watch for other traps we might run into."

Pickett just shook her head. "And I thought just going into storm sewers was scary enough."

"If this actually is a million dollar porn operation," Sarge said, "and they have kidnapped and maybe killed as many people as we think they have, the tunnels are going to be the least of our worries."

She knew he was right.

Completely right.

And she couldn't see another choice but to go right into it. They couldn't legally go in and search above ground. They had no evidence at all against anyone. So they had to go into the public areas below ground.

"I hope we are wrong about what is happening down there," Sarge said, staring off at the people around them in the restaurant going about their daily lives and vacations.

"Rather start back at square one to figure out all this?" Pickett asked.

"To be wrong on this I sure would," Sarge said, nodding.

"But you don't think we're wrong, do you?"

He shook his head.

And again, she agreed with him. All her years of being a detective told her they were right.

And that meant those tunnels were going to lead them straight into hell.

THIRTY-TWO

October 20th, 2016
Las Vegas, Nevada

MIKE DANS ARRIVED about the same time as Robin and joined them.

Mike looked ex-military all the way, with a shaved head, massive shoulders, and a panther-like walk. He just radiated power and confidence and Sarge loved that.

The introductions were great. Sarge introduced Robin and Pickett and then Pickett and Mike dropped into computer and job and security service shoptalk, ignoring both Sarge and Pickett.

Sarge found it funny and was glad they didn't talk about the coming mission until after they had all ordered lunch.

And it was clear to Sarge that both Robin and Pickett liked Mike almost instantly. That was good, considering what they were going to trust him with.

"So, Mike," Sarge said after the waitress left with their orders. "Any ideas of what we might be facing and how to do it?"

"I should have a little more idea any time now," Mike said. "I have a great friend with some pretty special ground-penetrating radar equipment taking a look in that area for us right now."

Sarge was shocked at that, as clearly was Pickett and Robin.

"GPR is only good for about sixty feet in this sandy soil," Robin said.

Mike smiled. "Regular GPR, yes. My friend has invented a way for the government to go much deeper by combining the waves off of a dozen GPRs at the same time, using a massive computer to sort out the details."

"How far down can he go?" Sarge asked.

Mike smiled. "Detail will only be empty spaces and pipes and tunnels and such, but he'll get us a pretty clear picture of that area if anything is down there."

"And the shaft going down if it's under the August Tux Shop area?" Robin asked.

"He's doing a complete search of that 25 block area at the level of those two tunnels," Mike said. "After lunch, if you don't mind, Sarge, we can go up to that secret room of yours and study the results."

"No problem," Sarge said. "So you think we can get in there without being seen?"

"Into the main tunnel down there, yes," Mike said. "And we can block any security cameras and trips they might have set up along the way."

Sarge could see that Mike wasn't saying something.

"But the problem is…" Sarge said, giving him his chance.

Mike nodded. "Getting into that closed-off tunnel. I have an expert who knows where that old tunnel connections to the new tunnel are and the concrete used to close it off."

Mike dug into a folder he had brought along and set on the booth beside him. "This is a picture of that old tunnel where it meets the new tunnel."

He slid the picture to Sarge who looked at it and could feel himself shudder. That was a nightmare.

He slid it to Pickett.

The picture showed clearly the square shape of the old tunnel, now filled with concrete. And in the very center of the fill was a small square hole on the floor that was clearly drainage for any water that got down into the old tunnel. The hole was black and it looked like some sort of slime had built up on the floor of the hole.

"How big is that hole?" Pickett asked as she passed the picture to Robin.

"I'll be able to squeeze through," Mike said. "But barely."

Robin just stared at the picture and shook her head.

"So one of the most hidden and inaccessible places in Las Vegas," Sarge said.

Mike nodded. "That old tunnel entrance there is a six mile walk from the main entrance to the newer tunnel. As far as we can tell, those holes in the ends are the only places to enter that old tunnel since all access drains were closed or diverted to the new tunnel."

"Wow," Robin said, still shaking her head.

Sarge could tell that Pickett looked like she was almost in shock as the reality of what they were thinking sank in. That picture just looked damned scary. He knew Pickett was one of the bravest people who had ever carried a badge. And he seldom backed down either, but right now he was having second thoughts as well.

"So anything closer than six miles that would still be safe?" Robin asked. "I have a hunch the main entrances to that tunnel will be monitored."

"They are," Mike said, nodding.

Sarge looked up at his friend, who was looking very serious. "My man who took that picture this morning also had equipment on him that could sense monitoring. That main tunnel is under surveillance and monitoring the entire length, all nineteen miles of it. And those old tunnel entrances both have major surveillance on them, including video. He snapped that picture while just walking past like an explorer."

Silence filled the booth. Around them the casino and dining room sounds seemed to just fade back and Sarge could almost hear his heart beating.

"We really are on to something big, aren't we?" Pickett said softly.

Mike nodded.

"Shit, just shit," Robin said.

Sarge just shook his head. He had so hoped that they were wrong about the tunnels and where all those people had gone. But there was more and more evidence pointing to the fact that they were not.

And they had nowhere near enough evidence to go in with a search warrant to the August Tux Shop and try to find the entrance. And even the ground-penetrating radar, if it showed a shaft going down, wouldn't be enough evidence to prove any crime.

Somehow they needed to get into that tunnel and find those people. Or at least their cars.

At that moment the waitress brought their lunches and all four of them put the task at hand away.

But Sarge wasn't sure he could eat that much at the moment.

Pickett reached over and put her hand on his leg, then smiled at him.

She looked worried in those wonderful brown eyes, but determined.

And with that smile he felt slightly better. And her touch made him feel even better. He smiled at her and nodded.

They were not tackling all this alone. They had the best help around them they could get.

And if the radar found more under there, they were going to need to bring in even more help.

THIRTY-THREE

October 20th, 2016
Las Vegas, Nevada

AFTER LUNCH THEY headed in three cars back to the Ogden and up to Sarge's apartment. Pickett hoped that they hadn't left any sort of evidence of their wonderful night draped over a chair or something silly like that. This morning she just hadn't cared and she doubted Sarge had as well.

But now with Robin and Mike with them, Pickett felt there was no point in being embarrassed. And then she realized how silly that thought was. She was a retired grown woman. She had a hunch Robin knew exactly what had happened last night. And that was fine.

So when they got to Sarge's condo, they all headed to his secret wine room with the incredible computer set-up.

Mike took the computer chair while the three of them stood behind him. The large screens were big enough and placed high enough that there was no problem seeing what he was doing.

Mike quickly, with his fingers moving faster than Pickett could imagine typing, brought up some sort of files.

"I've got all the preliminary scans," Mike said. "Here we go. First I'm going to run this like we are looking down through the ground from a plane flying overhead."

That made sense to Pickett until the image showed up.

"This is down to one hundred and twenty feet," Mike said, pointing to an indicator on the screen.

Pickett couldn't make sense out of what she was seeing. It seemed more like a bunch of blurry lines than anything.

"Oh, shit," Mike said softly, more to himself than anyone.

"You're going to have to help me read this," Sarge said.

"Me too," Pickett said. She glanced at Robin who seemed to have seen a ghost her face was so white.

"There are fifteen or twenty city blocks of tunnels and rooms down there," Mike said.

"City blocks?" Sarge asked.

Pickett just couldn't grasp what Mike had just said.

"City blocks," Mike said, clearly not happy with what he was seeing. "It's like a rat's nest of tunnels and rooms."

Mike ran his finger on the screen, showing lines of open spaces. Pickett could see what he was outlining and it still didn't make sense.

"From the looks of this," Mike said, "There is an open area in the center of all this, with what looks to be a dozen tunnels leading to complexes of rooms off the center area."

"Those are larger than rooms," Robin said, leaning forward and indicating some other things on the big screen. Clearly she could read this kind of image from ground penetrating radar. "Those are the size of two- and three- and four-bedroom homes dug out of the dirt. Looks like tunnels lead from the main room to them."

"And they go a long ways back," Mike said.

Pickett just wanted to be sick. The people kidnapped were being held in concrete rooms right under Las Vegas. Or at least some of them. How was this even possible?

"How big is the complex?" Sarge asked, his voice low and clearly shaken. "Can you tell?"

"Going to take some time to analyze all of these images," Mike said. "But at a glance, it's huge. Maybe upward of five or six thousand rooms carved from the ground. And all are square."

Robin pointed to the screen tracing her finger along a line. "Looks to me that the pattern is a complex of five rooms that has one door off a main tunnel leading into it, like a front door of a house."

Mike was nodding. "No other way out. Each suite could hold six people easily."

"This is insane," Pickett said.

Mike nodded and changed out the images. "This is a cut through the old storm tunnel," he said. "Looks like all the new rooms down there are about the same height as the old tunnel, all leading off to the west from the tunnel."

They all kept silent as Mike went through more images, explaining what they showed. They all confirmed that there was a massive complex down there.

Massive.

Picket wished she hadn't eaten lunch now. This was far, far larger than they could handle. But she doubted these images would be enough to stop all this either.

Finally, Mike got to an image and suddenly sat back.

"Oh, God," Robin said, shaking her head. "Can you switch that area to an eagle-eye view?"

Mike nodded and switched the view. A giant mass showed up on the screen.

It took a moment before Pickett's eye saw what they were looking at.

Thousands of cars.

A hundred feet underground.

"Where does the elevator leading down to that come to the surface?" Sarge asked a moment before Pickett could.

"In the back garage of the August Tux Shop," Mike said, turning and smiling at the three detectives.

"Now we have enough for a warrant," Robin said.

"But how do we keep those people in those rooms, if they are there, from being hurt if we raid on the top floor?" Pickett asked. "There has to be some major forms of communications with that area down there back to the surface somewhere."

"Especially if they are loading out porn videos," Sarge said. "All the

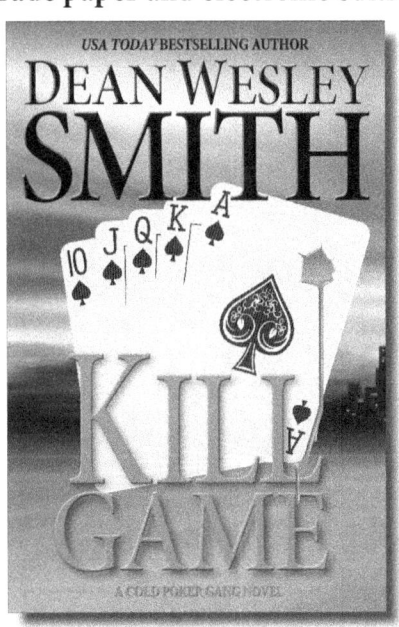

wedding rapes, all the voyeur videos and who knows what other things they are doing to those people. All have to be taken out of there somehow and loaded onto the dark web. Am I correct?"

Mike and Robin both nodded.

"He's right," Robin said. "We need to find that connection and control it first. I'll get Will and all our people on this."

She turned with the phone to her ear and moved out into the hallway.

Mike nodded and glanced at Sarge. "Can I use this computer? I'll get my people on this as well. You two need to talk with someone you can trust completely on this to get a warrant when we need it. We still go in tonight."

Pickett glanced at Sarge who was nodding.

"Thanks, Mike," Sarge said.

Then he and Pickett went out into the hallway and turned toward the kitchen. Pickett needed a glass of water, something to take the dry, desert feel out of her mouth.

Something to help her grasp the size of the evil they had just found.

THIRTY-FOUR
October 20th, 2016

Las Vegas, Nevada

SARGE FELT AS if his entire body was in shock. He remembered the feeling from a few different times over the years. Always after finding something so horrid that it was impossible to believe a human being could do such a thing.

But humans could. There was no way to ever overestimate the ability of humans to commit pure evil.

"Do you think most of the missing are still alive down there?" Pickett asked as they got bottles of water in the kitchen and stood facing each other across the island. Outside the sun was bright and the sky clear, adding an even stranger feeling to the bright kitchen considering what they had learned.

"I think the ones that didn't give up on hope of rescue are alive," Sarge said.

"So more than likely there are a lot of graves down there as well," Pickett said, her voice soft.

Sarge only nodded to that. He was sure she was right.

A lot of graves.

"We are dealing with mass murderers as well as kidnapping on a scale not seen in modern America," Sarge said. His mind felt numb; he felt numb.

How was any of this even possible?

"We're still missing a lot of things, aren't we?" Pickett asked after a few long moments of both of them just standing there lost in their own thoughts.

Sarge looked at the beautiful woman he was quickly falling for and his mind came back to the task at hand like a cloud vanishing letting the sun shine through again.

"You're right, we are," he said, nodding. "Sewer, water, power, ventilation, and a ton more. All has to be provided for and hidden. And on that scale, that can't be easy. And to say nothing of the amount of food needed and waste generated."

"How many people are involved here?" Pickett asked. "An operation of this scale can't just be a few people."

Sarge grabbed his notebook and jotted down all the questions he and Pickett had just come up with.

She was right, this had to be a fairly large operation, which meant people were being paid somehow. From the people who did the kidnapping to the tech people who cleaned up and loaded out the videos to the people who ran the supplies, not even counting the security forces.

"Who can we trust?" Pickett asked, staring at him with those deep brown eyes.

"Mike's people," Sarge said. "Robin and Will's people. Julia and Lott and Andor and Doc Hill and his people. That's a lot of highly trained help there."

Pickett nodded.

At that moment Robin joined them and dug out a bottle of water from the fridge and took a drink. "Will is as angry as I have ever seen him," Robin said. "I'm so disgusted at what we found, I am shaking."

Pickett just nodded and gave Robin a moment to take a drink and take a deep breath.

"Does Will know a judge he can trust to get the warrant on this?" Sarge asked.

Robin nodded. "My worry is the connection between the crew on the surface and the ones underground. The entire place could be rigged to explode and just kill and bury everyone."

"Shit," Sarge said. He hadn't even thought of that, but the type of people who could do this would think nothing of just burying all those people and trying to get away.

"So how do we make sure that can't happen?" Pickett asked.

Robin only shook her head and took another drink of water.

"Power," Sarge said, looking at both women. "Between lights, air, and everything else, that place has to be using the same amount of power as a decent-sized

hotel. We need to find how that is being fed into the place and cut the power."

"Damn, you're right," Robin said, her phone appearing at her ear almost instantly. "Tell Mike."

Robin turned to the living room while Sarge followed Pickett back toward his computer room.

It took them only a moment to explain their fear to Mike and he nodded and turned back to the screen, talking to someone through the computer. "Find the power source."

Mike's people found it just before Robin's people did. A small two-hundred room hotel just two blocks from the August Tux Shop was drawing about three times the power it would actually need. Normally that would never be noticed. But the hotel was owned by a corporation owned by the LaPine family. They also owned two small restaurants nearby under different corporation names.

"I'm betting those two restaurants order far more food than they sell to regular customers," Pickett said.

"So we cut the power," Sarge said. "Any thoughts on what we do next?"

"We get the warrant to hit all the above-ground locations and arrest the bastards there," Mike said, "including the owners of all this right out of their beds."

"Will and his people are on that," Pickett said. "They can make sure that will happen and have people they will vet and trust on the legal side."

"The rest of us go in the tunnels and try to get those people out of there that way," Mike said, still working the computer.

Sarge glanced at Pickett who looked pale, but was nodding.

Sarge didn't like the idea, but they had no choice at this point. And Mike and his trained men and women would be leading the way in.

Sarge nodded to Pickett. They could do this.

All that mattered now was getting all those people out of there and safe. If there really were people still alive down there.

THIRTY-FIVE

October 20th, 2016
Las Vegas, Nevada

PICKETT FELT SO at home in Sarge's place that when she ordered pizza for them, she first gave her condo address. Sarge corrected her with a smile. She really, really wanted this to be all over so that she and Sarge could just relax a little, as retired persons were supposed to do, and get to know each other even better.

Both of them had been spending the entire afternoon working over the plan for the evening rescue, trying to make sure that no detail was missed.

They had gone over and over all the tunnel diagrams and the ground penetrating radar images of the complex.

Pickett thought she could almost walk some of it in the dark which she might have to and that scared her more than the idea of a possible gun battle.

The plan, on the surface, seemed simple, which also bothered her.

Mike and his people were going to cut the power to the entire place and hope that there was no real backup power below. Or at least not enough backup power that

would allow them to blow up the entire place. That was a risk they were going to have to take.

Then Mike and his people would, at the same time as the power went down, block all surveillance in the entire area, both above ground and below.

Then Mike's people inside the new tunnel would open up the entrances to the old tunnel. And then they would go in and take care of what resistance there was in guards.

Mike said he didn't expect much, but they were going in strong from both ends to make sure no one got away.

Robin said that she and Will agreed. They didn't think there would be many guards at all underground, since with the layout of the complex and everything being recorded at all times, there was no real need.

Robin just wished they could find the feeds to those rooms being sent out, but so far no luck on that.

At the same time, Will's people with police they could trust would be taking

---

Now Available
**from all your favorite booksellers
in trade paper and electronic editions.**

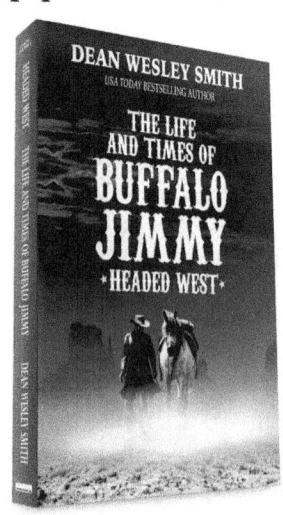

care of the arrests on the surface, including the entire LaPine family that owned the August Tux Shop, the hotel, and the restaurants.

Pickett and Sarge and Robin's job was to get the kidnapped victims out while Mike's people secured everything and made sure there were no traps or hidden explosives.

Pickett and Sarge and Robin had split up how they would take the large complex and what they would say to people as they went in.

Once the victims were on their way out, Will and the police would meet the victims at the mouth of the new tunnel and take them to a staging area and for medical attention.

Anyone not able to walk out on their own would be cared for by emergency techs as soon as the complete all-clear was given.

All effort was going to be made to keep the press from even getting a whiff of the fact that a lot of missing people had suddenly been found for at least a few days, until families could be notified.

At least Pickett hoped they were going to find a lot of missing people. They had no evidence but the huge cavern of cars to really back up their assumption that the missing would be down there.

But her gut said they would be right. She just hoped that a lot of the missing would be there and not in mass graves in some back cave.

The three of them had talked for almost an hour on what they would say to those being freed from the rooms. And what they might run into in a way of resistance of pure fear from the survivors. Some of those poor souls had been locked in those rooms for over eight or nine years. Being freed suddenly would not be an easy thing to grasp for them.

Pickett had no doubt about that. She couldn't imagine getting ready for the happiest day of your life, your wedding, and then suddenly being kidnapped and held in a concrete box with no windows and one locked door and no way to know where you were.

A horror story by any standards.

Part Six
DOWN INTO HELL

THIRTY-SIX

October 20th, 2016
Las Vegas, Nevada

SARGE CLIMBED OUT of Pickett's Jeep SUV and looked around the lower level of the concrete parking garage just one block off the strip. No cars were down this far and the place had a moldy smell.

Pickett climbed out of the driver's side and stretched and came around the car to him.

They both knew they were being monitored by the kidnappers. At the bottom level of this garage, about fifty paces from where they had parked, was a service access into the main storm drain just about a quarter mile from where the old tunnel was walled off.

They had to go down nine flights of stairs to get to it, but it was a logical way to go in.

As soon as Mike gave the word, all surveillance and all power to both the main areas above ground and the entire complex below ground would be cut.

At that point the police and Will's people would raid all the above ground property and make arrests.

Sarge glanced around, making sure he and Pickett were alone. He knew they weren't really alone because three of Mike's men were already staged on the floor above and another was pretending to be a homeless man sleeping in one corner with a shopping cart that happened to be full of weapons and other things needed underground.

All four were former Special Forces, as were the other five coming in near the other tunnel entrance. Robin was with them.

It was seven-fifty-eight in the evening. They had two minutes.

Pickett came up to Sarge, put her arms around his neck and pulled his head down and kissed him before he even had a chance to realize what she was doing.

That surprised him and pleased him more than he wanted to admit and he went with the kiss, pressing back into her and holding her as well.

They spent one of the two minutes in the kiss until she finally released him and pushed back, smiling.

He knew he was smiling as well. He could feel it.

"For luck?" he asked.

"More of a promise for later," she said, smiling.

"Let's be careful and make damn sure there is a later," he said.

She nodded to that. "That idea I like."

"Stand ready, everyone," Mike said in both their ears through their com links. "Mission is a go. Cutting power and surveillance in twenty seconds."

Both Sarge and Pickett nodded and smiled at each other as they waited.

It felt to Sarge like a very long twenty seconds.

Then Mike said, "Everyone go."

Sarge nodded to Pickett as they both turned back to the SUV.

Pickett clicked open the back hatch and both of them put on vests and grabbed their guns and some extra ammunition. Sarge didn't expect them to need the guns with Mike's people going in ahead, but they were taking them just in case.

Both made sure their badges were in clear view as well. The vests said Las Vegas Police on both front and back. They both wore helmets with LED lamps in the front and both carried first aid and extra small LED flashlights in small packs.

They had just finished and closed the latch when the three men from the level above headed for the door now guarded by the one man who had been pretending to be homeless.

Sarge and Pickett reached the door to the tunnel entrance as the first three men went through. One of Mike's men would follow them down for protection.

All four of Mike's men were in full combat gear and their faces were streaked black. All carried assault rifles and packs on their backs.

"It's clear of scanning," one man said and started down the metal staircase moving silently and quickly.

The staircase looked like a standard garage staircase with concrete walls and concrete on the runners. There were lights spaced evenly all the way down and only a couple had burnt out. Sarge felt like he was descending into hell and if this operation went south, that might be exactly what he was doing.

They all moved surprisingly silently until they reached the access door to the modern storm tunnel. At points, Sarge felt like he was tiptoeing to make sure he made no noise at all.

The man in the lead again checked a device on his arm, nodded, and then whispered, "Still clear."

Sarge watched as the guy opened the door and went through low and to the right while the man behind him went through low and to the left.

"Clear," the voice said softly and the third followed and Sarge and then Pickett followed, clicking on the LED lamps on their heads as they went.

All six of them had on their head lamps and had spread out.

The storm tunnel was all concrete on four sides, with water marks and debris along the center from the last floods. The ceiling was about eight feet overhead and Sarge could almost touch it. The entire thing was about as wide as a double car garage.

It smelled of damp earth and some rot and felt very claustrophobic and frightening with the shadows from their lights moving like bad dreams on the walls.

Sarge had not thought of himself as afraid of caves or tunnels, but at the moment, with the four special forces crew going up against some clearly smart and prepared enemies, being in this tunnel just flat scared him.

He glanced at Pickett as they headed off down the tunnel to the right. She seemed to be doing fine, but her eyes were large.

He had a hunch, his were as well.

THIRTY-SEVEN

October 20th, 2016
Las Vegas, Nevada

PICKETT COULDN'T REMEMBER another time in her long career that she had felt this afraid and this out of control. And being out of control scared her more than she wanted to think about.

And the tunnel and the creepy shadows their lights were casting made it worse.

Far worse.

They were a long ways from the bright lights and the excitement and people on the streets overhead. They might as well have been on another world down here.

It took them only a minute to reach the walled-up entrance to the old tunnel. As the picture they had studied showed, there was only a small hole about the size of an attic trap door at floor level. It was stained with black from the seepage of water over the decades.

The man with the scanning device moved up to the hole, stuck the device in and then said softly, "Clear. Mike, we are in position and setting charges."

"The other team is also in position at the other entrance," Mike said through their communications link. Picket was amazed at how clear his voice was in her ear. It was as if he was standing right beside her.

Two of the men quickly set devices in a rectangle about the size of a large front door while the other two took positions guarding up and down the tunnel in both directions.

Pickett and Sarge moved over with their back against the same wall and turned off their lights, not saying anything. The two guarding the tunnel in both directions had both turned off their lights as well, so now the only light was from the two working around the hole.

Seemed like time stretched at that point and she forced herself to take long, slow, deep breaths.

After a moment Sarge touched her arm and she put a hand on his hand and squeezed. This was all scaring her to death, and considering what she had seen in all her years of being a detective, that sort of surprised her.

And clearly Sarge was nervous as well. But the plan was solid and above them the police and Mike's people were taking down everyone associated with any of the businesses.

Will and the Chief of Police had presented a judge they had cleared of any chance of connection to the August Tux Shop family with the evidence they had all compiled. The judge gave the Chief a sweeping search and arrest warrant that covered above ground and below ground and all personal homes with the words, "Get these sons-of-bitches."

Mike and Will had convinced the Chief that they didn't dare let too many detectives in on the raid since there was no telling if any of them worked for these scum. And with the help of Sarge and Pickett, they had convinced the Chief it would be better if Mike's people with help from the Cold Poker Gang members took care of the underground threats first.

At the same time as the raid, Will's computer people would download all computer information to make sure there was no chances of anything being destroyed.

Pickett wondered how all the raids were going. But her priority, the most important thing she could think about was rescuing anyone who might still be alive down here.

She took another deep breath and squeezed Sarge's hand again. Even with trained fighting forces with them, this was still the scariest thing Pickett had ever done.

"Ready," one of the two men said as they stepped back away from the devices they had planted, pressing themselves against the wall on either side of the small hole.

"Ready," the other team said just a fraction of a second later.

"Blow them," Mike's voice said.

Pickett didn't have a chance to get her hands over her ears to muffle the explosion and it ended up she didn't need to. The sound was more like someone dropping something heavy on the ground right near where she was standing.

Very little sound.

Just a very solid thud.

Sarge squeezed her hand and let go as they started toward the door-sized hole in the concrete. They both clicked on their lights as they approached the light dust cloud rolling away from the new door-sized hole in the concrete. The two men who had set the charges were already through the hole.

"Clear," one of them said after a moment.

The concrete debris in the doorway was nothing more than powder now as Picket went through. Not even a piece left big enough to stumble over.

This older tunnel was lower and she could touch the ceiling easily. And a lot narrower and it smelled of rot and sewer and the air felt stale and heavy.

Three of Mike's people were at full run forward at this point with only one of the soldiers holding back with her and Sarge. That was the plan, for three to move in quickly the quarter mile along the old tunnel before she and Sarge and the fourth soldier came along as backup.

She had no doubt they wouldn't be needed as backup. It was to keep her and Sarge safe.

As they moved, as silently as they could, she kept expecting to hear gunshots ahead. The lights from the three had vanished around a slight bend in the tunnel.

Nothing.

They should be at the main area by now.

No gunshots.

Just the sound of her own breathing in her ears.

And the silence of a long-abandoned tunnel.

THIRTY-EIGHT

October 20th, 2016
Las Vegas, Nevada

SARGE MOVED AS quietly as he could down the tunnel. It felt claustrophobic even more than the larger tunnel they had just come from. He almost felt as if he would hit his head at times, so he walked slightly hunched over.

Ahead there was no sound at all.

He would have expected gunshots, but he knew the three men ahead would have switched over to night vision and might have just taken out anyone silently who might have been there guarding the tunnel.

From the images they had gotten, they knew that an artificial large room had been built off of one side of the old tunnel. And from there, the vast maze of rooms seemed to spread out through the ground.

The victim's cars were all off to the other side of the old tunnel in a massive room.

Beside him Pickett seemed to be doing better than he was. He had no idea that tunnels could bother him this much. Once this was done he hoped to live the rest of his life without ever going underground in a tunnel again.

Especially a tunnel that was only a few inches taller than he was and smelled of mold and busted sewer lines.

Suddenly, the word "Clear" sounded in his ear.

"Clear here as well," another said.

"Underground secured," another said. "No one was home."

Mike's voice came back in Sarge's ear loud and strong. "Well done. Wait for the detectives to arrive on scene before opening up any of the doors in the maze area. And stick with them."

"Copy that," the response came back.

Sarge glanced over at Pickett who looked intent as they picked up their pace to just under a jog.

Sarge was damned happy there was no one down here. They had all believed that might be the case. There would be no need to have anyone remain down here if all the doors were secured and there was no way for anyone to escape so far underground, especially if every inch of the place was monitored.

But they had had no choice but to go in expecting a force here.

Sarge and Pickett reached the large room that had been cut out of the tunnel just as Robin and her escort did from the other direction.

"Hold positions," Mike's voice said loudly in Sarge's ear. "We are bringing the lights back up and will be able to follow your progress on the monitors from here as you work your way into the maze area."

"That's great news," Robin said, nodding as she stood with Pickett and Sarge in the large open area. It looked like nothing more than a wide area in the tunnel and some garbage had been piled off to one side as if some homeless person was living there. One steel door blocked the way into the maze beyond.

Two of the special forces men were studying the door and then one said softly, "Mike, we have a problem here. Hold on bringing up the power."

"Copy," Mike said.

The other men in Mike's team quickly moved the three detectives back along the tunnel and out of direct sight of the door. Then the men spread out, moving silently and fading into the shadows almost like ghosts, leaving the detectives standing with their backs against the wall and alone.

Sarge had no idea what the two might have seen exactly at the big metal door, but if he had to bet, it would be explosives. The one thing they all had feared.

They stood in the tunnel for what seemed like an eternity, no one talking, until finally Mike's man said, "We have the door cleared. Let us go through and see what we find on the inside."

"Copy that," Mike said.

Sarge could hear a slight thump and then the sound of a heavy metal door opening slowly.

The sound was damn creepy in the old concrete tunnel.

Beside him Pickett actually shuddered, then laughed softly.

Then there was nothing again.

Silence.

And pure, complete silence in the small, underground concrete tunnel possibly filled with explosives was about as loud as anything Sarge had ever heard.

THIRTY-NINE

October 20th, 2016
Las Vegas, Nevada

PICKETT FOUND HERSELF almost holding her breath as the seconds of intense silence ticked on and on.

They were mostly standing in the dark and she knew the former Special Forces team were around them, but she couldn't see a one of them.

This was every nightmare she had ever had as a child and when that big metal door had opened with a scraping sound, it was everything she could do to just not bolt.

And then she had laughed at her own fear. She hoped not loud enough for anyone to hear. The laugh had helped.

After what seemed like the longest time, one of the Special Forces men said, "Mike, this entire place looks like it is rigged to explode."

Sarge looked at Pickett at the same time as she looked up at him in the dim light. She could see he was as worried as she felt, not for her own life but for all the victims they expected were in that place.

"All are set on two-hour timers and all the timers are going," the man said. "No motion detectors or any other problems. Just straight timers. No telling if we could find and disarm them all in time."

"We'll look for the security system up here to shut them down," Mike said, his voice clearly angry. "In the meantime, you work with the detectives to get anyone that is locked up down there out of there. Check each door as well for explosives."

"Copy that," the man said.

"People," Mike said, "we are switching to the backup plan and bringing everyone who can climb stairs up that nine-story stairwell into the parking garage. We'll stage medical and transportation help there. I have five more teams with detectives headed to help now in the evacuation, if there is one needed. Follow the search pattern we set up and detectives let my people clear an area before going into any space in that complex."

Pickett nodded. They had prepared for this and Mike was issuing orders clearly and calmly.

One of the former Special Forces men appeared next to Sarge and said, "Detective, you are with me. Stick close."

The guy was about as tall as he was and had huge shoulders and black on his face. Sarge knew better than to ask the man's name.

Sarge nodded and then smiled at Picket as one of Mike's men appeared in front of her and said the same thing. Her escort was as tall as Sarge and just as strong looking.

A moment later they were through the big metal door and into what looked like a modern living room with a low concrete

ceiling. In the lights from their headlamps, Pickett could see couches, a small kitchen, and a number of computer stations.

Considering they were nine stories underground, it felt comfortable and looked completely normal.

A dozen large hallways led off from the one main room and Pickett followed Mike's man down the one to the far right as they had planned.

Pickett knew the hallway branched a number of times and contained over three-dozen suites of room. They had figured in this instance, if they had to evacuate anyone down here quickly, they would start with the closest suite of rooms and work to the back.

Mike's man stopped at the first large steel door and did a quick inspection as Pickett watched from a few steps away, then ran a hand-held device over the entire door, then nodded.

"It's clear, detective. But explosives all along this hallway."

He pointed up at the small devices that looked like small smoke alarms and Pickett nodded. She couldn't think about that now.

Mike's man put a small device near the latch and there was a low thud and the door pushed inward.

Mike's man stayed to one side and Pickett stayed to the other, backs pressed against the wall. Nothing exploded and no gunfire, so Mike's man went in first, low and to the right and Pickett went in low and to the left.

What they faced in their lamp-light was a replica of a modern living room, right down to couches, chairs, television, paintings on the walls. There were even fake windows with blinds drawn.

A light carpeting covered the floor.

To one side sat a large modern kitchen and a dining area that could hold six. It was tiled in a modern-looking pattern.

There was no one in sight, but even in the dim light Pickett could see all the cameras in the upper corners of the rooms. These poor people had been recorded doing everything every moment of every day.

Pickett just shuddered. One of her worst nightmares.

Mike's man went silently down the hallway off the living room, checking for explosives before signaling the all clear.

"Suites are not rigged that I can tell," he said to Mike.

"Las Vegas Police!" Pickett shouted. "Anyone in here?"

She opened the first hallway door and was greeted by a man sitting up in bed, looking both shocked and scared. The room was large and well-furnished with a desk and computer and everything.

"Get dressed quickly," Pickett said. "We're getting you out of here. Wait for us by the kitchen."

The poor guy nodded and climbed out of bed.

Two more of the hallway doors opened and two women stuck their heads out to be met by Mike's man pointing a gun at them. Both were wearing pajamas.

"Las Vegas Police," Pickett said as Mike's man lowered his weapon. "Get on your robe, we're getting you out of here. Hurry."

There were three more in their rooms, all scared and surprised. But as far as Pickett could tell, they looked healthy.

By the time Pickett and Mike's man had them headed out of the door and into the main room and then out in to the drainage tunnel, ten minutes had passed.

Pickett knew that was far too long.

One of the men and two of the women were crying, but all looked unhurt, at least physically. Pickett didn't want to think about the mental damage this had done to them. She didn't want to know how long they had been locked up. She would find all that out later.

Sarge and Robin both had a group of six victims each as well and all of them seemed to converge on the main living room at the same time.

Eighteen victims in ten minutes.

They had less than ninety minutes left if Mike and his people couldn't get the explosives stopped.

That wasn't enough time to even begin to get out everyone that might be down here.

Not even close.

They needed a lot more help to get here very, very quickly.

Or they needed Mike to find a way to disarm those explosives.

Part Seven
COUNTING DOWN A VERY SHORT TIME

FORTY

October 20th, 2016
Las Vegas, Nevada

SARGE WASN'T LETTING himself think about the horror he had walked into. Six people, locked away in what looked like a large six-bedroom home, recorded every moment of every day.

The level of sickness here just made him want to stop, but he couldn't. They didn't have much time to rescue all the people that might be down here. Over the years this place had taken thousands. No telling how many still survived.

When he and Mike's man left the first group of rescues in the drainage tunnel and turned back into the main living room area, he said clearly, "Mike, we are going to need a lot more help."

"Seven teams are on the way now and will arrive in less than ten minutes, another ten teams will be on site in twenty with more following," Mike said. "And Will and I are working to find the connection to the explosives and try to shut it off when everyone is clear or our time is about to run out."

"Thank you," Sarge said, as he and the former Special Forces man assigned to him ran back down the hallway toward the next door to the next suite. Mike's man checked the door much quicker this time and blew it open and they didn't hesitate, but went in low and quick.

Again, as the first one they had gone into, the suite was a massive living room, with a kitchen off to one side and a dining room. It looked normal, like any home.

Disturbingly normal.

"Las Vegas Police," he shouted as they started down the hall.

A man looking angry opened one bedroom door right ahead of them. "What are you doing here?"

The guy had a gun at his side. Clearly he was one of the jailers spending a night with one of the victims.

"Drop the gun," Sarge said.

The guy just sneered and raised the gun.

Both Sarge and Mike's man fired, twice each.

147

The guy went down like the sack of shit he was, a shocked look on his face.

"We have some jailers in the apartments," Mike's man said into the general com link. "Go cautiously. One is down and won't be breathing anytime soon, but no telling how many more of these creeps are down here."

"Copy that," Mike said. "Be alert, people. Don't get sloppy and in too much of a hurry."

Sarge stepped over the pile of garbage they had just shot as the other bedroom doors opened and more victims looked out.

Sarge knew he had to be in a hurry, otherwise a lot of people were going to die.

And they had no idea how many.

One more thing he didn't want to think about at the moment.

FORTY-ONE

October 20th, 2016
Las Vegas, Nevada

PICKETT HEARD THE shots like a distant pop echoing through the corridors. She was relieved when she heard that Sarge and one of Mike's men had dropped a jailer. She just wished she could have put a bullet or two into the scum as well.

She and her partner had just pulled six more from another suite and were headed back down the hall toward the main room when Detective Sanders and a former Special Forces man either from Mike or Robin's people met them.

Detective Diana Sanders was tall, dark-haired, and as hard a cop as they came. But

Sanders' eyes were round and Pickett could see she was breathing hard, more than likely from the run here and from this horror show she had found herself in.

"Just leave the door open after you have cleared a suite of rooms," Pickett said to her. "We won't duplicate that way. But make sure everyone is out in case someone is too afraid to move."

Sanders nodded, staring at the six people in their pajamas and bathrobes heading down the hall past her.

"Be careful," Pickett said to her as she followed the six survivors out toward the main living room and the tunnel door.

Less than a half minute later, she and Mike's man were headed back into the tunnel just as Sanders and her partner went through a suite door shouting "Las Vegas Police."

She and her partner went to the next door in the seemingly endless hallway and had it open and through in less than thirty seconds.

And less than a minute later they were following Sander's group down the hall and toward safety.

Pickett and her partner had rescued 18 survivors of all this so far. They had less than 65 minutes left. There was no way they were going to get everyone before those bombs went off and brought all this down.

"Mike," Pickett said into her com link.

"Go ahead," Mike's calm voice came back.

"We're going to need to change up this plan a little to pick up speed. How about we clear a room and let the survivors just evacuate themselves back to the main room. We should be able to triple our speed."

Pickett noticed her partner nodding, but saying nothing.

Silence for a moment, then Mike said, "Seems like we have no choice."

There was a faint click.

"Listen up, people," Mike said. "Just clear the room, tell the survivors how to evacuate and then go to the next room. Jennings, I need you and Stevens in that big main room directing traffic out into the drainage tunnel. Carlson, you are in the tunnel pointing the way to the exit."

Pickett heard a couple of clicks as she and her partner headed at a run back up the tunnel. That might just get a bunch more out. But it was clearly more dangerous.

But after seeing all this, she was hoping against hope they would find a jailer so she could give him what he deserved: A bullet where his heart should be.

FORTY-TWO

October 20th, 2016
Las Vegas, Nevada

IT WAS ON the eighth suite Sarge and his partner had cleared that things turned worse, if that was possible. Until they went into that suite, Sarge would not have thought it could be worse.

And by that point they were under fifty minutes left.

They blew the lock and pushed it open and instantly Sarge knew something was wrong. The smell of death smacked him in the face like a hammer.

Mike's man ducked inside to the left, Sarge went in low to the right shouting "Las Vegas Police!"

Two people, one man, one woman came out of the dark at them. Both looked like they hadn't eaten in months and were nothing more than skin and bones. They were both naked from the waist up.

As they advanced, Sarge could see the knives in their hands. And both had a look of anger and hatred.

And insanity.

"Las Vegas police!" Sarge shouted.

Both of the people just growled and kept coming, knives held high.

"Stop! Now!" Sarge shouted.

Made no difference.

Sarge took the man coming at him with the knife raised and shot him twice.

Mike's man took down the woman the same way.

"We need to check the bedrooms and bathroom," the guy said.

Sarge only nodded and stepped around the insane couple and headed for the bedrooms.

Every room was a horror show. Blood everywhere, signs of fighting. Two bodies in their beds, clearly dead. Two more in the bathroom.

Sarge just felt himself go numb. He wasn't really seeing this. This wasn't possible.

He followed Mike's man out into the hallway and pulled the door closed.

Mike's man nodded and took out a marker and marked the door with a bright "X" that glowed in the dark. Then he wrote "Keep out!"

Sarge glanced at a couple of survivors going past him in the hallway. They looked fine.

"Mike," Sarge said. "You need to warn everyone that sometimes the survivors are dangerous as well."

"What happened?" Mike asked.

"We ran into a suite that two residents had clearly gone a little crazy and killed the others. We put them down when they attacked us. We closed the door and marked it."

Silence.

Then Mike said softly, "Jesus, sorry I asked."

Then he clicked on the com link to everyone and warned them of problems with survivors. "Stay alert, people."

Sarge took a deep breath, then nodded to his partner. "We got more to get out of here."

Thirty seconds later they were going through yet another door in this endless hallway of nightmares.

FORTY-THREE

October 20th, 2016
Las Vegas, Nevada

"**CLEAR THE AREA!**" Mike ordered.

"Shit, shit, shit," Pickett said to herself. They had just gone into a new suite and had two unable to walk.

"We have five minutes," Mike went on over the com link. "Get everyone out of that area and into the big tunnel. We're going to bring up the power in three minutes and try to defuse the bombs in four. Move it now, people. Now!"

Pickett swore again, then turned to two men who had been waiting for her orders and who had told her about the two women who couldn't walk. They were standing in one of the woman's bedroom.

"You two," Pickett said, "Pick her up between you and get going. We don't have time to wait for medical."

"Why?" one of them asked as they headed for the woman across her bedroom. She had wide brown eyes and looked scared out of her mind.

"The sick bastards who did this to you planted explosives. We're going to try to defuse them in a few minutes."

Both men nodded and then, as gently as they could, picked up the woman. They clearly liked her and more than likely had lived with her for a very long time.

Back in the suite hallway Mike's man had the other woman over his shoulder like carrying a light backpack. The other two women in the suite were already headed for the doorway into the hall as others streamed past, all in pajamas and bathrobes.

"We got anyone sweeping up behind us?" Pickett asked.

Her partner nodded. "Mike's got it covered."

She nodded.

But she didn't want to think about all the doors they hadn't made it to. The hallways past them just seemed to go on and on and branched.

If these hallways blew, this would turn into the most extensive rescue operation in history. Since the suites didn't have bombs set in them, the people in the suites would last for a short time. But not that long. Especially in the dark.

She just hoped Mike and Will and their computer experts had found the right way to stop this.

There were so many people in the hallway headed back toward the main room that it felt like a busy subway corridor at rush hour. Six teams had been opening doors along this hallway and then just pointing the survivors in the right direction. So some of the people were crying as they walked, others just sort of staggering along.

A few were helping others who didn't seem to be able to walk.

"Four minutes," Mike's voice came in strong.

Pickett flat couldn't remember how far down the hall they had gone. But she knew it was a distance and the one door into the drainage tunnel would be a jamming point as well.

She glanced back at her partner, who was carrying the woman over his shoulder like it was a normal day. Behind him she could see a couple dozen more people and then one of Mike's people bringing up the back.

This just seemed impossible, that such a horrible nightmare could be allowed to go on for so long. And right under the streets of Las Vegas.

She hoped that the Chief had arrested everyone responsible for this tragedy. And if lucky, they would all get small cells that never saw the light of day for the rest of their lives.

And even more sadly, every one of these people now moving down this corridor in their bathrobes and pajamas had once come to Las Vegas for the happiest day of their lives, only to find themselves down here like this.

Pickett had no doubt that some of these people had been in here for years and years, just holding on, living under the knowledge that every single moment of their day was being watched.

Pickett shook her head and then helped a man in a gray robe who had slowed down and was shaking. Clearly he was about ready to collapse.

"We need to get out of here," she said to him, giving him a shoulder to lean on even though he was considerably taller than she was.

He nodded. "Getting out of here is all I have been thinking about for three years."

"It's happening now, finally," Pickett said. "Just keep moving."

He nodded, clearly looking around and seeing everyone around him for the first time.

"They did this to this many people besides the six of us?" he asked, standing up and shaking himself slightly, seeming to come back into his mind.

"Far, far more than the ones you can see," Pickett said. "Far more."

"Oh, shit," the guy said.

Then he moved to help another man who was starting to slow.

"Three minutes," Mike said in Pickett's ear.

Three very short minutes.

FORTY-FOUR

October 20th, 2016
Las Vegas, Nevada

SARGE SAW PICKETT come out of a hallway one over from his. They had only two minutes and the lights should be coming up shortly.

The big living room was jammed with people as the tunnels came down trying to get through one doorway. Mike's men were helping people along as fast as they could, but it was going to be close.

Very close.

Behind him the last people they had gotten to made it out of the tunnel. Sarge had no idea how many they had rescued, but he knew it was far from everyone. The tunnel went on past the last door they had opened.

And he was sure that none of the other tunnels had reached the last people either.

Robin came out of a tunnel two over and moved to join Pickett.

"Lights coming up," Mike said.

There were so many lights in the big room from all of the police and Mike's men that when the lights did come up, it didn't seem that different.

But the lights down the hallways came on as well. Sarge didn't let himself look back. He didn't really want to think about how many people they had not gotten to.

The room was emptying quickly. Sarge moved over to Pickett and Robin. "You two all right?"

"I will be if we get a chance to get back down those tunnels for the rest of the survivors," Pickett said.

"I just want to wake up from this nightmare," Robin said.

Sarge nodded.

The people in the large living room were now down to the detectives and Mike's people.

"Let's get into the tunnel and away from this door," one of Mike's men said at the doorway.

They all moved quickly, and Sarge let Pickett and Robin go through ahead of him just as Mike said, "We're going to try to disarm the explosives in fifteen seconds. Get clear, people."

Sarge and Pickett and Robin headed to the right along the old drainage tunnel at a full run along with six or seven other detectives.

The last of Mike's men slammed the big metal door closed and followed them.

After about ten seconds, Sarge took Pickett's hand and the three of them crouched down, backs to the walls as Mike counted it down.

At one, Sarge knew he was holding his breath. He had no idea that, if that many explosives went off, the drainage tunnel they were in would even hold up.

The silence in the old drainage tunnel was intense as Las Vegas detectives and former Special Forces soldiers just waited.

Slowest few seconds Sarge could ever remember.

No explosion.

After a couple seconds, Pickett squeezed Sarge's hand.

He still didn't let himself take a breath. It wasn't over yet and they all knew it.

"We think we got it," Mike said, "but hold safe positions until we get past the full two hours. Another twenty seconds."

Sarge could only imagine how much stress there was up there with Mike and Will and all the computer people trying to disarm these explosives. Especially since Will's wife was down here.

Mike again counted it down.

Sarge again held his breath. He just couldn't help it.

After a few seconds past the final count, Mike said, "We're clear. Get the rest of those poor people out of there. Follow the procedure we have been doing and stay on guard."

Robin and Pickett and Sarge stood as their former Special Forces team members joined them, seeming to just appear out of the faint light in the tunnel.

Sarge nodded to them and all six of them turned and started back toward the big metal door that led to the cavern of horrors. Around them dozens of other teams were doing the same, this time walking instead of double-timing it.

The ticking clock was shut off.

They had survivors to rescue.

Part Eight
THE AFTERMATH

FORTY-FIVE

October 25th, 2016
Las Vegas, Nevada

FIVE OF THE longest days that Pickett could remember followed that long night in the underground hell. It had been almost ten in the morning before the teams started at the far end of the tunnels and checked every room and every closet for anyone remaining.

They had covered the body of the one jailer they had shot as they went past that suite and found no one else alive.

They also marked where they had found bodies in suites. Clearly people who couldn't hang on long enough and had killed themselves or died just days or hours before rescue was to arrive.

Sarge and two others found survivors hiding in closets too afraid to show themselves. And medical had to come for a few others.

Pickett and Robin and Sarge had finally climbed the stairs all the survivors had climbed to get up to the parking garage. There was no chance they were going to get Pickett's car out of the mass of tents and emergency vehicles set up there now, so Robin called Will and had him send someone to pick them up.

Pickett was fine with that. She wasn't sure she could have driven anyway. At that point all she really wanted was a long, hot shower and some breakfast and a bed.

As they had walked into the daylight to meet their ride, the warm morning air felt fantastic.

"I think I had forgotten what daylight felt like," Robin had said.

Pickett nodded.

Sarge said nothing.

"Imagine how all those poor souls held down there felt coming into the light," Robin had said, softly.

"We got them out," Sarge had said. "That's what matters at the moment."

Picket could only agree with that.

The long shower, a light breakfast, and a few hours sleep came four hours later after they reported in to the Chief.

About five in the evening, she and Sarge met and went to the Golden Nugget buffet for dinner, then they had headed to the large warehouse set up for survivors just a few blocks away.

The entire Cold Poker Gang had volunteered to help, talk with survivors, and get information. An entire computer center was set up to find relatives of the survivors. Mike's people and Will's people were all working full time to help the police on this.

And the FBI and Nevada State Police had been called in and were starting to bring in help as well.

Two of the women that Pickett had talked to had been in the same apartment for over six years. Sadly, both of their fiancés had found someone else and married during those six years.

Neither woman blamed the men, but Pickett had no doubt this was going to be difficult going home, if that was even going to be possible for many of the survivors.

On the third day they had learned that they had rescued over nine hundred missing persons from that hell in the ground.

Nine hundred people got to be reunited with the families. The largest missing persons case in history as far as they knew.

And the place where the dead had been buried had been found as well and was being worked on slowly to put closure on even more missing persons' cases.

On the fourth day the story had finally hit the papers, without any mention of the vast number of people being processed. The story was about how thirty-one people around Las Vegas had been arrested in connection to a massive kidnapping ring. Details would follow, but Pickett had been glad to see the mug shot of August LaPine, the owner of August Tux Shop on the front page of the paper.

The Chief had warned all the Cold Poker Gang members to not come back on the sixth day to help. That's when the press would be there. But over the three days Pickett had gotten to witness more reunions than she could ever imagine.

All of them full of tears of happiness and disbelief.

Pickett was glad that now, for her and Sarge and Robin, it was over.

But it was a long ways from being over for all the survivors and all their families.

For them, the recovery was just starting.

FORTY-SIX

October 25th, 2016
Las Vegas, Nevada

THAT NIGHT, FOR the first night in five days, he and Pickett found themselves alone in his apartment, sitting on his deck, sipping a white wine and staring out over the lights of the city.

Some Classic Poker Boy Stories
Available at your favorite booksellers.

Even with all the ugliness they had uncovered, he still loved the city spread out below him. Loved it more than he wanted to admit, actually.

And he knew for a fact he was in love with the wonderful woman sitting beside him.

"That was a great dinner," she said, holding up her wine glass in a toast. "Thanks."

"My pleasure," he said.

And it had been. They had stopped at the grocery store and bought a couple of steaks and some salad fixings and he had grilled steaks for them. It had turned out better than he had thought it would considering how tired and drained he felt.

"What are you thinking about?" she asked, "besides this fantastic view."

"Actually," he said, "wondering what we were going to do tomorrow, now that this case is over for us."

"I have no idea," she said, taking another sip of her wine. "But I do know what I would like to do tonight."

"And what might that be?" he asked.

"I'm thinking we go downstairs, take off all our clothes, crawl into that wonderful large shower of yours and then toddle off to bed together."

"Can I wash your back?" he asked, glancing over at her.

She smiled. "Please."

"Then I like that idea a great deal," he said, toasting her with his wine glass.

They sat for the next thirty minutes just sipping on their wine, mostly in silence, letting the cool night air and the wonderful view clear their minds of the last five days.

Then they headed for the shower and bed. They made love comfortably, not in a hurry, and she fell asleep in his arms just a moment before he dozed off as well.

Perfect.

And for the first night since going down into the tunnels, he didn't have a nightmare.

The next morning they ended up reading the papers over breakfast in the Golden Nugget Buffet. It seemed that the press was having a field day now and the national news led with the story.

Sarge felt very happy right now to be retired and out of it.

After a while Pickett put down her iPad and looked at Sarge. "No matter how ugly all that was, we saved a lot of people, didn't we?"

"We did," Sarge nodded.

"That feels wonderful," she said.

With that he could only agree. It did feel great, and he was going to stay focused on that instead of the nightmare they had seen and experienced underground.

"So how about we go rescue some more beings?" she asked, smiling at him.

"As long as I don't have to go underground," he said, knowing exactly what she meant.

"That I can promise," she said.

They walked leisurely back to the Ogden and took her car and headed out the old Boulder Highway.

Twenty minutes later they were standing in a large glassed-in room that held a number of cats and kittens in large cages while others ran loose. The cat shelter was clean and modern and the cats all looked happy and well-fed.

Almost in no time he found himself holding two ten-week-old orange kittens in his arms. Pickett had a black kitten in her arms from the same litter.

And he was smiling wider than he had smiled in a very long time.

The moment he had seen the two kittens he knew they had to come home with him.

Instant love at first sight.

And she had picked up the little black kitten first and hadn't put it down as well. There was no doubt the two of them had bonded instantly from the way the little kitten sort of cuddled on her arm and just looked around without fear.

"Don't you dare call those kittens Come and Go," she said, then laughed at how one of the kittens was climbing up his chest.

"Wouldn't think of it," he said, enjoying more than he wanted to admit the two kittens in his arms. "What are you thinking of naming that little sweetie?"

She held up the tiny kitten in front of her and then smiled. "Looks to me like he's going to be a long hair, so how about Harry."

"Well, that settles it," he said, smiling at her. He pointed to one of the orange kittens. "This is Dick and this one is Tom. That way if we ever live together the cats will be Tom, Dick, and Harry."

"Not a chance," she said, shaking her head and looking slightly horrified.

"No chance we won't live together?" he asked, knowing that wasn't what she meant.

"No chance we're going to name these cats any of those names," she said. "Let's get them home and let them tell us what their names are."

"I like that idea," he said, moving toward the front of the shelter with the two kittens. "But for the moment can I call them Pete and Repeat?"

"No!" she said.

"Spoilsport," he said, laughing.

"That's not what you said this morning in the shower," she said and gave him the arched eyebrow look.

"Did I actually say anything intelligent in the shower?" he asked, glancing at her and her new black kitten.

She laughed. "I'm not telling. But I honestly don't know since I was a little preoccupied."

"That's their names," Sarge said, smiling at her and pretending to be excited as they reached the shelter's front counter. "One is Pre and one is Occupied."

"No!" she said, her voice stern, her face slightly red. "Just no."

Then she reached over and scratched the chin of one of the orange kittens. "Trust me, little one, I'll save you."

Sarge laughed. He liked the sound of that and the promise of the future that it meant.

A wonderful future with a beautiful woman and three really cute cats. Didn't get much better than that in his book. As long as he stayed in his penthouse condo far, far above any tunnels under the city.

~

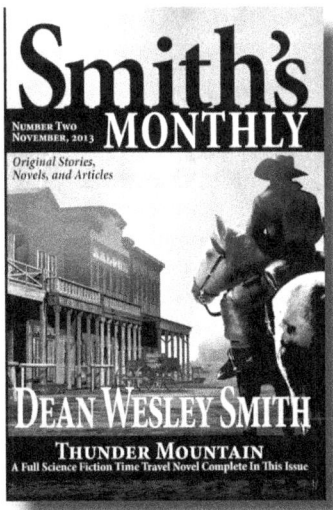

#4...January 2014

#5...February 2014

#6...March 2014

#7...April 2014

#8...May 2014

#9...June 2014

#10...July 2014

#11...August 2014

#12...September 2014

#13...October 2014

#14...November 2014

#15...December 2014

#16...January 2015

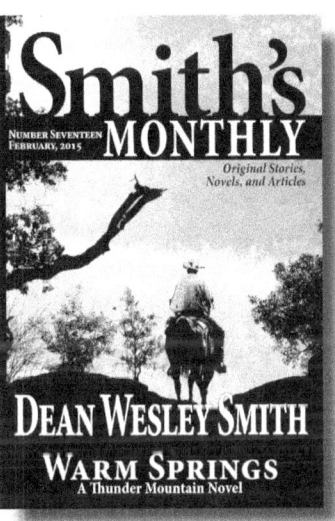

#17...February 2015

#18...March 2015

#19...April 2015

#20...May 2015

#21...June 2015

#22...July 2015

#23...August 2015

#24...September 2015

#25...October 2015

#26...November 2015

#27...December 2015

#28...January 2016

Don't Miss an Issue!

Subscribe to Smith's Monthly

Electronic or Paper Subscriptions Available.
For Full Subscription Information Go To:

www.SmithsMonthly.com

Thank You!!

I would like to thank the following wonderful people
who support my blog and my work through Patreon.
Your support is very important to me. Thanks!

Betsy Wilcox
Irette Y. Patterson
Kathryn Rooney
Wendy Lee Maddox
Jamie Curierre
Chris Cousino
Jane Lawson
Shantnu Tiwari
Miguel Angel Alonso Pulido
Nancy Hendrickson
Ryan M. Williams
Jacob Proffitt
Marian Goldeen
Gary Speer
Megan Bryce
Michelle Tatam
Ann Tucker
Kari Wolfe
Albert Lemke
Stacey Larson
Diane Darcy
Krystle Jones
Kari Gallagher
T. Thorn Coyle
Tasha Turner Lennhoff

Erick Lindman
Christopher Ridge
Terry Mixon
James Husun
Sherman Cox
Chong Go
Maria Grace
Grondpom
Fen
Robin Brande
J.R. Murdock
Kathleen McClure
Gunnar Gunderson
F.I. Goldhaber
Mary Jo Rabe
John Kilgallon
Dave Hendrickson
Jabberwocky
Eric Goebelbecker
Marsha Kessler
Scott Gordon
Martyn Folkes
John
Cj Lehi
Brenda Smith

www.ingramcontent.com/pod-product-compliance
Lightning Source LLC
Chambersburg PA
CBHW081150170626
46813CB00009B/3144